P9-CNH-355

All the Names

ALSO BY JOSÉ SARAMAGO IN
ENGLISH TRANSLATION

Baltasar and Blimunda

The Year of the Death of Ricardo Reis

The Gospel According to Jesus Christ

The Stone Raft

The History of the Siege of Lisbon

Blindness

The Tale of the Unknown Island

JOSÉ SARAMAGO

All the Names

———

Translated from the Portuguese
by Margaret Jull Costa

Harcourt, Inc.
New York   San Diego   London

This is a translation of *Todos os Nomes*.

www.harcourt.com

Library of Congress Cataloging-in-Publication Data
Saramago, José.
[Todos os nomes. English]
All the names / José Saramago; translated from the Portuguese by
Margaret Jull Costa.—1st U.S. ed.
p. cm.
ISBN 0-15-100421-8
I. Costa, Margaret Jull.   II. Title
PQ9281.A66 T6313 2000
869.3'42—dc21   00-036949

Text set in Dante MT
Designed by Lori McThomas Buley

First U.S. edition
A C E G I K J H F D B

Printed in the United States of America

For Pilar

You know the name you were given,
you do not know the name that you have.

The Book of Certainties

All the Names

Above the door frame is a long, narrow plaque of enamelled metal. The black letters set against a white background say Central Registry of Births, Marriages and Deaths. Here and there the enamel is cracked and chipped. The door is an old door, the most recent layer of brown paint is beginning to peel, and the exposed grain of the wood is reminiscent of a striped pelt. There are five windows along the façade. As soon as you cross the threshold, you notice the smell of old paper. It's true that not a day passes without new pieces of paper entering the Central Registry, papers referring to individuals of the male sex and of the female sex who continue to be born in the outside world, but the smell never changes, in the first place, because the fate of all paper, from the moment it leaves the factory, is to begin to grow old, in the second place, because on the older pieces of paper, but often on the new paper too, not a day passes without someone's inscribing it with the causes of death and the respective places and dates, each contributing its own particular smells, not always offensive to the olfactory mucous membrane, a case in point being the aromatic effluvia which, from time to time, waft lightly through the Central Registry, and which the more discriminating noses identify as a perfume that is half rose and half chrysanthemum.

Immediately beyond the main entrance is a tall, glazed double door, through which one passes into the enormous rectangular room where the employees work, separated from the public by a long counter that seamlessly joins the two side walls, except for a movable leaf at one end that allows people in and out. The room is arranged, naturally enough, according to a hierarchy, but since, as one would expect, it is harmonious from that point of view, it is also harmonious from the geometrical point of view, which just goes to show that there is no insurmountable contradiction between aesthetics and authority. The first row of desks, parallel with the counter, is occupied by the eight clerks whose job it is to deal with the general public. Behind them is a row of four desks, again arranged symmetrically on either side of an axis that might be extended from the main entrance until it disappears into the rear, into the dark depths of the building. These desks belong to the senior clerks. Beyond the senior clerks can be seen the deputy registrars, of whom there are two. Finally, isolated and alone, as is only right and proper, sits the Registrar, who is normally addressed as "Sir."

The distribution of tasks among the various employees follows a simple rule, which is that the duty of the members of each category is to do as much work as they possibly can, so that only a small part of that work need be passed to the category above. This means that the clerks are obliged to work without cease from morning to night, whereas the senior clerks do so only now and then, the deputies very rarely, and the Registrar almost never. The continual state of agitation of the eight clerks in the front row, who have no sooner sat down than they get up again, and are always rushing from their desk to the counter, from the counter to the card indexes, from the card indexes to the archives, tirelessly repeating this and other sequences and combinations to the blank indifference of their superiors, both immediate and distant, is an indispensable factor in understanding how it was possible, indeed shamefully easy, to commit the abuses, irregularities and forgeries that constitute the main business of this story.

In order not to lose the thread in such an important matter, it might be a good idea to begin by establishing where the card indexes and the archives are kept and how they work. They are divided, structurally and essentially, or, put more simply, according to the law of nature, into two large areas, the archives and card indexes of the dead and the card indexes and archives of the living. The papers pertaining to those no longer alive are to be found in a more or less organised state in the rear of the building, the back wall of which, from time to time, has to be demolished and rebuilt some yards farther on as a consequence of the unstoppable rise in the number of the deceased. Obviously, the difficulties involved in accommodating the living, although problematic, bearing in mind that people are constantly being born, are far less pressing, and, up until now, have been resolved in a reasonably satisfactory manner either by recourse to the physical compression of the individual files placed horizontally along the shelves, in the case of the archives, or by the use of thin and ultra-thin index cards, in the case of the card indexes. Despite the difficulty with the back wall mentioned above, the foresight of the original architects of the Central Registry is worthy of the highest praise, for they proposed and defended, in opposition to the conservative opinions of certain mean-minded, reactionary individuals, the installation of five massive floor-to-ceiling shelves placed immediately behind the clerks, the central bank of shelves being set farther back, one end almost touching the Registrar's large chair, the ends of the two sets of shelves along the side walls nearly flush with the counter, and the other two located, so to speak, amidships. Considered monumental and superhuman by everyone who sees them, these constructions extend far into the interior of the building, farther than the eye can see, and at a certain point darkness takes over, the lights being turned on only when a file has to be consulted. These are the shelves that carry the weight of the living. The dead, or, rather, their papers, are located still farther inside, in somewhat worse conditions than respect should allow, which is why it is so difficult to find anything when a relative, a notary or some agent of the law comes to the Central Registry to request certificates or copies of documents from other eras. The disorganisation in this part of the archive is caused and aggravated by the fact that it is precisely those people who died longest ago who are nearest to what is referred to as the active area, following immediately on the living, and constituting, according to the Registrar's intelligent definition, a double dead weight, given that only very rarely does anyone take an interest in them, only very infrequently does some eccentric seeker after historical trifles appear. Unless one day it should be decided to separate the dead from the living and build a new registry elsewhere for the exclusive use of the dead, there is no solution to the situation, as became clear when one of the deputies had the unfortunate idea of suggesting that the archive of the dead should be arranged the other way around, with the remotest placed farthest away and the more recent nearer, in order to facilitate access, the bureaucratic words are his, to the newly deceased, who, as everyone knows, are the writers of wills, the providers of legacies, and therefore the easy objects of disputes and arguments while their body is still warm. The Registrar mockingly approved the idea, on condition that the proposer should himself be the one responsible, day after day, for heaving towards the back of the building the gigantic mass of individual files pertaining to the long since dead, in order that the more recently deceased could begin filling up the space thus recovered. In an attempt to wipe out all memory of his ill-fated, unworkable idea, and also to distract himself from his own humiliation, the deputy felt that his best recourse was to ask the clerks to pass him some of their work, thus offending against the historic peace of the hierarchy, above as much as below. After this episode, the state of neglect grew, dereliction prospered, uncertainty multiplied, so much so that one day, months after the deputy's absurd proposal, a researcher became lost in the labyrinthine catacombs of the archive of the dead, having come to the Central Registry in order to carry out some genealogical research he had been commissioned to undertake. He was discovered, almost miraculously, after a week, starving, thirsty, exhausted, delirious, having survived thanks to the desperate measure of ingesting enormous quantities of old documents which neither lingered in the stomach nor nourished, since they melted in the mouth without requiring any chewing. The head of the Central Registry, who, having given the man up for dead, had already ordered the imprudent historian's record card and file to be brought to his desk, decided to turn a blind eye to the damage, officially attributed to mice, and immediately issued an internal order making it obligatory, at the risk of incurring a fine and a suspension of salary, for everyone going into the archive of the dead to make use of Ariadne's thread.

It would, however, be unfair to forget the problems of the living. It has long been known that death, either through innate incompetence or a duplicity acquired through experience, does not choose its victim according to length of life, a fact which, moreover, let it be said in passing, and if one is to believe the words of the innumerable philosophical and religious authorities who have pronounced on the subject, has, indirectly and by different and sometimes contradictory routes, had a paradoxical effect on human beings, and has produced in them an intellectual sublimation of their natural fear of dying. But, returning to the matter at hand, no one could ever accuse death of having left behind in the world some forgotten old man of no particular merit and for no apparent reason merely for him to grow ever older. We all know that, however long old people may last, their hour will always come. Not a day passes without the clerks' having to take down files from the shelves of the living in order to carry them to the shelves at the rear, not a day passes without their having to push towards the end of the shelves those that remain, although sometimes, by some ironic caprice of enigmatic fate, only until the following day. According to the so-called natural order of things, reaching the farthest end of the shelf means that fate has grown weary, that there is not much more road to be travelled. The end of the shelf is, in every sense, the beginning of the fall. However, there are files which, for some unknown reason, hover on the very edge of the void, impervious to that final vertigo, for years and years beyond what is conventionally deemed to be a sensible length for a human life. At first those files excite the professional curiosity of the clerks, but soon a feeling of impatience begins to stir in them, as if the shameless obstinacy of these Methuselahs were reducing, eating and devouring their own life prospects. These superstitious clerks are not entirely wrong, if we bear in mind the many cases of employees at every level whose files had to be prematurely withdrawn from the archive of the living, while the covers of the files of those obstinate survivors grew yellower and yellower, until they became dark, inaesthetic stains at the end of a shelf, an offence to the public eye. That is when the Registrar says to one of the clerks, Senhor José, replace those covers for me, will you.

Apart from his first name, José, Senhor José also has sur-names, very ordinary ones, nothing extravagant, one from his father's side, another from his mother's, as is normal, names legitimately transmitted, as we could confirm in the Register of Births in the Central Registry if the matter justified our inter-est and if the results of that inquiry repaid the labour of merely confirming what we already know. However, for some un-known reason, assuming it is not simply a response to the very insignificance of the person, when people ask Senhor José what his name is, or when circumstances require him to introduce himself, I'm so-and-so, giving his full name has never got him anywhere, since the people he is talking to only ever retain the first part, José, to which they will later add, or not, depending on the degree of formality or politeness, a courteous or famil-iar form of address. For, and let us make this quite clear, the "Senhor" is not worth quite what it might at first seem to promise, at least not here in the Central Registry, where the fact that everyone addresses everyone else in the same way, from the Registrar down to the most recently recruited clerk, does not necessarily have the same meaning when applied to the different relationships within the hierarchy, for, in the vary-ing ways that this one short word is spoken, and according to rank or to the mood of the moment, one can observe a whole range of modulations: condescension, irritation, irony, disdain, humility, flattery, a clear demonstration of the extent of expressive potentiality of two brief vocal emissions which, at first glance, in that particular combination, appeared to be saying only one thing. More or less the same happens with the two syllables of José, plus the two syllables of Senhor, when these precede the name. When someone addresses the above-named person either inside the Central Registry or outside it, one will always be able to detect a tone of disdain, irony, irritation or condescension. The caressing, melodious tones of humility and flattery never sang in the ears of the clerk Senhor José, these have never had a place in the chromatic scale of feelings normally shown to him. One should point out, however, that some of these feelings are far more complex than those listed above, which are rather basic and obvious, one-dimensional. When, for example, the Registrar gave the order, Senhor José, change those covers for me, will you, an attentive, finely tuned ear would have recognised in his voice something which, allowing for the apparent contradiction in terms, could be described as authoritarian indifference, that is, a power so sure of itself that it not only completely ignored the person it was speaking to, not even looking at him, but also made absolutely clear that it would not subsequently lower itself to ascertain that the order had been carried out. To reach the topmost shelves, the ones at ceiling height, Senhor José had to use an extremely long ladder and, because, unfortunately for him, he suffered from that troubling nervous imbalance which we commonly call fear of heights, and in order to avoid crashing to the ground, he had no option but to tie himself to the rungs with a strong belt. Down below, it did not occur to any of his colleagues of the same rank, much less his superiors, to look up and see if he was getting on all right. Assuming that he was all right was merely another way of justifying their indifference.

In the beginning, a beginning that went back many centuries, the employees actually lived in the Central Registry. Not inside it, exactly, in corporate promiscuity, but in some simple, rustic dwellings built outside, along the side walls, like small defenceless chapels clinging to the robust body of the cathedral. The houses had two doors, a normal door that opened onto the street and an additional door, discreet, almost invisible, that opened onto the great nave of the archives, an arrangement which, in those days and indeed for many years, was held to be highly beneficial to the proper functioning of the service, since employees did not have to waste time travelling across the city, nor could they blame the traffic when they signed in late. Apart from these logistical advantages, it was extremely easy to send in the inspectors to find out if they really were ill when they called in sick. Unfortunately, a change in municipal thinking as regards the urban development of the area where the Central Registry was located, meant that these interesting little houses were all pulled down, apart from one, which the proper authorities had decided to preserve as an example of the architecture of a particular period and as a reminder of a system of labour relations which, however much it may pain the fickle judgements of the modern age, also had its good side. It is in this house that Senhor José lives. This was not deliberate, they did not choose him to be the residual repository of a bygone age, it may have been a matter of the location of the house, in an out-of-the-way corner that would not disrupt the new plans, so it was neither punishment nor prize, for Senhor José deserved neither one nor the other, he was simply allowed to continue living in the house. Anyway, as a sign that the times had changed and to avoid a situation that could easily be interpreted as a privilege, the door that opened into the Central Registry was kept permanently closed, that is, they ordered Senhor José to lock it and told him that he could never go through it again. That is why, each day, even if the most furious of storms is lashing the city, Senhor José has to enter and leave by the main door of the Central Registry just like anyone else. It must be said, however, that his having to obey that principle of equality is a relief to his methodical nature, despite the fact that, in this case, the principle works against him, even though, to tell the truth, he wishes he was not always the one who had to climb the ladder in order to change the covers on the old files, especially since, as we have already mentioned, he suffers from a fear of heights. Senhor José has the laudable modesty of those who do not go around complaining about their various nervous and psychological disorders, real or imagined, and he has probably never mentioned his fear to his colleagues, for if he had, they would spend all their time gazing fearfully up at him when he was perched high on the ladder, afraid that, despite his safety belt, he might lose his footing on the rungs and plummet down on top of them. When Senhor José returns to earth, still feeling somewhat dizzy, but disguising as best he can the last remnants of his vertigo, none of the other officials, neither his immediate colleagues nor his superiors, has any idea of the danger they have been in.

The moment has arrived to explain that, even though he had to go the long way round in order to enter the Central Registry and to return home, Senhor José felt only satisfaction and relief when the communicating door was finally closed. He had never been one for receiving visits from his colleagues in the lunch hour, and on the few occasions when he had been ill enough to stay in bed, he, on his own initiative, had gone into work and presented himself before the deputy he worked under so that there would be no doubt about his honesty as an employee and so that they would not have to send the medical officer to his bedside. Now that the use of the door was forbidden to him, there was even less likelihood of an unexpected invasion of his domestic privacy, when, for example, he had accidentally left open on the table the project over which he had been labouring for many a long year, namely, his extensive collection of news items about those people in his country who, for good reasons and bad, had become famous. He was not interested in foreigners, however great their renown, for their papers were filed in far-off central registries, assuming that is what they call them there, and would be written in languages he would be unable to decipher, approved by laws he did not know, and he could never reach them, not even by using the longest of ladders. There are people like Senhor José everywhere, who fill their time, or what they believe to be their spare time, by collecting stamps, coins, medals, vases, postcards, matchboxes, books, clocks, sport shirts, autographs, stones, clay figurines, empty beverage cans, little angels, cacti, opera programmes, lighters, pens, owls, music boxes, bottles, bonsai trees, paintings, mugs, pipes, glass obelisks, ceramic ducks, old toys, carnival masks, and they probably do so out of something that we might call metaphysical angst, perhaps because they cannot bear the idea of chaos being the one ruler of the universe, which is why, using their limited powers and with no divine help, they attempt to impose some order on the world, and for a short while they manage it, but only as long as they are there to defend their collection, because when the day comes when it must be dispersed, and that day always comes, either with their death or when the collector grows weary, everything goes back to its beginnings, everything returns to chaos.

Now, since Senhor José's obsession is clearly wholly innocent, it's hard to understand why he takes such pains to prevent anyone's ever suspecting that he collects clippings from newspapers and magazines containing news and photos of famous people purely because they are famous, since he doesn't care whether they're politicians or generals, actors or architects, musicians or football players, cyclists or writers, speculators or ballerinas, murderers or bankers, con men or beauty queens. Yet he was not always so secretive. It is true that he never chose to talk about this hobby to the few colleagues whom he trusted,

11

but that was due to his natural reserve, not to a conscious fear that they might ridicule him. His concern with the jealous defence of his privacy came about shortly after the demolition of the other houses in which Central Registry employees had lived, or, to be more exact, after being told that he could no longer use the communicating door. This might just be coincidence, there are, after all, so many coincidences in life, for one cannot see any close or immediate relationship between that fact and a sudden need for secrecy, but it is well known that the human mind very often makes decisions for reasons it clearly does not know, presumably because it does so after having travelled the paths of the mind at such speed that, afterwards, it cannot recognise those paths, let alone find them again. Anyway, whether or not that is the explanation, late one night, while he was at home quietly working on updating his clippings about a bishop, Senhor José had an illumination that would transform his life. It is possible that a sudden, more disquieting awareness of the presence of the Central Registry on the other side of the thick wall, the enormous shelves laden with the living and the dead, the small, pale lamp hanging from the ceiling above the Registrar's desk, which was lit day and night, the thick shadows filling the aisles between the shelves, the fathomless dark that reigned in the depths of the nave, the solitude, the silence, it may be that all this, in an instant, following the same uncertain mental paths already mentioned, had made him realise that something fundamental was missing from his collection, that is, the origin, the root, the source, in other words, the actual birth certificate of these famous people, news of whose public doings he had devoted so much time to collecting. He did not know, for example, the names of the bishop's parents, nor who his godparents had been at baptism, nor where exactly he had been born, on which street, in which building, on which floor and, as for his date of birth, if indeed it happened to appear in one of his clippings, the official register in the Central Registry was the only one that could testify to the truth of that, rather than a random scrap of information in a newspaper, it might not even be right, the journalist might have misheard or copied it down wrongly, the copyeditor might have changed it back, it would not be the first time in the history of the *deleatur* that this had happened. The solution was within his grasp. The reason that the key to the communicating door was still in Senhor José's possession lay in the Registrar's unshakable belief in the absolute weight of his authority, in his certainty that any order uttered by him would be carried out with maximum rigour and scrupulousness, without the risk of capricious consequences or arbitrary digressions on the part of the subordinate who received it. Senhor José would never have thought of using it, he would never have taken it out of the drawer where he had placed it if he had not reached the conclusion that his efforts as a voluntary biographer would be of very little use, objectively speaking, without the inclusion of documentary proof, or a faithful copy, of the existence, not only real but official, of the subjects of those biographies.

Imagine now, if you can, the state of nerves, the excitement with which Senhor José opened the forbidden door for the first time, the shiver that made him pause before going in, as if he had placed his foot on the threshold of a room in which was buried a god whose power, contrary to tradition, came not from his resurrection, but from his having refused to be resurrected. Only dead gods are gods forever. The strange shapes of the shelves laden with papers seemed to burst through the invisible roof and rise up into the black sky, the feeble light above the Registrar's desk was like a remote, stifled star. Although he was familiar with the territory through which he would have to move, Senhor José realised, once he had calmed down sufficiently, that he would need the help of a light if he was to avoid bumping into the furniture, and, more important, in order not to waste too much time in finding the bishop's papers, first the record card and then his personal file. There was a small flashlight in the drawer where he had put the key. He went to get it and then, as if having a light to carry had filled him with new courage, he advanced almost resolutely between the desks to the counter, below which was the extensive card index pertaining to the living. He quickly found the bishop's card and, luckily, the shelf where the bishop's file was kept was within arm's reach. He therefore had no need to use the ladder, but he wondered fearfully what his life would be like when he had to ascend to the upper regions of the shelves, up there where the black sky began. He opened the cabinet containing the forms, took one of each sort and went back to his house, leaving the communicating door open. Then he sat down and, his hand still shaking, began to copy the identifying data about the bishop onto the blank forms, his name in full, with not a single family name or particular omitted, the date and place of birth, the names of his parents, the names of his godparents, the name of the priest who baptised him, the name of the employee at the Central Registry who had registered his birth, all the names. By the time he had completed this brief task, he was exhausted, his hands were sweating and shudders were running up and down his spine, he knew all too well that he had committed a sin against the esprit de corps of the civil service, indeed nothing so tires a person as having to struggle, not with himself, but with an abstraction. By plundering those papers, he had committed an offence against discipline and ethics, perhaps even against the law. Not because the information contained in them was confidential or secret, they were not, since anyone could go to the Central Registry and ask for copies or certificates of the bishop's documents without explaining why or for what purpose, but because he had broken the hierarchical chain by proceeding without the necessary order or authorisation from a superior. He considered turning back and correcting the irregularity by tearing up or destroying these impertinent copies, handing over the key to the Registrar, Sir, I would not want to be held responsible if anything should go missing from the Central Registry, and, having done that, forget what can only be described as the sublime moments he had just lived through. However, what prevailed was the pride and satisfaction he felt at now knowing everything, that was the word he used, Everything, about the bishop's life. He looked at the cupboard where he kept the boxes with his collections of clippings and smiled with inner delight, thinking of the work that lay ahead of him, the nighttime sallies, the orderly gathering of record cards and files, the copies made in his best handwriting, he felt so happy that he was not even cowed by the thought that he would have to climb the ladder. He returned to the Central Registry and restored the bishop's papers to their rightful places. Then, with a feeling of confidence that he had never before experienced in his entire life, he shone the flashlight around him, as if finally taking possession of something that had always belonged to him but that he had only now been able to recognise as his. He stopped for a moment to look at the Registrar's desk, haloed by the wan light falling from above, yes, that was what he should do, he should go and sit in that chair, and from now on, he would be the true master of the archives, and only he, if he wanted to, forced as he was to spend his days here, could also choose to spend his nights here, the sun and the moon turning tirelessly around the Central Registry, both the world and the centre of the world. When we announce the beginning of something, we always speak of the first day, when one should really speak of the first night, the night is a condition of the day, night would be eternal if there were no night. Senhor José is sitting in the Registrar's chair and he will stay there until dawn, listening to the faint rustle of the papers of the living above the compact silence of the dead. When the street lamps went off and the five windows above the main door turned the colour of dark ash, he got up from the chair and went into his house, closing the communicating door behind him. He washed, shaved, had some breakfast, filed away the bishop's papers, put on his best suit, and when it was time, he went out through the other door, the street door, walked around the building and went into the Central Registry. None of his colleagues noticed who had arrived, they responded to his greeting as they always did, Good morning, Senhor José, they said and they did not know to whom they were speaking.

Fortunately, there are not that many famous people. As we have seen, even using such eclectic, generous criteria of selection and representation as those employed by Senhor José, it is not easy, especially when one is dealing with a small country, to come up with a good hundred truly famous people without falling into the familiar laxness of anthologies of the one hundred best love sonnets or the one hundred most touching elegies, which so often leave us feeling perfectly justified in suspecting that the last to be chosen are only there to make up the numbers. Considered in its entirety, Senhor José's collection far exceeded one hundred, but, for him, as for the compiler of anthologies of elegies and sonnets, the number one hundred was a frontier, a limit, a ne plus ultra, or, to put it in ordinary language, like a litre bottle which, however hard you try, will never hold more than a litre of liquid. According to this way of thinking, the relative nature of fame could, we believe, be best described as "dynamic," since Senhor José's collection, necessarily divided into two parts, on the one hand, the hundred most famous people, on the other, those who have not quite got that far, is in constant movement in that area which we normally refer to as the frontier. Fame, alas, is a breeze that both comes and goes, it is a weather vane that turns both to the north and to the south, and just as a person might pass from anonymity to celebrity without ever understanding why, it is equally common for that person, after preening himself in the warm public glow, to end up not even knowing his own name. If one applies these sad truths to Senhor José's collection, one will see that it, too, contains glorious rises and dramatic falls, one person will have left the group of substitutes and entered the ranks, another will no longer fit in the bottle and will have to be disposed of. Senhor José's collection is very much like life.

Working with determination, sometimes long into the night until dawn, with the foreseeable negative consequences on the level of productivity he was obliged to reach in his normal work as a clerk, it took Senhor José less than two weeks to collect and transcribe the original data into the individual files of the one hundred most famous people in his collection. He experienced moments of indescribable panic each time he had to perch on the topmost rung of the ladder in order to reach the upper shelves, where, as if his suffering from vertigo were not enough, it seemed that every spider in the Central Registry had decided to go and weave the densest, dustiest, most entangling webs that ever brushed a human face. Repugnance, or, put more crudely, fear, made him wave his arms about wildly to free himself from that repellent touch, it was just as well that he was tied firmly to the rungs with his belt, but there were occasions when both he and the ladder came close to tumbling down, dragging with them a cloud of ancient dust and a triumphal rain of papers. In one such moment of affliction he even went so far as to consider detaching the belt and accepting the risk of an unbroken fall, this happened when he imagined the shame that would forever stain his name and memory if his boss should come in one morning and discover Senhor José caught between two shelves, dead, his head cracked open and his brains spilling out, ridiculously bound to the ladder by a belt. Then it occurred to him that untying the belt would save him from ridicule, but not from death, and that it was not, therefore, worth it. Struggling against the fearful nature with which he came into the world, and despite the fact that he had to carry out the work in near-darkness, towards the end of the task he managed to create and perfect a technique of locating and manipulating the files which allowed him to extract the documents he needed in a matter of seconds. The first time that he had the courage not to use the belt it was as if an immortal victory had been inscribed in his very modest curriculum vitae as clerk. He felt exhausted, in need of sleep, he had butterflies in the pit of his stomach, but he was happier than he had ever been in his entire life when the celebrity classified as number one hundred, now fully identified in accordance with all the rules of the Central Registry, took his place in the corresponding box, Senhor José thought then that, after such a great effort, he needed a bit of rest, and since the weekend began the following day, he decided to postpone until Monday the next phase of work, which involved giving full civil status to the forty or so famous people still waiting in the rearguard. He never dreamed that something more serious than simply falling from a ladder was about to happen to him. As a result of a fall he might have lost his life, which would doubtless have a certain importance from a statistical and personal point of view, but what, we ask, if that life were instead to remain biologically the same, that is, the same being, the same cells, the same features, the same stature, the same apparent way of looking, seeing and noticing, and, without the change even being registered statistically, what if that life became another life, and that person a different person.

He found it very hard to bear the abnormal slowness with which those two days dragged past, Saturday and Sunday seemed to him to last forever. He passed the time making clippings from newspapers and magazines, occasionally he opened the communicating door to contemplate the Central Registry in all its silent majesty. He felt that he was enjoying his work more than ever, for it allowed him to penetrate into the private lives of all those famous people, to know, for example, things that some went to great lengths to hide, for example, being the daughter of an unknown father or mother, or of unknown parentage, which was the case in one instance, or saying that they were from the capital of a district or province when in fact they had been born in some godforsaken village at a crossroads with a barbarous-sounding name, or even in a place that simply stank of manure and cowpens and barely deserved a name at all. With such thoughts, and others of a similarly sceptical cast, Senhor José arrived at Monday having just about recovered from the tremendous efforts he had made, and, despite the inevitable nervous tension caused by a permanent conflict between desire and fear, still determined to make further nocturnal excursions and further bold ascents. The day, however, began on a sour note. The deputy who was in charge of stores told the Registrar that, during the last two weeks, he had noticed that the number of record cards and file covers being used had risen considerably, and even taking into consideration the average number of administrative errors committed while filling them in, that number bore no relation to the number of new births registered. The Registrar wanted to know what measures the deputy had taken to discover the reasons for this strange increase in consumption and what other measures he intended taking to prevent its happening again. The deputy explained discreetly that he had taken no measures as yet, that he had not even allowed himself to have an idea, still less begin an initiative, without first explaining the matter to his superior for his consideration, as he was doing at that very moment. The Registrar replied in his usual brusque way, Now that you've explained, you can act, and I want to hear no more of the matter. The deputy returned to his desk in order to think and, after an hour, he returned to his boss with the draft of an internal memorandum, according to which the cabinet containing the forms would remain under lock and key, the key to remain permanently in his possession, as the person in charge of stores. The Registrar signed it and the deputy made a great show of locking the cabinet so that everyone would notice the change, and Senhor José, after his initial fright, breathed a sigh of relief because he had at least managed to complete the work on the most important part of his collection. He tried to remember how many record cards he had in reserve at home, twelve, perhaps fifteen. It wasn't that disastrous. When they ran out, he would copy onto ordinary paper the thirty that remained, the loss would only be an aesthetic one, You can't have everything, he thought to console himself.

As a possible pilferer of those forms, there was no reason why he should be considered any more suspicious than his other colleagues of the same rank, since only the clerks filled in the cards and the file covers, but all day Senhor José's fragile nerves made him fearful that the tremors of his guilty conscience might be seen and noticed from the outside. Despite this, he acquitted himself very well in the interrogation to which he was submitted. Adjusting his face and voice to suit the situation, he stated that he was always most scrupulous in his use of the forms, in the first place, because that was the way he was by nature, but above all, because he was conscious, at every moment, that the paper used in the Central Registry was paid for by public taxes, paid for over and over with the hard-earned money of taxpayers, and that he, as a responsible civil servant, had a strict duty to respect that and to make their money last. His declaration was well received by his superiors both for its form and for its content, so much so that the colleagues who were subsequently called for questioning repeated it with only minimal modifications of style, but it was thanks to the universal, tacit belief, inculcated in the staff over time by their chief's own peculiar personality, that, whatever happened, nothing in the Central Registry could be allowed to go against the interests of work, that no one even noticed that Senhor José had never uttered so many words consecutively since he had first started work there many years before. Had the deputy been versed in the investigatory methods of applied psychology, before you could say boo, Senhor José's deceitful speech would have collapsed around him, like a house of cards in which the king of spades had lost his footing, or like a vertigo sufferer on a ladder when that ladder is shaken. Fearful that, on reflection, the deputy in charge of the inquiry might suspect there was something fishy going on, Senhor José decided that to avoid further trouble he would stay home that night. He would not move from his corner, he would not go into the Central Registry, not even if someone were to promise him the extraordinary good fortune of discovering the document everyone has been looking for since the world began, nothing more nor less than the birth certificate of God. The wise man is only wise insofar as he is prudent, they say, and it must be acknowledged that Senhor José, despite recent irregularities in his conduct, did possess a kind of involuntary wisdom, albeit sadly lacking in precision and definition, the kind of wisdom that appears to have entered the body via the respiratory tract or from too much sun on the head, which is why it is not considered worthy of any particular applause. If prudence now counselled him to withdraw, he, wisely, would listen to the voice of prudence. A one- or two-week stoppage in his investigations would help erase from his face any vestige of fear or anxiety it might otherwise have borne.

After a meagre supper, as was his custom and as dictated by necessity, Senhor José found himself with a whole evening before him and with nothing to do. He managed to pass half an hour leafing through some of the more famous lives in his collection, even adding a few recent clippings, but his thoughts were elsewhere. They were wandering through the darkness of the Central Registry, like a black dog on the trail of the ultimate secret. He began to think that there would be no harm in simply using up the forms he had in reserve, even if there were only three or four of them, just to occupy some of the night and to be able to sleep peacefully afterwards. Prudence tried to hold him back, to grip him by the sleeve, but, as everyone knows, or should know, prudence is only of any use when it is trying to conserve something in which we are no longer interested, for what harm could it do to open the door, quickly search out three or four record cards, all right, five, a nice round number, but he would leave the files for another occasion and that way he wouldn't have to use the ladder. That was the idea that finally decided him. With the flashlight held in his trembling hand to light his path, he entered the vast cavern of the Central Registry and went over to the card index. He was more nervous than he had thought and kept turning his head this way and that as if afraid he was being observed by thousands of eyes hidden in the darkness of the aisles between the shelves. He had still not got over that morning's shock. As quickly as his anxious fingers would allow, he started opening and closing drawers, looking under the different letters of the alphabet for the cards he needed, making mistake after mistake, until he finally managed to gather together the five most famous people in the second category. Feeling really frightened now, he scurried back home, his heart pounding, like a child who has gone to steal a cake from the pantry and who leaves it pursued by all the monsters of the dark. He slammed the door in their faces and turned the key twice, he didn't even want to think about the fact that he would have to return that same night in order to replace those wretched cards. In an attempt to calm himself down, he took a sip of the brandy he kept for special occasions, both good and bad. In his haste and because he was unused to drinking, given that even good and bad had, until then, been rare occurrences in his insignificant life, the brandy went down the wrong way, he coughed, coughed again, almost choked, a poor clerk clutching five record cards, at least he thought there were five, he coughed so hard that he dropped them, and there weren't five, but six, scattered on the floor, as anyone could see and count, one, two, three, four, five, six, one sip of brandy didn't usually have that effect.

When he finally managed to catch his breath, he bent down to pick up the cards, one, two, three, four, five, there was no doubt about it, six, and as he picked them up he read the names on them, all of them famous, apart from one. In his haste and nervous agitation the intrusive card had got stuck to the one in front, the cards were so thin you barely noticed the difference in thickness. Now however much care and trouble you take over your handwriting, copying out five brief summaries of birth and life is not a long job. After half an hour, Senhor José could bring the evening to a close and again open the door. Reluctantly, he gathered together the six cards and got up from his chair. He did not feel at all like going back into the Central Registry, but there was no alternative, the following morning, the card index had to be complete and in its proper order. If anyone had to consult one of those cards and it was not in its place, the situation could become serious. Suspicion would lead to suspicion, investigation to investigation, and someone would inevitably remark that Senhor José lived right next door to the Central Registry, which, as we all know, does not even enjoy the elementary protection of a night watchman, someone might think to ask what had happened to the key that had never been handed in. What must be, will be, and there's nothing you can do about it, thought Senhor José rather unoriginally, and went over to the door. Halfway there, he suddenly stopped, It's odd, but I can't remember if the extra card belonged to a man or a woman. He turned back, he sat down again, he would thus delay a little longer before obeying the force of what must be. The card belongs to a woman of thirty-six, born in that very city, and there are two entries, one for marriage, the other for divorce. There must be hundreds, if not thousands of such cards in the index system, so it's hard to understand why Senhor José should be looking at it so strangely, in a way which, at first sight, seems intent, but which is also vague and troubled, perhaps this is the look of someone who, without making any conscious choice, is gradually losing his grip on something and has yet to find another handhold. Doubtless some will point out supposed, inadmissible contradictions in terms such as "troubled," "vague" and "intent," but they are people who take life as it comes, people who have never been brought face-to-face with destiny. Senhor José looks and looks again at what is written on the card, the handwriting, needless to say, is not his, it's in an old-fashioned hand, thirty-six years ago another clerk wrote the words you can read here, the name of the baby girl, the names of her parents and godparents, the date and hour of her birth, the street and the number of the apartment where she first saw the light of day and first felt pain, the same beginning as everyone else, the differences, great and small, come later, some of those who are born become entries in encyclopedias, in history books, in biographies, in catalogues, in manuals, in collections of newspaper clippings, the others, roughly speaking, are like a cloud that passes without leaving behind it any trace of its passing, and if rain fell from that cloud it did not even wet the earth. Like me, thought Senhor José. He had a cupboard full of men and women about whom the newspapers wrote almost every day, on the table was the birth certificate of an unknown person, and it was as if he had placed them both in the pans of a scale, a hundred this side, one the other, and was surprised to discover that all of them together weighed no more than this one, that one hundred equalled one, that one was worth as much as a hundred. If someone had gone into his house at that moment and, out of the blue, asked him, My dear sir, do you really believe that the one that you are is also worth the same as a hundred, that the hundred people in your cupboard, to be precise, are worth the same as you, he would have replied without hesitation, My dear sir, I'm just a clerk, just an ordinary fifty-year-old clerk, who has never even been promoted to senior clerk, if I thought that I was worth the same as even one of the people in there, or worth the same as any one of the five less famous people, I would never have started my collection, Then why is it that you keep staring at the card of that unknown woman, as if she were suddenly more important than all the others, Precisely, my dear sir, because she is unknown, Oh, come on, the card index in the Central Registry is full of unknown people, But they're in the card index, they're not here, What do you mean, I don't quite know, In that case, forget all these metaphysical thoughts for which your brain doesn't seem particularly well suited, go and put the card back in its place and get a good night's sleep, That's what I hope to do, as I do every night, the tone of his reply was conciliatory, but Senhor José had one more thing to add, As for the metaphysical thoughts, my dear sir, allow me to say that any brain is capable of producing them, it's just that we cannot always find the words.

Contrary to his desire, Senhor José did not have his customary, relatively peaceful night's sleep. He was pursuing through the confused labyrinth of his unmetaphysical head the trail of motives that had led him to copy out the details from the unknown woman's card, and he could not find a single one that could consciously have determined that unexpected action. He could only remember the movement of his left hand picking up a blank card, then his right hand writing, his eyes going from one card to the other, as if, in reality, they were the ones carrying the words from there to here. He also remembered how, to his surprise, he had walked calmly into the Central Registry, the flashlight grasped firmly in his hand, feeling not the least bit nervous or anxious, how he had put the six cards back in their places, how the last had been that of the unknown woman, lit until the last moment by the flashlight beam, then sliding down, disappearing, vanishing between the card bearing the previous letter and the card bearing the subsequent letter, a name on a card, that's all. In the middle of the night, worn out from not sleeping, he turned on the light. Then he got up, put his raincoat on over his underclothes and went and sat at the table. He fell asleep much later, his head resting on his right forearm and his left hand on the copy he had made of the record card.

Senhor José's decision appeared two days later. Generally speaking, we don't talk about a decision appearing to us, people jealously guard both their identity, however vague it might be, and their authority, what little they may have, and prefer to give the impression that they reflected deeply before taking the final step, that they pondered the pros and cons, that they weighed up the possibilities and the alternatives, and that, after intense mental effort, they finally made a decision. It has to be said that things never happen like that. Obviously it would not enter anyone's head to eat without feeling hungry, and hunger does not depend on our will, it comes into being of its own accord, the result of objective bodily needs, it is a physical and chemical problem whose solution, in a more or less satisfactory way, will be found in the contents of a plate. Even such a simple act as going down into the street to buy a newspaper presupposes not only a desire to receive news, which, since it is a desire, is necessarily an appetite, the effect of specific physico-chemical activities in the body, albeit of a different nature, that routine act also presupposes, for example, the unconscious certainty, belief or hope that the delivery van was not late or that the newspaper stand is not closed due to illness or to the voluntary absence of the proprietor. Moreover, if we persist in stating that we are the ones who make our decisions, then we would have to begin to explain, to discern, to distinguish, who it is in us who made the decision and who subsequently carried it out, impossible operations by anyone's standards. Strictly speaking, we do not make decisions, decisions make us. The proof can be found in the fact that, though life leads us to carry out the most diverse actions one after the other, we do not prelude each one with a period of reflection, evaluation and calculation, and only then declare ourselves able to decide if we will go out to lunch or buy a newspaper or look for the unknown woman.

It is for these reasons that, even if we were to submit him to the closest of cross-questionings, Senhor José would be at a loss to explain how and why the decision made him, let's hear the explanation he would give, All I know is that it was Wednesday night and I was at home, feeling so tired I couldn't even face having any supper, my head still spinning after all day spent at the top of that wretched ladder, my boss should realise I'm too old for such acrobatics, that I'm not a slip of a boy anymore, not to mention my problem, What problem, I suffer from giddiness, vertigo, fear of falling, whatever you want to call it, You've never complained about it, No, I don't like to complain, That's very considerate of you, go on, Well, I was considering getting into bed, no, I tell a lie, I'd just taken off my shoes, when suddenly I made a decision, If you made a decision, do you know why you made it, I don't think I did make it, the decision made me, Normal people make decisions, they're not made by their decisions, Until that Wednesday night that's what I thought too, What happened on that Wednesday night, What I'm telling you now, I had the unknown woman's record card on my bedside table and I started looking at it as if for the first time, But you'd looked at it before, At home I'd done little else since Monday, So you were mulling over the decision, Or it was mulling over me, Now don't start that again, Anyway, I put my shoes back on, pulled on my jacket and my raincoat and I went out, I didn't even remember to put on a tie, What time was it, About half past ten, Where did you go, To the street where the unknown woman was born, With what intention, I wanted to see the place, the building, the house, So you're finally ready to admit that there was a decision and that it was, as it should have been, made by you, No, sir, I merely became aware of it, For a mere clerk you certainly know how to argue, Generally speaking, clerks go unnoticed, people underestimate them, Go on, There was the building, there was a light on in the windows, You mean the house where the woman was born, Yes, What did you do next, I stayed there for a few minutes, Looking, Yes, sir, looking, Just looking, Yes, sir, just looking, And then, Then, nothing, You didn't knock on the door, you didn't go up, you didn't ask questions, Certainly not, it didn't even occur to me to do so at that hour of the night, What time was it, By then, it must have been about half past eleven, You walked there, Yes, sir, And how did you come back, I walked, You mean, there were no witnesses, What witnesses, The person who would have opened the door if you'd gone up, or the driver of a tram or a bus, for example, And what would they have been witnesses to, To the fact that you really did go to the street of the unknown woman, And what use would those witnesses be, They could prove that all this wasn't just a dream, I've told you the truth, the whole truth and nothing but the truth, I'm under oath, my word should be enough, It should be, perhaps, if it wasn't for one very telling detail, incongruous if you like, What detail, The tie, What's my tie got to do with it, A clerk from the Central Registry never goes anywhere without his tie on, it's impossible, it's against nature, As I've already told you, I wasn't myself, I was in the grip of a decision, That's just further proof that it was a dream, I don't see why, The choice is simple, if you admit that you made a decision, just like everyone else, then I'm prepared to believe that you went to the street of the unknown woman without a tie on, a disgraceful deviation from professional conduct which I choose not to examine just now, or else you continue to say that you were made by the decision, and that that, as well as the unavoidable matter of the tie, could only possibly occur in a dream state, I say again that I did not make a decision, I looked at the card, I put on my shoes and I went out, So you dreamed it, No, I didn't dream it, You lay down, went to sleep and dreamed that you went to the street of the unknown woman, I can describe the street to you, You would have to prove to me that you had never been there before, I can tell you what the building's like, Come now, all buildings are grey in the dark, They usually say that about cats, It's the same with buildings, So you don't believe me, No, Why, if you don't mind my asking, Because what you say you did doesn't fit with my reality and what doesn't fit with my reality doesn't exist, The body that dreams is real, therefore, unless there's some higher authority on the subject, the dream the body is dreaming must be real too, A dream only has reality as a dream, You mean my only reality was a dream, Yes, that was the only reality experienced by you, Can I go back to work now, You can, but prepare yourself, because we still have to deal with the matter of the tie.

Having acquitted himself well in the administrative inquiry into the disappeared forms, Senhor José, in order not to lose the dialectical ground he had won, invented in his mind the fantasy of this new dialogue, from which, despite the ironic, threatening tone of his opponent, he emerged the easy winner, as a second, more attentive reading will prove. And he did so with such conviction that he was even able to lie to himself and to maintain the lie with no sense of remorse, as if he would not be the first to know that he had in fact gone into the building and up the stairs, that he had put his ear to the door of the house where, according to the card, the unknown woman had been born. It's true that he did not dare ring the bell, he had told the truth about that, but he had remained for a few moments in the darkness of the landing, motionless, tense, trying to decipher the noises coming from within, so curious that he almost forgot his fear of being discovered and mistaken for a burglar. He could hear the squalling of a little baby, It must be her child, the gentle murmur of a woman rocking her baby, It must be her, then a man's voice said from the other side of the door, Doesn't that child ever shut up, Senhor José's heart skipped a beat out of sheer fear, what if the door were to open, as it very well might, perhaps the man was just about to go out, Who are you, what do you want, he would ask, What should I do now, Senhor José asked himself, poor thing, he didn't do anything, he stayed there, paralysed, defenceless, but he was in luck because the child's father did not share the old masculine habit of going out to the café after supper to chat with his friends. Then, when the only thing to be heard was the child's crying, Senhor José made his way slowly down the stairs, without putting on the light, gently sliding his left hand along the wall so as not to stumble, the curves of the bannister were too tight, at one point, he was almost overwhelmed by a wave of terror when he considered what would happen if another person, silent, invisible, were at that moment coming up the stairs, sliding his right hand along the wall, they would be certain to collide, the other man's head thudding into his chest, that would be even worse than being at the top of the ladder and having a spider's web tickle his face, it might be someone from the Central Registry who had followed him there in order to catch him in flagrante and thus be able to add to the disciplinary procedure, which was doubtless already under way, the incriminating, unanswerable piece of evidence that was still lacking. When Senhor José finally reached the street, his legs were trembling, sweat was dripping from his brow, Honestly, I'm a bundle of nerves, he said to himself angrily. Then, absurdly, as if his brain had suddenly run out of control and gone shooting off in all directions, as if time had collapsed everything, backwards and forwards, compressing everything into one compact moment, he thought that the child whom he had heard crying behind the door was, thirty-six years before, the unknown woman, that he himself was a boy of fourteen with no reason to go looking for anyone, much less at that time of night. Standing on the pavement, he looked at the street as if he had never seen it before, thirty-six years ago the street lamps shone more dimly, the road wasn't tarmacked, it was cobbled, the sign over the corner shop said it was a shoe shop, not a fast-food place. Time moved, began to expand slowly, then faster, it seemed to buck violently, as if it were inside an egg struggling to get out, the roads succeeded one another, became super-imposed, the buildings appeared and disappeared, they changed colour, shape, everything was jockeying anxiously for position before the light of day came to change it all back. Time started counting the days from the very beginning, using a multiplication table to make up for the delay, and it did this so accurately that Senhor José was once again fifty years old when he reached home. As for the tearful child, it was only an hour older, which just goes to show that, even though the clock would like to convince us otherwise, time is not the same for everyone.

Senhor José had yet another difficult night to add to other recent nights that had been no better. Meanwhile, despite the intense emotions experienced during his brief nocturnal excursion, he had just pulled the top part of the sheet over his ears, as was his custom, and had already fallen into a sleep which, at first glance, any other person would have described as deep and restful, when he was jerked into wakefulness again, as if some disrespectful, inconsiderate person had shaken him by the shoulder. He was woken by an unexpected idea that erupted into the middle of his sleep in such a devastating fashion that there wasn't even time for a dream to become woven about it, the idea that perhaps the unknown woman, the one on the card, was in fact the woman he had heard rocking the child, the one with the impatient husband, in which case his search would have ended, foolishly, at the very point when it should begin. His throat tightened with sudden anxiety, while his beleaguered reason tried to resist, it wanted him not to care, to say, Just as well really, that'll mean less work for me to do, but the anxiety would not let go, it continued to tighten and tighten its grip, and now it was his anxiety asking his reason, What's he going to do if he can't carry out this plan of his, He'll do what he always did, he'll collect newspaper clippings, photographs, news items, interviews, as if nothing had happened, Poor thing, I don't think he'll be able to, Why not, Because anxiety, when it comes, isn't that easy to get rid of, He could choose another record card and go in search of that person instead, Chance doesn't choose, it proposes, it was chance that brought him the unknown woman, and only chance has any say in these matters, There's no shortage of strangers in the files, But he has no reason to choose one rather than another, one in particular, and not just one of many, It doesn't seem a very good rule in life to let yourself be guided by chance, Regardless of whether it's a good rule or not, whether it's convenient or not, it was chance that put that card in his hands, And what if that woman is the same one, If she is, then that was what chance offered, With no further consequences, Who are we to speak of consequences, when out of the interminable line of consequences that come marching ceaselessly towards us we can only ever distinguish the first, Does that mean something could still happen, Not just something, everything, I don't understand, It's only because we live so sunk in ourselves that we don't notice that what is actually happening to us leaves intact, at every moment, what might happen to us, Does that mean that what might happen is constantly being regenerated, It's not only being regenerated, it's multiplying, you just have to compare the events of two consecutive days, I never thought of it like that, These are things known only to the angst-ridden.

As if this conversation had nothing to do with him, Senhor José tossed and turned in bed unable to get back to sleep, If she is the woman on the card, he repeated, if, after all this, she is the same woman, I'll tear up that wretched card and think no more about it. He knew he was merely trying to disguise his disappointment, he knew that he could not bear to return to his usual gestures and thoughts, it was as if he had been on the point of setting off to discover a mysterious island and, at the last moment, with his foot already on the gangplank, someone had come up to him holding an outspread map, There's no point in your going now, the unknown island you wanted to find is here, look, on latitude so-and-so, longitude such and such, it's got ports and cities, mountains and rivers, all with their names and histories, you'd better just resign yourself to being who you are. But Senhor José did not want to resign himself, he continued to stare out at the horizon that appeared to be lost, and suddenly, as if a black cloud had lifted and allowed the sun to shine through, he realised that the idea which had woken him was misleading, he remembered that there were two entries on the card, one for marriage, the other for divorce, and the woman in that apartment was certainly married, if it was the same woman, there should be another entry on the card for a second marriage, of course, the Central Registry did sometimes make mistakes, but Senhor José preferred not to think about that.

Alleging personal reasons of irresistible force majeure, which he begged leave not to have to explain, bearing in mind, anyway, that in twenty-five years of dutiful and always punctual service, this was the first time he had ever done so, Senhor José asked permission to leave an hour early. In accordance with the regulations governing the complex hierarchical relationships in the Central Registry, he began by making his request to the senior clerk in his wing of the Registry, on whose good or bad mood would depend the terms in which the request was transmitted to the corresponding deputy, who, in turn, by the omission or addition of words, by emphasising one syllable or muting another, could, up to a point, influence the final decision. On this matter, however, there are far more doubts than there are certainties, because the reasons that lead the Registrar to allow or refuse this or other authorisations are known only to him, and because there is no memory or record, in all the years of the Central Registry's existence, of a single report, either written or verbal, giving the necessary background information. It will never be known, therefore, why Senhor José was authorised to leave half an hour earlier instead of a whole hour earlier as he had requested. It is perfectly legitimate to imagine, although it is gratuitous, unverifiable speculation, that first the senior clerk or later the deputy, or both of them together, had pointed out that such a prolonged absence would have a deleterious effect on the service, it is much more likely that the boss had merely decided to take advantage of the occasion to humiliate his subordinates yet again with one of his displays of discretionary authority. Informed of the decision by the senior clerk, to whom it had been transmitted by the deputy, Senhor José calculated the time allowed and concluded that, if he was not to arrive late at his destination, if he did not want to come face-to-face with the man of the house, already back from work, he would have to take a taxi, a luxury almost unknown to him. No one was expecting him, there might not even be anyone home at that hour, but what he wanted to avoid was having to deal with the husband's impatience, it would be far more awkward trying to satisfy the suspicions of a person like that than replying to the questions of a woman with a child in her arms.

No man appeared at the door nor did he hear his voice inside the house, so he must still have been at work or on his way home, and the woman was not carrying the child in her arms. Senhor José realised at once that the unknown woman, whether married or divorced, could not possibly be the one who stood before him. However well preserved she might be, however kind time might have been to her, it would be unnatural for someone with thirty-six years behind her to look less than twenty-five. Senhor José could simply have turned his back, come up with some instant excuse, say, for example, I'm sorry, I made a mistake, I was looking for someone else, but, in one way or another, the end of his Ariadne's thread was there, to use the mythological language of the Central Registry, not forgetting, too, the reasonable probability that other people lived in the house, among whom might be the object of his search, although, as we know, Senhor José's spirit vehemently rejects such a hypothesis. He took the record card out of his pocket, as he said, Good afternoon, madam, Good afternoon, what can I do for you, asked the woman, I work for the Central Registry and I've been charged with investigating certain doubts that have arisen about the file of a person who we know was born in this house, Neither I nor my husband was born here, only our daughter, and she's only three months old now, I don't suppose it's her, No, of course not, the person I'm looking for is a woman of thirty-six, Well, I'm twenty-seven, You're obviously not the same person then, said Senhor José, and went on, What's your name. The woman told him, he paused to smile, then asked, Have you lived here long, Two years, Did you know the people who lived here before, these people, he read her the name of the unknown woman and the names of her parents, We don't know anything about them, I'm afraid, the apartment was empty, and my husband sorted out the lease with the agent, Is there an older resident in the building, There's a very old lady in the ground-floor apartment on the right, and I've heard people say that she's the oldest resident, It's unlikely she was here thirty-six years ago though, people today move around so much, I couldn't really say, you'd better talk to her, but I have to go now, my husband's about to arrive and he doesn't like to see me talking to strangers, besides, I have to make supper, As I said, I work for the Central Registry, so I'm not really a stranger, and I did come here on official business, I'm very sorry to have troubled you though. Senhor José's wounded tones softened the woman, No, no, it was no trouble, I just meant that if my husband had been here, he would have immediately asked you for your credentials, I can show you my identity card from work, look, Oh right, your name's Senhor José, but when I said credentials I meant some official document giving details of the case you've been charged with investigating, It didn't occur to the Registrar that anyone would be suspicious, Everyone's different, the woman who lives on the ground floor, for example, she doesn't open her door to anyone, I'm different, I like talking to people, Well, I'm very grateful to you for your help, I'm only sorry I can't be of more use to you, On the contrary, you've been a great help, you mentioned the lady downstairs and the matter of the credentials, Well, I'm glad you feel like that about it. The conversation looked set to continue for a few more minutes, but the peace in the house was suddenly interrupted by the crying of a child, who must have woken up, It's your little boy, said Senhor José, It's not a little boy, it's a little girl, I told you before, smiled the woman, and Senhor José smiled too. At that moment, the street door banged and the light on the stairs came on, It's my husband, I recognise the way he comes in the door, whispered the woman, go away and pretend you didn't speak to me. Senhor José did not go down the stairs. Noiselessly, on tiptoe, he went rapidly up to the landing above and stayed there, pressed against the wall, his heart pounding as if he were living through some dangerous adventure, while the young man's firm steps grew louder as they approached. The bell rang, between the opening and shutting of the door he could still hear the baby crying, then a great silence filled the stairwell. After a moment, the light went out. It was only then that Senhor José realised that almost the whole of his dialogue with the woman had taken place in the conspiratorial shadows of the stairway, as if both of them had something to hide, "conspiratorial" was the unexpected word that came into his head, What were we conspiring about, why "conspiratorial," he wondered, the fact is that she hadn't turned the light on again when it went out shortly after they had exchanged their first words. At last, he began to go back down the stairs, cautiously to begin with, then quickly, he paused only for a moment to listen outside the door of the ground-floor apartment, he could hear a sound inside that must be the radio, he decided not to ring the bell, he would leave that new investigation for the weekend, for Saturday or Sunday, but this time he would not be caught out, he would present himself with his credentials in his hand, invested with a formal authority that no one would dare to question.

They would be false credentials, of course, but, they would bear the irresistible force of an official stamp and impress, and they would save him the task of having to dispel suspicions before getting down to business. As for the chief's signature, he felt absolutely no qualms, it was hardly likely that the old lady in the ground-floor apartment would ever have seen the Registrar's signature, whose curlicues, when he thought about it, precisely because of their fantastic, ornamental nature, would not prove particularly difficult to imitate. If all went well this time, as it was bound to, he would continue to make use of the document whenever he encountered or foresaw difficulties in future investigations, because he was sure that his search would not end in that ground-floor apartment. Even if the woman had been there when the unknown woman's family had lived in the building, they might not have known each other, in the old lady's weary memory, it might all come down to a few vague recollections, it would depend on how many years had passed since the family on the second floor had moved somewhere else in the city. Or somewhere else in the country or even the world, he thought anxiously, once he was out in the street again. Wherever the famous people in his collection went, they always had a newspaper or a magazine following in their tracks and sniffing around them for just one more photograph, one more question, but nobody wants to know about ordinary people, no one is really interested in them, no one cares what they're up to, what they think, what they feel, even when they try to make you believe otherwise, it's all pretence. If the unknown woman had gone to live abroad, she would be beyond his reach, she might as well be dead, Full stop, end of the story, murmured Senhor José, then, he thought, that might not be the case, for when she departed, she would at least have left a life behind her, perhaps only a brief life, four years, five, almost nothing, or fifteen, or twenty, a meeting, an infatuation, a disappointment, a few smiles, a few tears, which seem, at first sight, the same for everyone but which are, in fact, different for us all. And different each time too. I'll go as far as I can, concluded Senhor José, with unaccustomed serenity. As if this were the logical conclusion to what he had thought, he went into a stationer's and bought a thick notebook with lined pages, like the ones students use to make notes on their school subjects, believing that they are actually learning them as they do so.

It didn't take him long to forge some credentials. Twenty-five years of daily calligraphic practice beneath the vigilance of zealous senior clerks and demanding deputies had left him with complete mastery of fingers, wrist and palm, absolute confidence in executing both curved lines and straight, an almost instinctive feel for thick and thin strokes, a consummate awareness of the degree of fluidity and viscosity of various inks, which, put to the test on this occasion, resulted in a document capable of resisting the scrutiny of the most powerful of magnifying lenses. The only incriminating features were his fingerprints and the invisible traces of sweat that clung to the paper, but the likelihood of either of these being examined was, of course, negligible. The most competent graphologist called to testify would swear that the document in question was written by the Registrar himself and was as authentic as if it had been written in the presence of appropriate witnesses. In support of his worthy colleague's opinion, a psychologist would add that the content of the letter, the style and the vocabulary offer ample proof that its author is an extremely authoritarian person, with a harsh, inflexible, secretive nature, convinced of the rightness of his own views, scornful of other people's opinions, as even a child would conclude from reading the text, which says, In the name of the authority conferred on me and which, under oath, I uphold, apply and defend, I, as Registrar of the Central Registry, declare to all those, be they civil or military, private or public, who might see, read and examine this letter written and signed by my own hand, that Senhor so-and-so, a clerk in my service and in the service of the Central Registry which I direct, govern and administer, has received directly from me the order and commission to find out and investigate everything regarding the life, past, present and future, of so-and-so, born in this city on such and such a date, daughter of so-and-so and such and such, and it should be recognised, with no further proof being required, that, for the duration of the investigation, he is in possession of the absolute powers which I, in this document and to this end, delegate to him. This is the express wish of the Central Registry and of my own will. So be it. Trembling with fear, having barely managed to read to the end of this impressive bit of paper, the above-mentioned child took refuge on her mother's lap, wondering how a clerk like Senhor José, so timid by nature, so mild in his manners, could possibly have conceived of, imagined, invented this expression of, to say the very least, despotic power, with no previous model to use as a guide, since there is no norm nor was there any technical need for the Central Registry ever to have written such a letter of authority. The frightened child will have to eat a lot of bread and a lot of salt before she begins to learn from life, by then, she will no longer be surprised to discover that, when the occasion arises, even the good can become hard and tyrannical, even if only in order to write a letter of authority, forged or otherwise. They will say to excuse themselves, That wasn't me, I was just writing, acting in the name of someone else, and they are probably just trying to delude themselves, for, in truth, whether visible or not, that hardness and despotism, not to say cruelty, came from within them, not from someone else. Even so, judging what has happened up until now by its effects, it is unlikely that the world will be seriously damaged by Senhor José's intentions and future actions, therefore let us provisionally suspend judgement until other events, more enlightening, in both the good and the bad senses, draw us a definitive portrait.

On Saturday, wearing his best suit, with his shirt washed and ironed, his tie almost matching and more or less correct, the envelope bearing the official seal and containing the letter of authority safe in his inside jacket pocket, Senhor José took a taxi to the door of the house, not in order to gain time, the day was his, but because it looked like rain, and he didn't want to appear before the lady in the ground-floor apartment with rain dripping from his ears, and with the bottoms of his trousers all spattered with mud, running the risk that she would slam the door in his face before he even had a chance to explain why he was there. It filled him with excitement to imagine how the old lady would receive him, what the effect would be on the old girl, the pejorative term sprang unbidden to his mind, of reading a stern, solemn document like that, some people don't react at all as you would expect, he just hoped she wouldn't be one of them. Perhaps the expressions he had used were too hard and despotic, although verisimilitude demanded that it should be true to both the character and the calligraphy of the Registrar, besides, everyone knows that while it is true that you catch no flies with vinegar, it is no less true that some you can't even catch with honey. We'll see, he sighed. The first thing he saw shortly afterwards, having replied to the insistent questions from within, Who is it, What do you want, Who sent you, What's that got to do with me, was that the lady in the ground-floor apartment was not, after all, as ancient as he had imagined, those bright eyes, that straight nose, those firm, thin lips with no downward curve at the corners, did not belong to an old lady, her great age was noticeable only in the loose skin on her throat, he probably fixed on that because he had already started to notice in himself that unmistakable sign of physical decline, and he was only fifty. The woman would not open the door completely, she said repeatedly that she was not interested in the affairs of her neighbours, a perfectly reasonable response given that Senhor José, taking a wrong tack, had begun by saying that he was looking for someone on the second floor. The confusion seemed to end when he finally mentioned the name of the unknown woman, then the door opened a little more, only to return to its former position, Do you know the lady, asked Senhor José, Yes, I did, said the woman, I'd like to ask you a few questions about her, But who are you, As I already told you, I'm an authorised official from the Central Registry, And how am I supposed to know if that's true or not, I have a signed letter of authority from the Registrar, Look, I'm in my own home and I don't want to be disturbed, I'm afraid you have to cooperate with the Central Registry in cases such as this, What cases, The resolution of certain outstanding matters at the Central Registry, Why don't you go and ask her, We don't have her present address, if you know it, perhaps you could tell me, and I won't need to trouble you any further, It must be about thirty years since I heard from her, She must have been a child then, Yes. With that one word, the woman appeared to consider the conversation at an end, but Senhor José did not give up, he might as well be hanged for a sheep as for a lamb. He drew the envelope from his pocket, opened it and, with a slowness that must have seemed threatening, removed the letter, Read it, he ordered. The woman shook her head, No, I won't read it, it's nothing to do with me, If you don't read it, I will return accompanied by the police, and it will be all the worse for you. The woman resigned herself to taking the document he held out to her, she turned on the light in the corridor, put on the glasses she wore hanging round her neck and read it. Then she gave it back to him and, standing to one side, said, You'd better come in, they'll probably be listening to us from behind the door over there. Given the implicit alliance that the personal pronoun "us" seemed to represent, Senhor José realised that he had won that round. In a certain indefinable way, this was the first objective victory of his whole life, true it was an extremely fraudulent one, but there are so many people out there preaching that the ends justify the means, who was he to argue. He entered humbly, like a victor whose generosity prevents him from giving in to the easy temptation of humiliating the vanquished, but who would, nevertheless, appreciate his greatness being noticed.

The woman led him to a small, neat, clean room, decorated according to the taste of a different age. She offered him a chair, sat down herself and, without giving her visitor time to ask any further questions, she said, I was her godmother. Senhor José had expected all kinds of revelations, but not that. He had gone there as a mere civil servant carrying out the orders of his superiors, and therefore without any involvement of a personal nature, at least, that was how the woman sitting opposite him should see him, but only he knew the effort it took not to break into a smile of beatific delight. From his other pocket he drew a copy of the record card, he looked at it for a long time as if memorising all the names on it, then he said, And your husband was the godfather, Yes, Can I speak to him too, I'm a widow, Ah, in that quiet exclamation there was as much genuine relief as there was feigned emotion, that was one less person with whom he would have to do battle. The woman said, We got on well, I mean, the two families, ours and theirs, we were real friends, and when the little girl was born they invited us to be her godparents, How old was the girl when they moved, She was about eight I think, You said a little while ago that it's nearly thirty years since you heard from her, That's right, Could you explain, Shortly after they'd moved I received a letter, Who from, From her, What did she say, Nothing much, it was the kind of letter that a child of no more than eight, with the few words she knows, would write to her godmother, Have you still got it, No, And the parents, did they never write, No,

Didn't you find that strange, No, Why, That's a very personal matter, not for general consumption, As far as the Central Registry is concerned there are no personal matters. The woman looked at him hard, Who are you, My letter of authority tells you who I am, It just told me your name, Senhor José, isn't it, That's right, Senhor José, So you can ask me all the questions you want, and I can't ask you any, The only person who can question me is an official of the Central Registry of superior rank, You're a happy man, then, you can keep your secrets, Happiness does not, I believe, consist merely in being able to keep your secrets, Are you happy, It doesn't matter what I am, as I've already told you, only someone higher up in the hierarchy is authorised to ask me questions, Have you got any secrets, I won't answer that, But I have to answer, It's best if you do, What do you want me to tell you, What were these personal matters. The woman drew a hand across her forehead and slowly lowered her lined eyelids, then, without opening her eyes, she said, The girl's mother suspected I was having an affair with her husband, And was that true, It was, it had been going on for a long time, Was that why they moved, Yes. The woman opened her eyes and asked, Do you like my secrets, They're only of interest to me insofar as they have to do with the person I'm looking for, besides, I wasn't authorised to find out anything else, So you don't want to know what happened next, Not officially no, But personally perhaps, I'm not in the habit of prying into other people's lives, said Senhor José, forgetting about the hundred and forty or so that he had in his cupboard, then he added, But probably nothing very extraordinary happened, since you're a widow you say, You've got a good memory, It's a fundamental quality for anyone working at the Central Registry, just to give you an idea, my boss, for example, knows by heart all the names that exist or ever have existed, all the names and all the surnames, What's the point of that, The Registrar's brain is like a duplicate of the Central Registry, I don't understand, Since he's capable of making every possible combination of name and surname, my boss's brain knows not only the names of all the people who are now alive and of all those who have died, he would also be able to tell you the names of all those who will be born from now until the end of the world, You know more than your boss, Never, beside him I'm nothing, that's why he's the Registrar and I'm just a clerk, You both know my name, That's true, But that's all he knows about me, You're right there, the difference is that he already knew it before, whereas I only knew it after I'd been given this job to do, And in one bound you were ahead of him, here you are in my house, you can see my face, hear me say that I deceived my husband, and, in all these years, you are the only person I've ever told, what more proof do you need that beside you, your boss is an ignoramus, Don't say that, it's not right, Have you any further questions to ask me, What questions, For example, if I was happy in my marriage after what happened, It's irrelevant to the matter in hand, Nothing is irrelevant, just as all the names are in your boss's head, so one person's life is everyone's life, You're very wise, So I should be, I've lived a long time, Compared with you I know nothing and I'm fifty, You'd be amazed how much you learn between fifty and seventy, Is that how old you are, A bit more actually, Were you happy after what happened, So you are interested, It's just that I don't know much about other people's lives, Just like your boss, just like your Central Registry, Yes, I suppose so, Well, I was forgiven, if that's what you mean, Forgiven, Yes, it often happens, forgive one another, as they say, The usual phrase is love one another, It comes to the same thing, you forgive each other because you love each other, you love each other because you forgive each other, you're just a child, you have a lot to learn, So I see, Are you married, No, You've never lived with a woman, No, I couldn't really say I've lived with one, Just passing relationships, temporary, Not even that, I live

47

alone, when I feel the need, I do what everyone else does, I look for a woman and I pay, You do realise that you're answering my questions, Yes, but I don't mind now, perhaps that's how you learn, by answering questions, Now I'm going to tell you something, Go on, I'll begin by asking you if you know how many people there are in a marriage, Two, a man and a woman, No, there are three people in a marriage, there's the woman, there's the man, and there's what I call the third person, the most important, the person who is composed of the man and woman together, I've never thought of that, For example, if one of the two commits adultery, the person who is most hurt, who receives the deepest cut, however incredible it may seem, is not the other person, but that other "other" which is the couple, not one person, but two, And can you really live with that person made up of two people, I have enough trouble living with myself, The most common thing in marriage is to see the man or the woman, or both, each in their own way, trying to destroy the third person that they form together, the one that resists, that wants to survive regardless, The arithmetic's too complicated for me, Get married, find a woman, and then you'll see, Oh, no, it's too late for me, Don't bet on it, who knows what you might find when you reach the end of your mission, or whatever you called it, The doubts I was ordered to clear up are the Central Registry's doubts not mine, And what doubts are those, if you don't mind my asking, It's a confidential matter, I can't tell you, A fat lot of good your confidentiality does you, Senhor José, you'll soon have to leave, and you'll do so knowing exactly what you knew when you came, nothing, That's true, and Senhor José shook his head despondently.

The woman looked at him as if she were studying him, then she asked, How long have you been involved in this investigation, Well, to be honest, I only started today, but the Registrar is going to be furious when I turn up empty-handed, he's a very impatient person, That would be a most unfair way to treat a clerk who, it seems, doesn't mind working on Saturdays, Well, I had nothing else to do, it was a way of catching up on my work, You didn't do much catching up, I'm going to have to think about it, Ask your boss's advice, that's why he's a boss, You don't know him, he doesn't allow people to ask him questions, he just gives the orders, So, what now, Like I said, I'm going to have to think about it, Then think, You really don't know anything, where they went to live when they left here, the letter you received must have had the sender's address on it, it must have, Yes, but that letter doesn't exist anymore, You didn't answer the letter, No, Why, Given the choice between killing something and letting it die, I chose killing, in the figurative sense, of course, It seems I've come to a dead end, Perhaps not, What do you mean, Give me a piece of paper and something to write with. Senhor José passed her a pencil with trembling hands, You can write here, on the back of the card, it's a copy. The woman put on her glasses and scribbled a few words, There you are, it's not their address or anything, it's just the name of the road where the school was that my goddaughter used to go to after they moved, perhaps you'll find out what you need to know there, assuming the school still exists of course. Senhor José's mind was divided between personal gratitude for the favour and official irritation because it had taken so long. He dealt with the gratitude by saying Thank you, and nothing more, and then in a moderate tone, he allowed his irritation to show, I can't understand why you took so long to give me the address of the school, knowing that any information, however insignificant, would be of vital importance to me, Don't exaggerate, Nevertheless, I'm very grateful to you and I say that on my own behalf and on behalf of the Central Registry which I represent, but I insist on knowing why you took so long to give me that address, It's very simple, I don't have anyone to talk to. Senhor José looked at the woman, she was looking at him, there's no point wasting words in explaining the expression in their eyes, all that matters is what he managed to say after a silence, Neither do I. Then the woman got up out of her chair, opened the drawer of the sideboard behind her and took out what seemed to be an album, Photographs, thought Senhor José, startled. The woman opened the album and leafed through it, in a few seconds she found what she was looking for, the photograph wasn't stuck in, it was only held in place by four little cardboard corners, Here you are, take it, she said, it's the only one I have of her, just don't ask me if I've got any photographs of the parents, I won't. Senhor José held out a tremulous hand and received a black-and-white photo of a girl of eight or nine, a small, thin, probably pale face, serious eyes beneath eyebrow-length bangs, a mouth trying to smile but failing, and fixed like that. Senhor José, being a sensitive soul, felt his own eyes fill with tears, No one would think you worked for the Central Registry, said the woman, Well, I do, he said, Would you like a cup of coffee, That would be very nice.

They didn't talk much while they were drinking their coffee and nibbling biscuits, just a few words about how quickly cruel time passed, It passes and we don't even notice, It was morning only a moment ago and now it's nearly dark, in fact, the afternoon was drawing to a close, but perhaps they were talking about life, about their lives, about life in general, that's what happens when we listen to a conversation and don't pay attention, the most important things always escape us. The coffee was finished, the words were finished, Senhor José got up and said, I must be going, thank you for the photograph and the address of the school, the woman said, Well, if you're ever passing this way again, then she accompanied him to the door, he held out his hand, and said, Thank you very much, and like a gentleman from another age, he raised her hand to his lips, it was then that the woman smiled mischievously and said, It might be a good idea to try looking her up in the phone book.

Such was the force of this blow that, once his disoriented feet were out in the street again, it took Senhor José a while to realise that a very fine, almost diaphanous rain was falling on him, the sort of rain that soaks you vertically and horizontally, and from every other angle as well. It might be a good idea to try looking her up in the phone book, the old girl had remarked slyly as they said goodbye, and each of those words, innocent in themselves, incapable of offending even the most susceptible of creatures, was transformed in an instant into an aggressive insult, a proof of insufferable stupidity, as if, throughout that conversation, so rich in emotions after a certain point, she had been observing him coldly and had come to the conclusion that this awkward official sent by the Central Registry to seek out things both distant and hidden was incapable of seeing what was right in front of his eyes and within reach of his hands. Having no hat or umbrella, Senhor José received the fine spray of water directly on his face, the swirling confusion of drops resembling the disagreeable thoughts coming and going inside his head, but all of them, he noticed, were circling round one central point, still barely discernible, but which, little by little, was becoming clearer. It was true that he hadn't even thought of doing something as simple and everyday as consulting the telephone book in order to find out both the telephone number and the address of the person whose name they were listed under. If he wanted to discover the unknown woman's whereabouts, that should have been his first action, in less than a minute he would have found out where she was, then, on the pretext of clearing up some imaginary query in her file at the Central Registry, he could arrange to meet her at her home, saying that he wanted to save her having to pay a bit of tax, for example, and then, immediately afterwards, risking everything with one bold gesture, or days later, when he had gained her confidence, saying to her, Tell me about your life. He hadn't done that, and although he was fairly ignorant of the arts of psychology and the secrets of the unconscious, he was beginning now, with considerable accuracy, to understand why he hadn't. Let's imagine a hunter, he was saying to himself, let's imagine a hunter who has lovingly gathered together his equipment, the rifle, the cartridge belt, the bag of provisions, the canteen of water, the net bag to collect his booty in, his walking shoes, let's imagine him setting out with his dogs, de-termined, confident, prepared, as one should be on these hunt-ing expeditions, for a long day, and then, as he turns the next corner, he comes across a flock of partridges right by his house, ready and willing to be killed, and although they take flight, however many of them are brought down, they still don't actually fly away, to the delight and surprise of the dogs, who have never in their lives seen manna fall from heaven in such quantities. What interest could such an easy kill have for the hunter, with those partridges offering themselves up, so to speak, to his gun, wondered Senhor José, and he gave the obvi-ous answer, None. That's what has happened to me, he added, inside my head, and probably inside everyone's head, there must be a kind of autonomous thought that thinks for itself, that decides things without the participation of any other thought, it is the thought we have known for as long as we have known ourselves and which we address familiarly as "tu," the one that allows itself to be guided by us in order to take us where we think we consciously want to go, but that, in the end, might be being led along an entirely different path, in another direction, and not towards the nearest corner, where a flock of partridges is waiting for us all unknowing, although we know that it is the search that gives meaning to any find and that one often has to travel a long way in order to arrive at what is near. The clarity of this thought, whether the former or the latter, the special thought or the habitual one, the truth that, once you've arrived, it matters little how you arrived there, was so dazzling that Senhor José stopped, stunned, in the middle of the pavement, wrapped in the misty drizzle and in the light of a street lamp that happened to come on at that very moment. Then, from the depths of a contrite and grateful soul, he regretted the evil, unmerited thoughts, those all too conscious thoughts he had heaped upon the kind old lady in the ground-floor apartment, when in truth he was in her debt, not only for the address of the school and for the photo, but also for the full and perfect explanation of a process that apparently had no explanation. And since she had left hanging in the air that invitation to go back and see her, If you're ever passing this way again, those were her words, clear enough for her not to bother with the rest of the phrase, he promised himself that he would knock on her door again one of these days, both to tell her how his researches were going and to surprise her with the revelation of his real reason for not consulting the phone book. Obviously this would mean having to confess to her that the letter of authority was false, that the search had not been ordered by the Central Registry, but was his own idea and, inevitably, tell her about everything else too. Everything else was his collection of famous people, his fear of heights, the age-blackened documents, the spiders' webs, the monotonous shelves of the living, the chaos of the dead, the frowsty smell, the dust, the despair, and finally, the record card which, for some reason, had got stuck to the others, So that it and the name it bore would not be forgotten, The name of the little girl I have with me, he realised, and had not the powdery rain continued to fall from the skies, he would have taken the photo out of his pocket to look at it. If he was ever to describe to anyone what the Central Registry was like inside, it would be to that lady in the ground-floor apartment. It's a matter that only time can resolve, thought Senhor José. At that precise moment, time brought him the bus that would take him near to his house, it was full of drenched people, men and women of various ages and shapes, some young, some old, some younger, some older. The Central Registry knew them all, knew their names, where they had been born and who their parents were, it counted up and counted off their days one by one, that woman, for example, with her eyes closed, the one with her head resting on the window, must be what, thirty-five, thirty-six, that was all Senhor José needed for his imagination to take wing, And what if she's the woman I'm looking for, it wasn't, in fact, impossible, in this life we meet strangers all the time, and you just have to resign yourself to it, we can't go around asking everyone, What's your name, and then produce a record card from our pocket to see if that is the person we want. Two stops later, the woman got off, then she stood on the pavement waiting for the bus to continue its journey, she probably wanted to cross to the other side of the road and, since she wasn't carrying an umbrella, Senhor José could see her face full on despite the tiny raindrops clinging to the bus windows, there was a moment when, perhaps impatient because the bus was taking a while to draw away, she looked up, and that was when her eyes met his. Both he and she stayed like that until the bus set off again, they stayed like that for as long as they could see each other, Senhor José craning and turning his neck, the woman following his movements from where she was standing, perhaps asking herself, I wonder who that is, he saying to himself, It's her.

It wasn't very far from Senhor José's stop to the Central Registry, a most praiseworthy show of consideration on the part of the transport services for the people who had to go to the Central Registry to deal with various papers, but despite that, Senhor José arrived home soaked from head to foot. He quickly took off his raincoat, changed his trousers, socks and shoes, rubbed his dripping hair with a towel, and, while he was doing all this, continued his interior dialogue, It's her, It's not her, It could be, It could, but it wasn't, But what if it was, You'll know that when you find the woman on the card, If it was her, I'll say we've already met, that we saw each other on the bus, She won't remember, If I find her soon, she's bound to remember, But you don't want to find her soon, perhaps not even later, if you really wanted to you would look up her name in the telephone book, that's where you should start, I forgot, The phone book's in there, I don't feel like going into the Central Registry just now, You're afraid of the dark, Not at all, I know that darkness like the back of my hand, You don't even know the back of your hand, If that's what you think, then just let me wallow in my own ignorance, after all, the birds don't know why they sing, but they still sing, You're very poetic, No, just sad, Hardly surprising considering the life you lead, Imagine the woman on the bus was the woman on the card, imagine I never find her again, that that was the one and only time, that my destiny was there and I let it slip by, You have one way of finding out, What, Do what the old girl in the ground-floor apartment said, Watch your tongue, please, But she is an old girl, She's just getting on a bit, Oh, enough of your hypocrisy, we're all getting on a bit, the question is how much, if it's not much, you're young, if it's a lot, you're old, the rest is just idle twaddle, Oh, forget it, All right, Anyway, I'm going to look in the phone book, That's what I've been telling you to do for the last half hour. In pyjamas and slippers and wrapped in a blanket, Senhor

José went into the Central Registry. His unusual outfit made him feel rather uneasy, as if he were being disrespectful to the venerable archives, to that eternal yellowish light which, like a moribund sun, hovered above the Registrar's desk. The telephone book was there, on one corner of the table, you were not allowed to consult it without permission, even if it was an official call, and now, as he had done before, Senhor José could sit down at the desk, it's true that he had done so only once before, in a peerless moment that had seemed to him triumphant and glorious, but this time he didn't dare, perhaps because he was improperly dressed, out of an absurd fear that someone might surprise him like that, but what other living being, apart from him, wandered about there after hours. He thought it might be best to take the phone book with him, he would feel more comfortable at home, without the threatening presence of those towering shelves that seemed about to hurl themselves down from the shadowy ceiling, up there where the spiders weave and gorge. He shuddered as if the dusty, sticky webs really were falling on him and he very nearly made the rash mistake of picking up the phone book without first taking the precaution of measuring exactly the distances that separated it, above and to the side, from the edge of the table, and not just the distances, the precise angles too, fortunately, though, the Registrar's geometrical and topographical inclinations showed a clear preference for right angles and parallel lines. He returned home in the certainty that, shortly afterwards, when he replaced the phone book, it would be in exactly the right place, to the millimetre, and that the Registrar would not have to give orders to his deputies to find out who had used it, how, when and why. Up until the very last moment, he was still expecting something to happen that would prevent him from taking the book, a murmur, a suspicious creaking, a bright light emerging suddenly out of the mortuary depths of the archives, but there was absolute quiet, not even the sound of the woodworm's tiny grinding jaws.

Now, Senhor José, with the blanket round his shoulders, is sitting at his own table, in front of him is the telephone book, he opens it at the beginning and lingers over the instructions, the codes, the price tariffs, as if that were what he was looking for. After a few moments, a sudden, unwitting impulse makes him leaf rapidly through the pages, forwards and backwards, until he stops on the page where the name of the unknown woman should be. Either it isn't there or his eyes won't see it. No, it's not there. It should come after that name, and it doesn't. It should come before that name, and it doesn't. Just as I said, thought Senhor José, and it wasn't true that he had said any such thing, that's just a way of proving oneself right in the eyes of the world, of giving expression, in this case, to joy, any police investigator would have shown his irritation by thumping the table, not Senhor José, Senhor José wears the ironic smile of someone who, having been sent to look for something he knew did not exist, returns from the search with these words on his lips, Just as I said, either she hasn't got a phone or she doesn't want her name to appear in the book. He was so pleased that, immediately after that, without bothering to weigh the pros and cons, he looked for the name of the unknown woman's father, and that was there. Not a fibre of his being trembled. On the contrary, determined now to burn all his bridges, drawn on by an impulse known only to the true researcher, he looked for the name of the man whom the unknown woman had divorced, and he was there too. If he had a map of the city he would be able to mark the first five established staging posts, two in the street where the girl in the photo had been born, another at the school, and now these, the beginning of a design made up, like that of all lives, of broken lines, crossings, intersections, but never bifurcations, because the spirit never goes anywhere without its legs, and the body would be incapable of moving without the wings of the spirit. He noted down the addresses, then what he would need to buy, a large map of the city, a thick piece of cardboard of the same size on which to fix it, a box of pins with coloured heads, red so they could be seen from a distance, for lives are like paintings, you always need to look at them from four paces away, even if one day you manage to touch their skin, catch their smell, taste them. Senhor José was quite calm, he wasn't troubled by the fact that he now knew where the unknown woman's parents and former husband lived, the husband, curiously enough, lived quite close to the Central Registry, obviously, sooner or later, Senhor José would go and knock at their doors, but only when he felt the moment had arrived, only when the moment told him, Now. He closed the phone book, returned it to the boss's desk, to the exact place where he had taken it from, and he went back home. According to the clock, it was suppertime, but the emotions of the day must have distracted his stomach, which gave no signs of impatience. He sat down again, pulled the blanket around him, tugging at the corners so as to cover his legs, and took up the notebook he had bought at the stationer's. It was time to begin making notes on how the search was going, the people he had met, the conversations he had had, his thoughts, his plans and tactics for an investigation that promised to be complex, The steps taken by someone in search of someone else, he thought, and the truth is, that although the process was only in its early stages, he already had a lot to say, If this were a novel, he murmured as he opened the notebook, the conversation with the lady in the ground-floor apartment would be a chapter in itself. He picked up a pen to begin, but stopped halfway, his eyes caught the paper on which he had written down the addresses, there was something he hadn't considered before, the perfectly plausible hypothesis that the unknown woman, after she got divorced, had gone to live with her parents, the equally possible hypothesis that her husband had left the apartment, leaving the telephone in his name. If that was so, and bearing in mind that the street in question was near the Central Registry, the woman on the bus might well have been the same one. The inner dialogue seemed to want to start up again, It was, It wasn't, It was, It wasn't, but this time, Senhor José paid no heed to it and, bending over the notebook, he began to write the first words, Thus, I went into the building, went up the stairs to the second floor and listened at the door of the apartment where the unknown woman was born, then I heard a little baby crying, it could be her child I thought, and, at the same time, I heard a woman crooning to it softly, It must be her, later, I found out that it wasn't.

Contrary to what people might think when viewing these things from the outside, life is not necessarily easy in a government department, certainly not in this Central Registry of Births, Marriages and Deaths, where, since time which cannot be described as immemorial simply because the Registry contains a record of everything and everyone, thanks to the persistent efforts of an unbroken line of great Registrars, all that is most sublime and most trivial about public office has been brought together, the qualities that make of the civil servant a creature apart, both usufructuary and dependent of the physical and mental space defined by the reach of his pen nib. Put simply, and with a view in this preamble to a more exact understanding of the general facts considered in the abstract, Senhor José has a problem to solve. Knowing how difficult it had been to squeeze out of the rule-bound reluctance of the hierarchy one miserable half hour off, which meant that he was not caught in flagrante by the husband of the young woman in the second-floor apartment, we can imagine his current distress as, night and day, he racks his brain for some convincing excuse that would allow him to ask for not one hour, but two, not two, but three hours, which is probably the amount of time he will need if he is to carry out a useful search of the school's archives. The effects of this constant, obsessive disquiet soon revealed themselves in mistakes at work, in lack of attention, in sudden bouts of drowsiness during the day due to insomnia, in short, Senhor José, until then considered by his various superiors to be a competent, methodical and dedicated civil servant, began to be the object of severe warnings, reprimands and calls to order that only served to confuse him all the more, and, needless to say, the way he was carrying on, he could be absolutely sure of a negative response if, at some point, he could actually bring himself to ask for the longed-for time off. Things reached such a pitch that, after fruitless analysis by senior clerks and deputies in turn, they had no option but to bring the matter to the notice of the Registrar, who, at first, found the whole business so absurd that he could not understand what all the fuss was about. The fact that a civil servant should have so grievously neglected his duties made any benevolent tendency towards reaching an exculpatory decision impossible, it constituted a grave offence against the working traditions of the Central Registry, something that could only be justified by some grave illness. When the delinquent was brought into his presence, that was exactly what the Registrar asked Senhor José, Are you ill, I don't think so, sir, Well, if you're not ill, how do you explain your recent poor standard of work, I don't know, sir, perhaps it's because I haven't been sleeping well, In that case, you are ill, No, it's just that I'm not sleeping very well, If you're not sleeping well, it's because you're ill, a healthy person always sleeps well, unless he has something weighing on his conscience, some reprehensible mistake, the sort that your conscience cannot forgive, for conscience is most important, Yes, sir, If your errors at work are caused by insomnia and if your insomnia is being caused by a guilty conscience, then we have to discover what your mistake was, I haven't made any mistakes, sir, Impossible, the only person here who doesn't make mistakes is me, but what's wrong, why are you staring at the telephone book, Sorry, sir, I got distracted, A bad sign, you know perfectly well that you must always look at me when I'm talking to you, it's in the disciplinary regulations, I'm the only one who has the right to look away, Yes, sir, Now what was your mistake, I don't know, sir, That only makes matters worse, forgotten mistakes are always the worst ones, I've fulfilled all my duties, The information I have regarding your conduct is satisfactory, but that only serves to show that your recent poor professional performance was not the consequence of some forgotten mistake, but of a recent mistake, one you have only just made, My conscience is clear, Consciences keep silent more often than they should, that's why laws were created, Yes, sir, Now I have to make a decision, Yes, sir, Indeed, I already have, Yes, sir, I'm giving you a day's suspension, Is that just a suspension of salary, sir, or is it also a suspension from work, asked Senhor José, seeing a glimmer of hope, Of salary, of course, we can't have work being any more disrupted than it already has been, only a while ago I gave you half an hour off, you surely weren't expecting your bad behaviour to be rewarded with a whole day's leave, No sir, For your sake, I hope this serves as a lesson, and that, in the interests of the Central Registry, you soon go back to being the punctilious worker you always have been up until now, Yes, sir, That's all, you may go back to your desk.

Desperate, close to tears, his nerves in tatters, Senhor José did as he was told. During the few minutes that the difficult conversation with his boss had lasted, the work had piled up on his desk, as if the other clerks, his colleagues, taking advantage of his precarious disciplinary situation, had chosen to punish him on their own account. There were also several people waiting their turn to be served. They were standing before him not by chance nor because they thought, when they came into the Central Registry, that the absent clerk would perhaps be a kinder, more welcoming sort than the others they could see behind the counter, but because the other clerks had told them to go there. Since staff regulations stated that attending to clients had absolute priority over any work you might have on your desk, Senhor José approached the counter, knowing that, behind him, papers would continue to rain down. He was lost. Now, after the Registrar's angry warning and subsequent punishment, even if he were to invent the impossible birth of a child or the dubious death of a relative, he could abandon any hopes he might have had that, in the near future, they would give him permission to leave early or to arrive late, even if it were only a matter of an hour, half an hour, even a minute. In this house of archives, memory is tenacious, slow to forget, so slow that it will never entirely forget anything. Ten years hence, should Senhor José suffer a lapse of concentration, however insignificant, you can be sure that someone will immediately remind him, in detail, of these unfortunate days. Probably that was what the Registrar meant when he said that the worst errors are those that are apparently forgotten. For Senhor José, frantic with work, tormented by thoughts, the rest of the day was utter torture. While one part of his conscious mind was giving clear explanations to members of the public, filling in and stamping documents, filing away record cards, the other part was monotonously cursing the chance or coincidence that had somehow transformed into morbid curiosity something that would not even cause a flicker in the imagination of a sensible, well-balanced person. The boss is right, thought Senhor José, the interests of the Central Registry should come before all else, if I led a proper, normal life, I certainly would not, at my age, have started collecting actors, ballerinas, bishops and football players, it's stupid, useless, ridiculous, a fine legacy I'll leave when I die, just as well I haven't got anyone to leave it to really, it probably all stems from living alone, now if I had a wife. When he reached this point, his thoughts stopped, then took another route, a narrow, uncertain path, at the start of which he could see the picture of a little girl, at the end of which she would be, if she were there, a real person, a grown-up woman, an adult, thirty-six and divorced, What do I want her for, what would I do with her if I met her. The thought broke off again and abruptly retraced its steps, And how exactly do you think you're going to find her, if they won't give you time off to go and look for her, it asked him, and he didn't reply, at that precise moment he was busy telling the last person in the queue that the death certificate he had asked for would be ready the following day.

Some questions, however, are very determined, they don't give up, and this one returned to the attack when, weary in body, exhausted in spirit, Senhor José finally went home. He had thrown himself down on the bed like a rag, he wanted to sleep, to forget his boss's face, the unfair punishment, but the question came and lay down next to him, insinuating in a whisper, You can't go looking for her, they won't let you, this time it was impossible to pretend he was busy talking to a member of the public, he still tried to ignore it, though, he said he'd have to find a way and that if he didn't, then he would just give up, but the question would not let go, You give in awfully easily, if that's the case, then it wasn't worth forging a letter of authority and making that nice, unhappy lady in the ground-floor apartment talk about her sinful past, it shows a lack of respect for other people visiting their homes like that and probing into their intimate lives. The allusion to the letter made him suddenly sit up on the edge of the bed, frightened. He had it in his jacket pocket, he had been walking around with it all these days, just imagine if for some reason or other he had dropped it, or, with the state his nerves were in, if he had fainted, become unconscious, and one of his colleagues, not with any ill intention, had, as he unbuttoned his jacket to let him breathe, seen the white envelope with the official Central Registry stamp on it, and said, What's this, and then a senior clerk and then a deputy and then the director. Senhor José didn't want to think about what would happen next, he leapt up, went over to his jacket, which was hanging on the back of a chair, took out the letter, and, looking anxiously about him, wondered where the devil he could possibly hide it. None of the furniture could be locked, all his sparse belongings were within easy reach of any interfering busybody who might enter. It was then that he noticed his collections lined up in the wardrobe, there lay the solution to this difficulty. He found the bishop's file and stuck the envelope inside, a bishop never excites much curiosity however pious his reputation, not like a cyclist or a Formula One racing driver. Relieved, he went back to bed, but the question was there waiting for him, You didn't resolve anything, the problem isn't the letter, it makes no difference whether you hide it or show it, that won't lead you to the woman, Look, I said I'll find a way, I doubt it, the boss has got you bound hand and foot, he won't let you take a step, Then I'll wait until things calm down, And then, I don't know, I'll think of something, You could resolve the matter right now, How, You could phone her parents, say that you're phoning on behalf of the Central Registry and ask them to give you her address, I can't do that, Tomorrow you go to the woman's house, what kind of conversation you'll have I can't imagine, but at least you'll get your peace of mind back, I probably won't want to talk to her when she's there in front of me, Well, in that case, why are you looking for her, why are you investigating her life, I collect articles about the bishop too, but I don't particularly want to talk to him either, That seems absurd to me, It is absurd, but it's about time I did something absurd in my life, Do you mean to tell me that if you do manage to find this woman, she won't even know you were looking for her, Probably, Why, I can't explain, Anyway, you're not even going to get to visit the girl's school, schools are like the Central Registry, they're closed on weekends, I can go into the Central Registry whenever I want, That's hardly a remarkable achievement given that the door of your house opens on to it, You've obviously never had to go in there yourself, I go wherever you go and see whatever you see,

Do continue, I will, but you are not going to get into that school, We'll see. Senhor José got up, it was time for supper, if the extremely light meals he usually ate at night merited the name. While he was eating, he was thinking, then, still thinking, he washed the plate, the glass and the cutlery, gathered up the crumbs fallen on the tablecloth, and, as if that gesture had been the inevitable conclusion to his thoughts, he opened the door that led out into the street. Opposite him, on the other side of the pavement, was a telephone box, a stone's throw away if you like, just twenty paces and he would reach the end of a thread that would carry his voice to her, the same thread would bring him an answer, and there, in one way or another, his search would end, he could calmly go back home, win back his boss's trust, and then the world, spinning in its own invisible tracks, would resume its usual orbit, the deep peace of someone who simply awaits the hour when all things will be done, always supposing that those words, so often spoken and repeated, have any real significance. Senhor José did not cross the road, he put on his jacket and his raincoat and went out.

He had to change buses twice before he reached his destination. The school was a long, two-storey building with dormer windows, separated from the street by high railings. The intervening space, a strip of land with a sprinkling of rather small trees, was probably used as a playground by the pupils. There was no light anywhere. Senhor José looked about him, even though it wasn't that late, the street was deserted, that's the good thing about these out-of-the-way places, especially if it's not the weather to have your windows open, the locals huddle inside their houses, and besides, there's nothing to see outside. Senhor José walked to the end of the road, crossed to the other sidewalk and walked slowly back towards the school like someone out enjoying a stroll in the evening cool and who has no one at home waiting for him. Right by the main door, he bent down as if he had just noticed that his shoelace had come untied, a tired old trick, no one's fooled by it, but it can still be used for want of something better when the imagination can't come up with any alternative. With his elbow, he nudged the gate, which moved a little, it wasn't locked. Methodically, Senhor José tied a second knot over the first, got up, stamped his foot on the ground to test the firmness of the knots, and continued on his way, more briskly now, as if he had suddenly remembered that he did, in fact, have someone waiting for him.

Senhor José lived through the days until the weekend as if he were watching his own dreams. In the Central Registry no one saw him make a single mistake, he was never distracted, he never once muddled one document up with another, he got through enormous quantities of work which, at any other time, would have made him protest, silently of course, against the inhuman treatment of which clerks have always been victims, and all this was carried out and borne without a word, without a murmur. The Registrar glanced at him a couple of times from a distance, we know that he was not in the habit of looking at subordinates, far less at subordinates of such lowly rank, but Senhor José's spiritual concentration reached such a degree of intensity that it was impossible not to notice it in the perennially paralysed atmosphere of the Central Registry. On Friday, when the office was closing, the Registrar, with no prior warning, broke all the rules, scorned all the traditions, leaving the staff in a state of shock, for, as he passed Senhor José on his way out, he asked him, Are you feeling better. Senhor José said that he was, that he was much better, that he had not suffered from insomnia again, and the Registrar said, That conversation of ours must have done you good, he looked as if he were going to add something more, some idea that had suddenly occurred to him, but he closed his mouth and left, he had said quite enough, to cancel the punishment that had been imposed would be to subvert discipline. The other clerks, the senior clerks and even the deputies looked at Senhor José as if seeing him for the first time, the director's few words had made him a different person, it was rather like what happens when a child is taken to be baptised, one child is taken there, quite another child is brought back. Senhor José finished tidying his desk, then awaited his turn to leave, the rule was that the first to leave was always the longest-serving deputy registrar, then the senior clerks, then the clerks, always in order of length of service, it was left to the other deputy to close the door. Unusually, Senhor José did not immediately walk around the Central Registry building in order to go into his house, he set off into the nearby streets, he went to three different shops and in each of them he made a purchase, half a kilo of lard in one, a soft towel in another, and a third small object, a mere trifle, that fitted in the palm of his hand, and this he put in his jacket pocket because there was no need for it to be wrapped. Only then did he go home. It was long past midnight when he went out again. At that hour, there were few buses around, only very infrequently would one appear, which is why, for the second time since he had encountered the unknown woman's card, Senhor José decided to take a taxi. He felt a kind of vibration in the pit of his stomach, like a hum, a frenzy, but his mind remained calm, or rather, he was incapable of thought. There was a moment when Senhor José, hunched in the back of the taxi as if afraid of being seen, still tried to imagine what might happen to him, the consequences it could have for his life, if the action he was about to undertake should go wrong, but the thought hid behind a wall, I'm not coming out, it said, then he understood, because he knew himself well, he knew that the thought wanted to protect him, not from fear, but from cowardice. When they neared his destination, he asked the taxi to stop, he would walk the remaining short distance. He had his hands in his pockets, holding beneath his buttoned-up raincoat the packages containing the lard and the towel. Just as he was turning the corner into the street where the school was, a few drops of rain fell on him, which, when he was almost at the gate, immediately became a great torrent raking noisily along the pavement. It has been said, from classical times onwards, that fortune favours the bold, in this case, the intermediary charged with that responsibility was the rain, or, in other words, heaven, anyone passing at that late hour would certainly be more concerned with trying to avoid a sudden drenching than watching the actions of a man in a raincoat who, given his apparent age, had escaped from the shower with quite unexpected speed, he was there a minute ago, now he's gone. Sheltering beneath one of the trees inside the railings, his heart beating wildly, Senhor José was breathing hard, amazed at the agility with which he had moved, he who, when it came to physical exercise, went no further than climbing to the top of the ladder in the Central Registry, and God knows he hated that. He was out of sight of the street, and he believed that, by moving cautiously from tree to tree, he could reach the school door without anyone outside seeing him. He had persuaded himself that there was no guard inside, in the first place, because of the absence of light, both the other day and now, and in the second place, because schools, except for certain very particular, exceptional reasons, are not places that are deemed to be worth burgling. His reasons were definitely exceptional and particular, which is why he had gone there armed with half a kilo of lard, a towel and a glass cutter, for that was the object that had not required wrapping. Meanwhile, he had to think carefully about what he was going to do. Gaining entry at the front would be imprudent, someone living in one of the upper storeys on the opposite side of the street might be peering out at the rain that was still falling heavily and see a man breaking one of the school's windows, there are plenty of people who wouldn't lift a finger to prevent a violent act being carried out, on the contrary, they would let the curtain fall and return to bed, saying, That's their business, but there are other people who would save the world if only the world would let them, they would immediately call the police and rush out onto the verandah shouting, Stop thief, a harsh epithet which Senhor José does not deserve, at worst forger, but only we know about that. I'll go around to the rear of the building, it might be easier there, thought Senhor José, and perhaps he was right, so often the backs of buildings are badly cared for, with piles of old junk, boxes awaiting re-use, empty paint cans, broken bricks from building work, all that anyone wanting to improvise a ladder, reach a window and climb in could possibly desire. In fact, Senhor José did find some of these useful objects, but, as he could tell by touch, they were all very neatly arranged underneath the porch, against the wall, in the darkness, and it would take too much time and effort to select and carry away the things that would best suit the structural needs of the pyramid he would have to scale. If I could just get onto the roof, he muttered, and, in principle, the idea was an excellent one, since there was a window about two feet above where the porch joined the wall, Even so, it's not going to be easy, the roof is very steep and with this rain it's bound to be slippery, treacherous, he thought. Senhor José felt himself beginning to lose heart, that's what happens when someone has no experience in burgling, when someone has not had the benefit of lessons from master climbers, he hadn't even thought to come and inspect the place beforehand, he could have done so the other day when he noticed that the gate wasn't locked, he must have thought himself so fortunate on that occasion that he preferred not to push his luck. He had in his pocket the small flashlight that he had used in the Central Registry to be able to read the record cards, but he didn't want to turn it on here, a shape in the darkness that might pass more or less unseen is one thing, a moving circle of light betraying his presence is quite another, quite different, much worse, declaring Look, here I am. He took shelter under the porch, he could hear the rain drumming tirelessly on the roof, and he didn't know what to do. There were trees on this side too, taller and leafier than those in the front, if there were any other buildings hidden behind them, he couldn't see them from where he was standing, Therefore, they can't see me either, thought Senhor José, and after hesitating a moment longer, he turned on his flashlight and moved it rapidly from side to side. He had been absolutely right, the objects in the school junkyard were very carefully disposed and arranged, like neatly dovetailing bits of machinery. He turned on the flashlight again, this time pointing the beam upwards. Lying across the junk but apart from the other things, as if it were something that was occasionally put to use, was a stepladder. Either because of the unexpected nature of the discovery, or because of a sudden, random memory of the heights he had to scale in the Central Registry, Senhor José felt a rush, a popular and expressive phrase in current usage that removes the need for the word "vertigo" to be articulated by mouths not born for it, and thus aids communication. The stepladder wasn't long enough to reach the window, but it would do to climb onto the porch and, from then on, he was in God's hands.

Thus invoked, God decided to help Senhor José out of his difficulty, which is not so very extraordinary when one considers the enormous number of burglars who, ever since the world began, have been fortunate enough to return from their burglaries, not only laden with goods, but also unharmed, that is, having suffered no divine punishment. Providence determined that the corrugated concrete sheets that formed the roof of the porch, as well as having a rough finish, also had on the lower edges a projecting edge whose attractive, ornamental qualities the factory designer had, imprudently, been unable to resist. Thanks to this, and despite the steepness of the porch roof, Senhor José, with a foot here, a hand there, moaning, sighing, catching his fingernails, scuffing the toes of his shoes, managed to drag himself up. Now all he had to do was get in.

The moment has come to reveal that the methods used by Senhor José, as cat burglar and housebreaker, are completely outmoded, not to say antiquated, even archaic. A long time ago, not even he can remember in which book or newspaper, he had read that lard, a soft towel and a glass cutter were the essential tools for anyone trying to enter through a window with malicious intent, and, in blind faith, he had equipped himself with these unusual aids. He could, of course, in order to hasten the task, have simply smashed the glass, but he was afraid, when he was planning the break-in, that the unavoidable sound of splintering glass would alarm the neighbourhood, and although it was true that the bad weather, with its own natural noises, might diminish the risk, it would be best to keep strictly to the discipline of the method. So, resting his feet on that providential edge, his knees digging into the rough ridges of the roof, Senhor José started cutting the glass with the diamond blade, along the frame. Then, breathing hard from the effort and the awkwardness of his position, he wiped the glass as best he could with his handkerchief, to assist the desired adhesive qualities of the lard, or, rather, what remained of the lard, since his violent efforts in climbing the steep slope had left the package a shapeless, sticky mass with inevitable consequences for the cleanliness of the clothes he had on. Even so, he managed to spread an acceptably thick layer of lard all over the window, then over that, as carefully as possible, he laid the towel which, after endless contortions, he finally managed to extract from his raincoat pocket. Now he would have to calculate precisely the force of the blow required, not so weak as to require repetition, nor so strong that the glass would fail to cling to the towel. Holding the upper part of the towel against the window frame with his left hand so that it would not slip, Senhor José made a fist of his right hand, brought his arm back and dealt the glass a sharp blow that fortunately produced only the dull muted sound of a gun fitted with a silencer. He had got it right the first time, a notable achievement for a beginner. One or two small fragments of glass fell inside, nothing more, but that didn't matter, there was no one in there. For a few seconds, despite the rain, Senhor José lay stretched out on the porch roof, recovering his strength and savouring his triumph. Then, straightening up, he reached in, fumbled for and found the window catch, dear God, the risks burglars take, opened it wide and, grasping the windowsill, his feet frantically scrabbling for non-existent footholds, he managed to lift himself up, raise one leg, then the other, and finally drop through to the other side, as lightly as a leaf falling from a tree.

Respect for the facts, and a simple moral obligation not to offend the credulity of anyone prepared to accept as plausible and coherent the difficulties of such an extraordinary exploit, demand immediate clarification of that last statement: Senhor José did not drop as lightly from the windowsill as a leaf falling from a bough. On the contrary, he fell very heavily, the way an entire tree would fall, when he could perfectly easily have lowered himself gradually down from his temporary seat until his feet touched the ground. The fall, given the thud with which he hit the ground and the subsequent succession of painful collisions, revealed to him, before his eyes could confirm the fact, that the place he had landed in was like a prolongation of the porch outside, since both places were used as a storage space for things no longer needed, although it had probably happened the other way around, this place came first and, only later, when there was no more room here, did they resort to the porch outside. Senhor José sat there for a few moments, waiting for his breathing to return to normal and for his arms and legs to stop shaking. Then he turned on the flashlight, being careful to shine it only on the floor in front of him, and he saw that, between the piled-up furniture on either side, there was a path that led to the door. It troubled him to think that the door might be locked, in which case he would have to break it down despite having none of the necessary implements and despite the ensuing noise. Outside it was still raining, everyone must be asleep, but we can't be sure, there are people who sleep so lightly that even the whine of a mosquito is enough to wake them, then they get up, go to the kitchen for a glass of water, look casually out of the window and see a black rectangular hole in the wall of the school, and perhaps think, They're awfully careless at that school, imagine leaving a window open in weather like this, or, If I remember rightly, that window was closed, it must have been blown open by the wind, no one is going to think there's a thief inside, besides, they'd be quite wrong, because Senhor José, may we remind you once again, has not come here to steal. It has just occurred to him that he should close the window so that no one outside will notice the break-in, but then he has doubts, he wonders if it wouldn't be better to leave it as it is, They'll think it was the wind or carelessness on the part of some employee, if I close it they'll immediately notice that there's no glass in it, especially since the glass is opaque, almost white. Convinced that the rest of the world follows the same deductive paths as he does, he decided to leave the window open and then began to crawl past the furniture to the door. It wasn't locked. He gave a sigh of relief, from then on, there should be no further obstacles. Now what he needed was a comfortable chair, or, even better, a sofa, to spend what remained of the night resting, if his nerves would let him sleep. As an experienced chess player, he had calculated the moves, indeed, when you're reasonably sure of the immediate objective causes, it's not that difficult to think through the range of probable and possible effects and their transformation into causes, all in turn generating effects causes effects and causes effects causes, and so on into infinity, but we know that Senhor José has no need to go quite that far. To prudent people it will seem foolish for the clerk to have walked straight into the lion's den, and then, as if that were not audacious enough, to remain there calmly for what remained of the night and all of tomorrow, with the risk of being caught in flagrante by someone with far greater deductive powers than his in the matter of open windows. It must be recognised, however, that it would have been even less sensible to have gone walking from room to room putting on lights. The combination of an open window and a light, when everyone knows that the legitimate users of a house or a school are absent, is a mental leap that anyone can make, however trusting they may be, they usually call the police.

Senhor José ached all over, he had skinned his knees, which were possibly bleeding, the discomfort caused by his trousers rubbing against them could mean nothing else, apart from that, he was soaked to the skin and dirty from head to foot. He removed his dripping raincoat and thought, If there was an inner room here, I could turn on the light, and a bathroom, a bathroom where I could have a wash, or at least wash my hands. Feeling his way, opening and shutting doors, he found what he was looking for, first, a small, windowless room lined with shelves containing stationery for school and office, pencils, notebooks, loose paper, pens, erasers, bottles of ink, rulers, set squares, bevel squares, protractors, drawing sets, tubes of glue, boxes of staples, and other things he couldn't see. With the light on he could at last examine the damage caused by his adventure. The wounds to his knees were not as bad as he had imagined, they were only superficial grazes, although still painful. In the morning, when he would no longer need to turn on lights, he would look for something that can be found in every school, the white first-aid cabinet, disinfectant, alcohol, peroxide, cotton wool, bandages, compresses, plasters, not all of which he would need. None of those remedies would be of any help to his raincoat, which is suffering from terminal grime, the lard having impregnated the fabric, Perhaps I could get the worst of it off with alcohol, thought Senhor José. Then he went in search of a bathroom, and he was lucky, he didn't have to walk very far before he found one which, to judge by its tidiness and cleanliness, must have been used by the teachers. The window, which also opened onto the back of the school, apart from having frosted glass, obviously more necessary here than in the storeroom through which he had entered, had internal wooden shutters, thanks to which Senhor José could at last turn on the light, have a wash and be able to see what he was doing. Then, more or less clean, his strength restored, he went in search of a place to sleep. Although, as a student, he had not been in a school like this, so luxurious and spacious, he knew that every school has a head teacher, and that every head teacher has a study, and that all such studies have a sofa, which was exactly what his body was crying out for. He continued to open and close doors, he looked inside rooms to which the diffuse light from outside gave a ghostly air, where the students' desks looked like lines of tombs, where the teacher's desk was like a sombre sacrificial altar, and the blackboard the place where everyone would be called to account. He saw, pinned to the walls, like the vague stains that time leaves behind on the skins of people and things, maps of the sky, of the world and of different countries, hydrographic and orographic maps of the human body, the channelling of the blood, the digestive tract, the ordering of the muscles, the communication network of the nervous system, the framework of the bones, the bellows of the lungs, the labyrinth of the brain, the section of the eye, the tangle of the genitals. The classrooms followed one after the other, along corridors that circled the school, everywhere there was the smell of chalk, almost as old as that of bodies, there are even those who believe that God, after shaping the clay from which he later made them, began by drawing a man and a woman with a stick of chalk on the surface of the first night, which is where we get the one certainty we have, that we were, are and will be dust, and that we will be lost in another night as dark as that first night. In some places the darkness was thick, absolute, as if swathed in black cloths, but in others, there hovered the vibrant shimmer of an aquarium, a phosphorescence, a blue-tinged luminosity that could not possibly come from the street lamps, or, if it did, it was transformed as it came in through the glass. Remembering the pale lamp eternally suspended above the Registrar's desk, and which the surrounding shadows always seemed about to devour, Senhor José murmured, The Central Registry is different, then he added, as if requiring a response to his own remark, Probably the greater the difference, the greater the similarity, and the greater the similarity, the greater the difference, at that moment he did not yet know how right he was.

There were only classrooms on that floor, the head teacher's study was doubtless upstairs, removed from voices, from irksome noises, from the hubbub of students entering and leaving their classes. There was a skylight above the staircase and, as he went up the stairs, he moved from darkness into light, which, in the circumstances, had no other meaning than the prosaic one of allowing us, at last, to be able to see where we are putting our feet. Chance ordained that during this new search, before he found the head teacher's study, Senhor José should first enter the school secretary's office, a room with three windows that looked out onto the street. The room contained the usual furniture found in offices of this type, there were a few desks and an equal number of chairs, as well as cupboards, filing cabinets, card indexes, Senhor José's heart leapt to see them, that was what he had come looking for, files, index cards, records, statements, notes, the history of the unknown woman when she had been a girl and an adolescent, always assuming that there were no other schools in her life after this one. Senhor José opened a card-index drawer at random, but the light coming in from the street was not bright enough for him to see what kinds of records it contained. I've got plenty of time, thought Senhor José, what I need now is to sleep. He left the office, and two doors farther along, he finally found the head teacher's study. Compared with the austerity of the Central Registry, it would be no exaggeration here to speak of luxury. The floor was carpeted, the window was hung with heavy curtains, which were drawn shut, there was a large, old-fashioned desk and a modern chair in black leather, all this Senhor José discovered because, when he opened the door and found himself in complete darkness, he did not hesitate to turn on first his flashlight, and then, the centre light. Since you could see no light coming in from the outside, no one outside would be able to see light coming from inside. The head teacher's chair was comfortable, he could sleep there, but even better was the long, broad, three-seater sofa that seemed charitably to be opening its arms to him in order to welcome and comfort his weary body. Senhor José looked at his watch, it was a few minutes before three. Seeing how late it was, for he hadn't even noticed time passing, he felt suddenly very tired, I've had enough, he thought, and, unable to contain himself, out of pure nervous exhaustion, he began to sob, to weep uncontrollably, almost convulsively, standing there, as if he were once again the little first-year student, in another school, who had committed some mischief and been summoned by the head teacher to receive his just punishment. He threw his drenched raincoat down on the floor, took his handkerchief out of his trouser pocket and raised it to his eyes, but the handkerchief was just as wet as everything else, for his entire being, from head to foot, he realised now, seemed to be oozing water, as if he were nothing but a wrung-out rag, his body was filthy, his spirit bruised, and both felt equally wretched, What am I doing here, he asked himself, but he preferred not to answer, he was afraid that, once laid bare, the reason that had brought him to this place would strike him as absurd, ridiculous, crazy. A sudden shiver ran through him. I've caught a cold already, he said out loud and immediately sneezed twice, and then, while he was blowing his nose, he found himself following the capricious paths of a thought which goes where it chooses without offering any explanation, and remembering those film actors who are constantly plunging into water fully clothed or getting drenched by torrential rain, and who never catch pneumonia, or even a simple cold, as happens every day in real life, at most, they wrap themselves up in a blanket over their wet clothes, which would seem a ludicrous thing to do if we did not know that filming is about to be interrupted so that the actor can withdraw to his dressing room, take a hot bath and don his monogrammed dressing gown. Senhor José began to take off his shoes, then he removed his jacket and shirt, pulled off his trousers and hung them on a tall hat stand that he found in one corner, now all he needed was to wrap himself up in that film's inevitable blanket, a difficult accessory to find in a head teacher's study, unless the head teacher was an elderly person, the sort whose knees get cold when he's been sitting down for any length of time. Senhor José's deductive powers led him once more to the correct conclusion, the blanket lay carefully folded on the seat of the chair. It wasn't a large blanket, it didn't cover him completely, but it would be better than lying naked all night. Senhor José turned off the centre light, used the flashlight to guide himself back to the sofa and, sighing, stretched out on it, but then immediately curled up tight in order to fit his whole body beneath the blanket. He was still shivering, he had kept on his underclothes and they were still damp, probably with sweat, from the physical effort, the rain couldn't possibly have penetrated that far. He sat up on the sofa, slipped off his vest and pants, removed his socks, then wrapped the blanket around him as if he were trying to make of it a second skin, and thus, rolled up like a wood louse, he let himself sink into the darkness of the study, waiting for a little merciful warmth that would transport him into the mercy of sleep. Both took a long time to come, driven away by a thought that would not leave him, What if someone walks in and finds me in this state, I mean, naked, they would call the police, they would handcuff him, they would ask him his name, his age and his profession, the head teacher would be the first to arrive, then the Registrar, and both would look at him with harsh, condemnatory eyes, What are you doing here, they would ask, and he would have no voice to reply with, he couldn't explain to them that he was looking for an unknown woman, they would probably all just burst out laughing, and then ask again, What are you doing here, and they would keep asking until he confessed everything, the proof of this was that they were still repeating it in his dreams when, as morning was returning to the world, Senhor José finally managed to abandon his exhausting vigil, or it abandoned him.

He woke up late, dreaming that he was back on the porch roof with the rain pounding down on him as loudly as a waterfall, and the unknown woman, in the shape of a film actress from his collection, was sitting on the window ledge with the head teacher's blanket folded in her lap, waiting for him to complete his climb, at the same time saying to him, Wouldn't it have been better to have knocked at the front door, to which he, panting, replied, I didn't know you were here, and she, I'm always here, I never go out, then, just as it seemed she was about to bend towards him in order to help him up, she suddenly disappeared, the porch disappeared with her, and only the rain remained, falling, falling without cease upon the chair belonging to the Registrar, where Senhor José saw himself sitting. His head ached slightly, but his cold didn't seem to have got any worse. A sliver of greyish light slipped in between the curtains, which meant that, contrary to appearances, they had not been completely closed. No one will have noticed, he thought, and he was right, the light of a star is brighter than bright, but not only is the greater part of it lost in space, a mere mist is enough to hide the excess light from our eyes. Even if those living on the other side of the street had come to peer out the window to see what the weather was like, they would think that the luminous thread undulating between the drops sliding down the windowpane was just the rain glittering. Still wrapped in the blanket, Senhor José slightly parted the curtains, it was his turn to find out what the weather was like. It wasn't raining at that moment, but the sky was covered by a single dark cloud, so low it seemed to touch the rooftops, like a huge tombstone. Just as well, he thought, the fewer people out in the street the better. He went over and felt the clothes he had taken off, to see if they were in a fit state to be put back on. His shirt, vest, underpants and socks were reasonably dry, his trousers rather less so, but his jacket and raincoat would take many more hours to dry. To avoid the damp-stiffened cloth rubbing against his grazed knees, he put everything on except his trousers and set off in search of the first-aid cabinet. Logically, it must be on the ground floor, near the gymnasium and the accidents that tend to happen there, next to the playground where, between classes, in games of greater or lesser violence, the students go to work off their energy and, more important, the tedium and anxiety provoked by study. He was right. After washing his wounds with peroxide, he dabbed them with some disinfectant that smelled of iodine and carefully bandaged them, using so many plasters that it looked as if he were wearing knee pads. He was still able, though, to flex his joints enough to walk. He put on his trousers and felt like a new man, although not new enough to forget the general malaise affecting his whole body. There must be something here for colds and headaches, he thought, and soon afterwards, having found what he needed, he had two pills in his stomach. He did not need to take any precautions to avoid being seen from outside, since, as one would expect, the window in the first-aid room was also made of frosted glass, but from then on, he would have to pay attention to every move he made, he couldn't afford any mistakes, he must keep well away from the windows and, if he absolutely had to go over to a window, then he would have to do so on all fours, he must behave, in short, as if he had never done anything in his life but burgle houses. A sudden burning in his stomach reminded him that it had been a mistake to take the pills unaccompanied by food, even if only a biscuit, Right, where would I find biscuits here, he asked himself, realising that now he had a new problem to solve, the problem of food, since he wouldn't be able to leave the building until it was dark, Very dark, he added. Although, as we know, he is easily satisfied when it comes to food, he would have to eat something to dull his appetite until he got home, Senhor José, however, replied to that necessity with these stoical words, It's only one day, no one ever died from not eating for a few hours. He left the first-aid room, and although the secretary's office, where he would go to do his research, was on the second floor, he decided, out of sheer curiosity, to take a turn about the rooms on the ground floor. He immediately found the gymnasium, with its cloakrooms, its wall bars and other apparatus, the beam, the box, the rings, the pommel horse, the springboard, the mattresses, in his day, schools didn't have all this sports equipment, nor would he have wanted them to, being, as he had been then and as he continued to be, what is generally termed a bit of a wimp. The burning in his stomach was getting worse, a wave of bile rose into his mouth, pricking his throat, if only he could get rid of his headache, It's the cold, I've probably got a fever, he thought, as he opened another door. Blessed be the spirit of curiosity, it was the refectory. Then Senhor José's thoughts grew wings, he rushed off in search of food, Where there's a refectory, there's a kitchen, where there's a kitchen, he didn't need to complete the thought, the kitchen was there, with its oven, its pots and pans, its plates and glasses, its cupboards, its huge fridge. He headed straight for it, flung open the door, and there was the food all lit up, once more may the god of the curious be praised, as well as the god of burglars, in some cases no less deserving. A quarter of an hour later, Senhor José was definitely a new man, restored in body and soul, with his clothes almost dry, his knees bandaged and his stomach working on something rather more nutritious and substantial than two bitter anti-cold pills. Around lunchtime, he would return to this kitchen, to this kindly fridge, but now he must go and investigate the card indexes in the secretary's office, to advance a step further, whether a large step or a small one he had yet to find out, in probing the circumstances of the unknown woman's life thirty years ago, when she was just a little girl with serious eyes and bangs down to her eyebrows, she would have sat down on that bench to eat her afternoon snack of bread and jam, perhaps sad because she had blotted her fair copy, perhaps glad because her godmother had promised her a doll.

The label on the drawer was explicit, Students in Alphabetical Order, other drawers were marked differently, First-year Students, Second-year Students, Third-year Students and so on up to the final year of school. Senhor José took a quiet professional pleasure in the archive system, organised in such a way as to facilitate access to the cards of students by two convergent and complementary routes, one general, the other particular. A separate drawer contained the teachers' record cards, as one could tell from the label, Teachers. Seeing that label immediately set in motion, in Senhor José's mind, the gears of his highly efficient deductive mechanism, If, as it is logical to suppose, he thought, the teachers in this drawer are those currently teaching in the school, then the student cards, out of mere archivistic coherence, must refer to the current student population, besides, anyone can see that the record cards of thirty years' worth of students, and that's a low estimate, could never fit in these half-dozen drawers, however thin the cards.

With no hope of finding the card, but merely to soothe his conscience, Senhor José opened the drawer where, according to the alphabet, the card belonging to the unknown woman would be found. It wasn't there. He closed the drawer and looked around him, There must be another card index for former pupils, he thought, they can't possibly destroy them when they come to the end of their course, that would be a crime against the most elementary rules of archivism. If such a card index existed, however, it wasn't there. Nervously, and knowing full well that the search would be fruitless, he opened the cupboards and the drawers in the desk. Nothing. As if it could not bear the disappointment, his headache intensified. What now, José, he asked himself. We must look elsewhere, he replied. He left the secretary's office and looked up and down the long corridor. There were no classrooms here, therefore the rooms on this floor, apart from the head teacher's study, must have other uses, one of them, as he saw straightaway, was the staff room, another seemed to be a storeroom for redundant school material, and the other two contained, at last, what seemed to be, what must be, the school's historic archive, arranged in boxes on large shelves. Senhor José was at first exultant, but, and this is the advantage of someone with experience in his line of work, or, given his suddenly dashed hopes, the painful disadvantage, only a few minutes sufficed for him to realise that what he wanted wasn't there either, the files were of a purely bureaucratic nature, letters received, duplicates of letters sent, statistics, attendance records, progress charts, rule books. He searched again, twice, in vain. Feeling desperate, he went out into the corridor, All this effort for nothing, he said, and then, again, forcing himself to obey logic, It's impossible, those wretched record cards must be somewhere, if these people keep all those years of correspondence that is of no use to anyone, they must have kept students' record cards, which are vital documents for biographies, it wouldn't surprise me in the least if some of the people in my collection were students at this school. In other circumstances, it might have occurred to Senhor José that, just as he had enriched his collection of clippings with copies of the relevant birth certificates, it would also be interesting to add documents regarding attendance and success at school. However, that would never be anything but an impossible dream. It was one thing having the birth certificate in hand in the Central Registry, quite another having to wander the city breaking into schools in order to find out if so-and-so got an eight or a fifteen in math in the fourth year, and if someone else really was such an unruly pupil as he claimed to have been in interviews. And if, in order to get into each of those schools, he had to suffer as much as he had suffered breaking into this one, then it would be better to remain in the peace and quiet of his home, resigned to knowing of the world only what the hands can grasp without actually leaving the house, words, images, illusions.

Determined to get to the bottom of things once and for all, Senhor José went back into the archive, If there's any logic in this world, then the record cards must be here, he said. He went through the shelves in the first room, box by box, bundle by bundle, with a fine-tooth comb, a turn of phrase that must have its origins in the days when people needed to comb their hair with what was also called a nit comb in order to catch what a normal comb missed, but the search again proved vain, there were no record cards. That is, there were, placed higgledy-piggledy in a large box, but only from the last five years. Convinced now that all the other record cards had been destroyed, torn up, thrown into the rubbish, if not burned, it was with a feeling of hopelessness, with the indifference of someone merely fulfilling a useless obligation, that Senhor José went into the second room. However, his eyes, if the expression is not entirely inappropriate, took pity on him, however hard you try you will find no other explanation for the fact that they immediately placed before him a narrow door between two shelves, as if they knew, from the start, that the door was there. Senhor José thought he had reached the end of his work, the crowning moment of all his efforts, indeed the opposite would reveal an unforgivable harshness on the part of fate, there must be some reason why ordinary people persist in saying, despite all life's vicissitudes, that bad luck is not always waiting just behind the door, behind this one, anyway, as in the old stories, there must be a treasure, even if, in order to reach it, it might still be necessary to fight the dragon. This one does not have furious, drooling jaws, it does not snort smoke and fire through its nostrils, it does not roar loud as any earthquake, it is simply a waiting, stagnant darkness, thick and silent as the ocean deeps, there are reputedly brave people who would not have the courage to go any farther, some would even run away at once, terrified, fearful that the obscene beast would grab them round the throat with its claws. Although not a person whom one could give as an example or model of bravery, Senhor José, after his years in the Central Registry, has acquired a knowledge of the night, of shadows, obscurity and darkness that makes up for his natural timidity and now permits him, without excessive fear, to reach his arm into the body of the dragon in search of the light switch. He found it, he flicked it on, but there was no light. Shuffling forwards so as not to stumble, he advanced a little until he barked his right shin on something hard. He bent down to feel the obstacle and, just as he realised that it was a metal step, he felt the shape of the flashlight in his pocket, in the midst of so many contradictory emotions, he had completely forgotten about it. Before him was a spiral staircase that ascended into an even thicker darkness than that on the threshold and which swallowed up the beam of light before it could show him the way upwards. The staircase has no bannister, exactly what a chronic vertigo sufferer does not need, on the fifth step, if he manages to get that far, Senhor José will lose all notion of the real height he has reached, he will feel that he's going to fall helplessly to the ground, and he will fall. But that is not what happened. Senhor José is being ridiculous, but it doesn't matter, only he knows just how absurd and ridiculous what he is doing is, no one will see him drag himself up that staircase like a lizard recently awoken from hibernation, clinging anxiously to the steps, one after the other, his body trying to follow the apparently never-ending, spiralling curve, his knees again bearing the brunt. When Senhor José's hands finally touched the smooth floor of the attic, his physical strength had long since lost the battle with his frightened spirit, which is why he could not immediately get up, he lay down there, his shirt and face resting on the dust covering the floor, his feet hanging over the steps, what torments people have to go through when they leave the safety of their homes to become embroiled in mad adventures.

After a few moments, still lying facedown, because he was not so foolish as to attempt to stand up in the midst of the darkness, running the risk of taking a false step and plunging back into the abyss from which he had come, Senhor José managed, with difficulty, to turn around and to remove the flashlight he had put in his back trouser pocket. He switched it on and shone it over the floor immediately ahead of him. There were scattered papers, cardboard boxes, some of them burst, all of them thick with dust. A few yards ahead he could see what seemed to be the legs of a chair. He raised the beam slightly, it was a chair. It seemed in good condition, the seat, the back, and above it, hanging from the low ceiling, was a bare lightbulb, Just like in the Central Registry, thought Senhor José. He directed the beam around the room and saw the fleeting shapes of shelves that seemed to cover every wall. They were not high shelves, nor could they be, given the steepness of the roof, and they were weighted down with boxes and shapeless bundles of paper. I wonder where the light switch is, thought Senhor José, and the reply was as expected, It's downstairs and it doesn't work, I don't think I can find the record cards with only this flashlight, besides I'm beginning to think the battery might be getting low, You should have thought of that before, Perhaps there's another switch in here, Even if there is, we already know that the bulb's burned out, We don't know that, It would have come on otherwise, The only thing we know is that we tried the switch and the light didn't come on, Exactly, It could mean something else, What, That there's no bulb downstairs, So I'm right, the bulb here has burned out too, But there's nothing to say that there aren't two switches and two bulbs, one on the stairs and the other in the attic, now the one downstairs has burned out, but we still don't know about the one upstairs, If you're clever enough to deduce that, then find the switch. Senhor José abandoned the awkward position in which he was still lying and sat up, My clothes will be in a dreadful state by the time I leave here, he thought, and pointed the beam at the wall nearest the opening onto the stairs, If there is a switch, then it will be here. He found it at the precise moment when he was reaching the discouraging conclusion that the only switch was indeed downstairs. As he shifted his free hand on the floor in order to get more comfortable, the light went on, the switch, one of those button switches, had been installed in the floor, so that it would be within immediate reach of anyone coming up the stairs. The yellowish light from the bulb barely reached the wall at the back, there was no sign of footprints on the floor. Remembering the record cards that he had seen on the floor below, Senhor José said out loud, It's at least six years since anyone came in here. When the echo of his words had faded, Senhor José noticed that there was a vast silence in the attic, as if the silence that had been there before contained a larger silence, the woodworms must have stopped their excavating work. From the ceiling hung spiders' webs black with dust, their owners must have died long ago from lack of food, there was nothing here that would attract a stray fly, especially not with the door shut downstairs, and the moths, the silverfish and the woodworms in the beams had no reason to exchange the galleries of cellulose, where they lived, for the outside world. Senhor José got up, vainly trying to brush the dust from his trousers and shirt, his face looked like the face of some eccentric clown, with a great stain on one side only. He went and sat down on the chair, underneath the bulb, and started talking to himself, Let's look at this rationally, he said, if the old record cards are here, and everything indicates that they are, it is highly unlikely that they are going to be grouped student by student, that is, that the record cards of each student will be all together, so that you can see at a glance the whole of their scholastic career, it's more likely that, at the end of each school year, the secretary bundled up all the record cards corresponding to that year and placed them here, I doubt she would even have gone to the trouble of putting them in boxes, or perhaps she did, we'll have to see, I hope, if she did, she at least thought to write the relevant year on them, but one way or another, it will just be a question of time and patience. This conclusion had not added greatly to his initial premise, from the very beginning of his life, Senhor José has known that he only needs time in order to use patience, and from the very beginning he has been hoping that patience will not run out of time. He got up, and faithful to the rule that, in all searches, the best plan is to start at one point and proceed from there on with method and discipline, he set to work at the end of one of the rows of shelves, determined to leave no piece of paper un-turned, always checking that there wasn't another piece of paper hidden between top and bottom sheets. Each movement he made, opening a box, untying a bundle, raised a cloud of dust, so much so that in order not to be asphyxiated, he had to tie his handkerchief over his nose and mouth, a preventive measure that the clerks were advised to follow each time they went into the archive of the dead in the Central Registry. In a matter of moments his hands were black and the handkerchief had lost any remaining trace of whiteness, Senhor José had become a coal miner hoping to find in the depths of the mine the pure carbon of a diamond.

He found the first file after half an hour. The girl no longer had bangs, but, in this photograph taken at fifteen, her eyes had the same air of wounded gravity. Senhor José placed it carefully on the chair and continued his search. He was working in a kind of dream state, meticulous, feverish, moths fluttered out from beneath his fingers, terrified by the light, and little by little, as if he were rummaging in the remains of a tomb, the dust became grafted onto his skin, so fine that it penetrated his clothing. At first, when he picked up a bundle of record cards, he went straight to what really interested him, then he began to linger over names, images, for no reason, just because they were there and because no one else would go into this attic to remove the dust covering them, hundreds, thousands of faces of boys and girls, looking straight at the camera, at the other side of the world, waiting, for what exactly they didn't know. It wasn't like that in the Central Registry, in the Central Registry there were only words, in the Central Registry you could not see how faces had changed or continued to change, when that was precisely what was most important, the thing that time changes, not the name, which never changes. When Senhor José's stomach began to rumble, there were seven record cards on the chair, two of them with identical pictures, her mother must have said, Take this one from last year, there's no need to go to the photographer again, and she took the picture, sad that she wouldn't have a new photograph this year. Before going down to the kitchen, Senhor José went to the head teacher's bathroom to wash his hands, he was amazed by what he saw in the mirror, he hadn't imagined that his face could possibly get into this state, filthy, furrowed with lines of sweat, It doesn't even look like me, he thought, and yet he had probably never looked more like himself. When he had finished eating, he went up to the attic as fast as his knees would allow, it occurred to him that if the light failed, something to bear in mind after all this rain, he would not be able to complete his search. Assuming that she hadn't repeated a year, he only had five more record cards to find, and if he were now to be plunged into darkness, all his efforts would be in part lost, since he would never be able to get back into the school. Absorbed in his work, he had forgotten about his headache, his cold, and now he realised that he was feeling worse. He went downstairs again to take another two pills, then went back up, making a supreme effort, and resumed his work. The afternoon was drawing to a close when he found the last record card. He turned off the light in the attic, closed the door and, like a sleepwalker, put on his jacket and raincoat, removed as best he could any sign of his passing and sat down to wait for night to come.

The next morning, almost as soon as the Central Registry had opened and when everyone else was at their desk, Senhor José half-opened the communicating door and said *pst-pst* to attract the attention of the nearest clerk. The man turned and saw a flushed face and blinking eyes, What do you want, he asked, in a low voice so as not to disturb anyone, but with a note of ironic recrimination in his words, as if the scandal of absence only confirmed the worst suspicions of one already scandalised by Senhor José's lateness, I'm ill, said Senhor José, I can't come to work. Annoyed, his colleague got up, took three steps in the direction of the senior clerk in charge of his wing, and said, Excuse me, sir, Senhor José is over there saying he's ill. The senior clerk also got up, took four steps in the direction of the respective deputy and told him, Excuse me, sir, the clerk Senhor José is over there saying he's ill. Before taking the five steps that separated him from the Registrar's desk, the deputy went over to ascertain the nature of the illness, What's wrong with you, he asked, I've got a cold, said Senhor José, A cold has never been a reason not to come to work, I've got a fever, How do you know you've got a fever, I used a thermometer, What are you, a few degrees above normal, No sir, my temperature's well over 100, You never get a fever like that with an ordinary cold, Then maybe I've got flu, Or pneumonia, Thanks very much, It's just a possibility, I'm not saying you've actually got pneumonia, No, I know you're not, And how did you get in this state, Probably because I got caught in the rain, Imprudence always has its price, You're right, Any illness contracted for non-work-related reasons should simply not be considered, Well, I wasn't, in fact, at work when it happened, I'll tell the Registrar, Yes, sir, Don't shut the door, he might want to give you further instructions, Yes, sir. The Registrar did not give any instructions, he merely looked over the bent heads of the clerks and made a gesture with his hand, a brief gesture, as if dismissing the matter as insignificant or as if postponing any attention he might give it until later, at that distance, Senhor José could not tell, always supposing that his red, streaming eyes could see that far. Anyway, it seems that Senhor José, terrified by that look and not realising what he was doing, opened the door wider, thus revealing himself full-length to the Central Registry, an old dressing gown over his pyjamas, his feet in a pair of down-at-heel slippers, the shrunken look of someone who has caught a terrible cold, or a malignant form of flu, or a fatal strain of bronchopneumonia, you never know, it happens often enough, a gentle breeze can so easily turn into a raging hurricane. The deputy came over to him to say that today or tomorrow he would be visited by the official doctor, but then, oh miracle, he uttered some words that no lowly clerk in the Central Registry, neither he nor anyone else, had ever had the joy of hearing before, The Registrar hopes that you will soon feel better, and the deputy himself didn't quite seem to believe what he was saying. Dumbstruck, Senhor José still had sufficient presence of mind to look across at the Registrar in order to thank him for his unexpected good wishes, but the Registrar had his head down, as if he were hard at work, which, knowing as we do the work habits of this particular Central Registry, is most unlikely. Slowly, Senhor José closed the door, and, trembling with excitement and fever, got back into bed.

He had been drenched not only by the rain that fell on him while he slithered about on the porch roof, struggling to get into the school. When night came and he finally left through the window and reached the street, he could not, poor thing, have imagined what awaited him. The extremely tortuous circumstances of his ascent, but, above all, the dust accumulated in the attic archive, had left him, from head to foot, in an indescribably grimy state, his hair and face were smeared with black, his hands were like charred stumps, not to mention his clothes, his raincoat was like an old rag impregnated with lard, his trousers looked as if he had been rubbing them with tar, his shirt as if it had been used to clean a chimney thick with centuries of soot, even a vagabond living in the most extreme poverty would have sallied forth onto the street with more dignity. When Senhor José was two blocks away from the school, by which time it had stopped raining, he hailed a taxi to take him home, and the inevitable happened, the driver, seeing that black figure emerge suddenly from the depths of the night, took fright and accelerated, and that was not the only time, Senhor José hailed three other taxis and they all disappeared round the corner as if pursued by the devil himself. Senhor José resigned himself to having to walk home, he certainly wasn't going to get onto a bus, oh well, it would be just one more weariness to add to the one that barely allowed him to drag his feet along, but the worst thing was that, shortly afterwards, the rain started again and didn't stop throughout the whole of that interminable walk, streets, sidewalks, squares, avenues, through a city that seemed deserted, apart from that lone man, dripping water, without even the partial protection of an umbrella, you can understand why, no one takes an umbrella along when they go burgling, no more than you would when going to war, he could have taken shelter in a doorway and waited for a break in the clouds, but it wasn't worth it, he couldn't get any wetter than he was. When Senhor José reached home, the only reasonably dry part of his clothing was a pocket in his jacket, the inside pocket on his left side, where he had placed the school record cards of the unknown girl, he had kept them covered with his right hand all the time, to protect them from the rain, anyone who saw him would have thought he had something wrong with his heart, especially given the pained look on his face. Shivering, he took all his clothes off, wondering confusedly how he would solve the problem of getting that pile of clothes on the floor washed, he didn't have so many suits, shoes, socks and shirts that he could afford to send it all off to the dry cleaners, as if he were a man of means, a complete suit, he was bound to need one of those items of clothing when he had to put his remaining clothes on tomorrow. He decided to worry about that later, now he just had to get the filth off his body, the worst thing was that the heater didn't work very well, the water sometimes came out boiling hot, sometimes ice cold, just the thought of it made him shudder, and then, like someone trying to convince himself, he murmured, Perhaps it would do my cold good, a blast of hot water followed by cold, or so I've heard. He went into the cubicle that served him as a bathroom, looked in the mirror and realised why the taxi drivers had been frightened. He would have felt exactly the same and fled from this hollow-eyed phantom with a kind of black drool running from the corners of his mouth. The heater didn't behave too badly this time, it unleashed only a couple of cold lashes at the beginning, and the rest of the time it was comfortingly warm, besides, a quick scalding blast from time to time even helped dissolve the dirt. When he got out of the shower, Senhor José felt reinvigorated, like new, but as soon as he got into bed, he started shivering again, it was then that he thought of opening the drawer in his bedside table, where he kept his thermometer, and shortly afterwards, was saying, One hundred, if I feel the way I do now tomorrow morning, I won't be able to go to work. Whether it was the effects of fever or exhaustion, or both, this thought did not trouble him, the abnormal idea of being absent from work did not seem strange to him, for at that moment, Senhor José did not seem like Senhor José, or, rather, there were two Senhor Josés lying in bed, with the blankets up to their nose, one Senhor José who had lost all sense of responsibility, another to whom this was all a matter of complete indifference. He dozed for a few moments with the light on and then woke with a start when he dreamed that he had left the record cards on the chair in the attic, that he had left them there deliberately, as if during this whole adventure his sole aim had been merely to seek them out and find them. He also dreamed that someone went into the attic after he had left, saw the pile of thirteen record cards and asked, What mystery is this. Half-dazed, he got up and went to look for them, he had put them on the table when he emptied out his jacket pockets, and then returned to bed. The record cards were smeared with black fingermarks, some even bore the clear impress of his fingerprints, he would have to wipe them off tomorrow to foil any attempt at identification, How stupid, he thought, we leave fingerprints on everything we touch, if I clean those off I'll just leave others, the difference is that some are visible and others are not. He closed his eyes and shortly afterwards fell asleep again, the hand barely grasping the record cards fell limply onto the bedcover, some slipped to the floor, there were the pictures of a girl at different ages, from child to adolescent, wrongfully brought here, no one has the right to carry off photos that don't belong to them, unless they were a gift, carrying a photo of someone in your pocket is like carrying a little bit of their soul. Senhor José's dream, from which this time he did not awake, was a different one now, he saw himself wiping away the fingerprints he had left at the school, they were everywhere, on the window through which he had entered, in the first-aid room, in the secretary's office, in the head teacher's study, in the refectory, in the kitchen, in the archive, he decided it wasn't worth worrying about the ones in the attic, no one was likely to go in there and ask, What mystery is this, the trouble was that the hands that wiped away the visible traces left behind them an invisible trace, if the head teacher at the school were to report the burglary to the police and there was a serious investigation, Senhor José would go to prison, as sure as two and two are four, imagine the dishonour and the shame that would forever stain the reputation of the Central Registry. In the middle of the night, Senhor José woke up burning with fever, apparently delirious, saying, I didn't steal anything, I didn't steal anything, and it was true that, strictly speaking, he hadn't stolen anything, however much the head teacher might search and investigate, however many verifications, counts and comparisons he made, inventory in hand, ticking off one item after the other, his conclusion would be the same, There has been no theft, at least not what you could call theft, doubtless the person in charge of the kitchen would remind him that there was food missing from the fridge, but, supposing that this had been the only crime committed, stealing in order to eat, according to a fairly widely held view, is not theft, even the head teacher is in agreement there, the police, of course, are of a different opinion, on principle, they, however, would have no option but to go away, grumbling, There's some mystery there, no one burgles a school just to grab a spot of breakfast. In any event, since the head teacher's formal written statement, in which he said that nothing valuable or non-valuable was missing from the school, the police had decided not to take any fingerprints, as routine demanded, We've got more than enough work as it is, said the one in charge of the investigation squad. Despite these tranquillising words, Senhor José could not get back to sleep again all night, fearful that the dream would be repeated and that the police would return with their magnifying glasses and their special dust.

He has nothing in the house that might help reduce his fever and the doctor will only come later in the afternoon, he might not even come today, and he won't bring any medicine with him, he'll merely write out the usual prescription for cases of cold and flu. The dirty clothes are still in a heap in the middle of the room and Senhor José looks at the heap from the bed, with a perplexed air, as if it didn't belong to him, only a remnant of common sense stops him from asking, Who was it who came in here and took off all their clothes, and it was the same common sense that forced him to think, at last, about the complications, both personal and professional, that would result if a colleague came through the door to find out how he was, on instructions from the Registrar or on his own initiative, and came face-to-face with all that filth. When he stood up, he felt as if someone had suddenly planted him at the very top of a ladder, but the dizziness he felt this time was different, it was a result of fever, as well as physical weakness, because what he had eaten at the school, apparently sufficient at the time, had served more as a comfort to his nerves than as nourishment to his body. Supporting himself against the wall, he managed, with some difficulty, to reach a chair and sit down. He waited for his head to return to normal before considering where he could hide his dirty clothes, not in the bathroom, doctors always have to wash their hands when they leave, and he certainly couldn't hide them under the bed, which was one of those old-fashioned, long-legged beds, anyone would be able to see the clothes, even without bending down, and they wouldn't fit in the cupboard where he kept his famous people, and besides it wouldn't be right, the sad truth is that, although his brain had now stopped spinning, it was still not working properly, the only place where the dirty clothes would be safe from prying eyes was the place where they usually hung when they were clean, that is, behind the curtain covering the niche that he used as a wardrobe, only the most impertinent of colleagues or doctors would go poking their nose in there. Pleased with himself for having reached a conclusion after such lengthy deliberation, a conclusion which, in other circumstances, would have been more than obvious, Senhor José started shunting the clothes towards the curtain with his foot in order not to get his pyjamas dirty. There was a great damp stain left on the floor which would take several hours to disappear completely, if someone came in before then and asked questions, he would say that he had knocked some water over or that there had been a stain on the floor and he had tried to get rid of it. From the moment he got up, Senhor José's stomach had been begging him for the charity of a cup of coffee with milk, a biscuit, a slice of bread and butter, anything to pacify his suddenly awoken appetite, now that his worries about the immediate fate of his clothes had disappeared. The bread was dry and hard, only a scraping of butter was left, he was out of milk, all he had was some rather mediocre coffee, as we know, a man who had never found a woman who would love him enough to agree to join him in this hovel, such a man, apart from rare exceptions which have no place in this story, will never be more than a poor devil, it's odd that we always say poor devil and never poor god, especially when he was unfortunate enough to turn out as disastrously as this one, we are referring, by the way, to the man not the god. Despite the meagre and unconsoling food, Senhor José felt well enough to have a shave, after which he judged he was looking considerably better, so much so that he ended up saying to the mirror, My fever seems to have subsided. This reflection led him to wonder whether it would be a good, prudent policy to turn up for work anyway, it was only a few steps away, he would say, The work of the Central Registry comes first, and the Registrar, bearing in mind how cold it was outside, would forgive him for not having taken the long way around as was the rule, and might even record such clear proof of esprit de corps and dedication to work in Senhor José's file. He thought about it, but decided against it. His whole body ached, as if someone had knocked him down, beaten him and shaken him, his muscles ached, his joints ached, and it wasn't because of the physical effort of climbing and breaking in, anyone could see that these aches and pains were different, This is flu, he concluded.

He had just got into bed when he heard someone knock on the door that opened into the Central Registry, it must be some charitable colleague, taking seriously the Christian precept of visiting the sick and the imprisoned, no, it couldn't be a colleague, it was still hours until lunchtime, and good works could only be done out of hours, Come in, he said, it's only on the latch, the door opened and the deputy whom he had told about his illness appeared in the doorway, The Registrar asked me to find out if you're taking anything while you're waiting for the doctor to come, No, sir, I haven't got anything suitable in the house, Then have these pills, Thank you very much, I'll pay you later if you don't mind, just so that I don't have to get up, how much do I owe you, It was an order from the Registrar, you don't ask the Registrar how much you owe him, I realise that, I'm sorry, You'd better take a pill now, and the deputy came in without waiting for an answer, All right, thank you, that's very kind of you, Senhor José could not stop him from coming in, he could not say Halt, you cannot come in here, sir, this is a private house, in the first place, because you don't speak like that to a superior, in the second place, because there was no memory in the oral tradition of the Central Registry nor any record in the written annals of a Registrar's ever having taken such an interest in the health of a clerk to the point of sending someone to bring him some pills. The deputy himself was perplexed with the novelty of it all, he would never have done it on his own initiative, however, he did not allow himself to be distracted, he behaved like someone who knew perfectly well what he was about and was familiar with every corner of the house, which is not to be wondered at, before the town planners went to work on the neighbourhood, he too had lived in a house like this. The first thing he noticed was the large damp stain on the floor, What's that from, a leak, he asked, Senhor José was tempted to say yes, simply in order not to give any further explanations, but he preferred to put it down to an accident of his own making, as he had at first thought, he didn't want the plumber coming to the house and then writing a report to the Registrar saying that the pipes, although old, were in no way responsible for the appearance of that damp stain on the floor. The deputy approached bearing a glass of water and a pill, his mission as designated nurse had softened his normally authoritarian features, but that look soon returned, accentuated by something that could be described as wounded surprise, when, as he approached the bed, he noticed the unknown girl's school records lying on the bedside table. Senhor José noticed the other man's surprise as soon as it happened and it was as if his whole world collapsed about him. His brain instantaneously sent an order to the arm muscles on that side, Get that off there, you idiot, but immediately, with the same speed, electrical impulse after electrical impulse, it changed its mind, if I may put it that way, like someone who has just recognised his own stupidity, Please, don't touch them, pretend you haven't noticed. That is why, with an agility totally unexpected in someone in the grip of the physical and mental depression which is the first known consequence of flu, Senhor José sat on the edge of the bed pretending he wanted to help the deputy in his charitable efforts, he reached out a hand to receive the pill, which he put in his mouth, as well as the water to help it down his tight, anxious throat, at the same time, taking advantage of the fact that the mattress on which he was lying was at the same height as the bedside table, he covered the cards with the elbow of his other arm, dropping his forearm forwards, with the palm of his hand imperatively open, as if he were saying to the deputy Stop right there. What saved him was the photograph stuck to the record card, that is the most notable difference between school records and those of birth and life, it would be impossible for the Central Registry to receive a new picture every year of all those whose names were inscribed in the archive of the living, and it wouldn't be every year, it would be every month, every week, every day, a photograph per hour, my God, how time passes, and the work it would generate, how many clerks would they have to recruit, a photograph a minute, a second, the amount of glue, the wear and tear on scissors, the care in the selection of staff, so as to exclude dreamers who might sit staring eternally at one picture, letting their minds wander, like idiots watching the clouds drift by. The deputy's face now bore the expression he wore on his worst days, when papers were piling up on all the desks and the Registrar called him over to ask if he was really quite sure he was doing his job properly. Thanks to the photograph, he did not think that the record cards on top of his subordinate's bedside table belonged to the Central Registry, but the speed with which Senhor José had covered them up made him suspicious, especially since Senhor José had done so as if by chance or distractedly. The damp stain on the floor had already aroused his distrust, now it was some record cards of an unknown nature with a photograph attached, a photograph of a child, as he could just make out. He couldn't count the cards, since they were placed one on top of the other, but from the thickness, there must have been at least ten of them, Ten record cards with photos of children on them, how odd, what can they be doing there, he thought, intrigued, and he would have been even more intrigued if he had known that the cards, in fact, all belonged to the same person and that the pictures on the last two were of an adolescent girl, with a grave but pleasant face. The deputy placed the packet of pills on the bedside table and withdrew. As he was leaving, he looked back and saw Senhor

José still there with his elbow covering the cards, I'd better talk to the chief, he said to himself. As soon as the door had closed, Senhor José, with a brusque movement, as if afraid of being caught out, thrust the record cards under the mattress. There was no one there to tell him it was too late, and, besides, that was something he preferred not to think about.

It's flu, said the doctor, you'd better start by taking three days'
sick leave. Head swimming, legs weak, Senhor José had got
out of bed to open the door, Forgive me for keeping you waiting outside, Doctor, that's what happens when you live alone,
the doctor came in grumbling, Terrible weather, closed his
dripping umbrella and left it in the hall, What seems to be the
problem, he asked when Senhor José, teeth chattering, had just
got back between the sheets, and then, without waiting for him
to reply, he said, It's flu. He took his pulse, told him to open his
mouth, briskly applied his stethoscope to his chest and back,
It's flu, he said again, you're very lucky, it could easily have
turned into pneumonia, but it's flu, you'd better start by taking
three days' sick leave, and then we'll see. He had just sat down
at the table to write a prescription when the communicating
door opened, it was only on the latch, and the Registrar appeared, Good afternoon, Doctor, You mean bad afternoon,
don't you, sir, it would be a good afternoon if I were sitting
nice and cosy in my consulting rooms rather than wandering
the streets in this ghastly weather, How's our patient, asked the
Registrar, and the doctor replied, I've given him three days' sick
leave, it's just a bout of flu. At that moment, it wasn't just a
bout of flu. With the bedclothes up to his nose, Senhor José was
trembling as if he were suffering from malaria, so much so that
the iron bedstead on which he was lying shook, however, that

irrepressible trembling was not the result of fever, but of sheer panic, a complete disorientation of the mind, The Registrar, here, he was thinking, the Registrar in my house, the Registrar asking him, How are you feeling, Better, sir, Did you take the pills I sent you, Yes, sir, Did they help at all, Yes, sir, Well, now you can stop taking those and take the medicine the doctor has prescribed, Yes, sir, Unless they're the same ones, let me see now, yes, they are, plus a couple of injections, I'll take care of this. Senhor José could hardly believe that the person who, before his very eyes, was folding up the prescription and putting it carefully away in his pocket really was the Registrar. The boss whom he had grown to know only with great difficulty would never behave in this way, he would never come in person to ask about his health, and the idea of his wanting to take charge of buying the medicine of a mere clerk was simply absurd. And he'll need a nurse to give him the injections, said the doctor, leaving the problem to be resolved by someone who was ready or able to do so, not the poor, scrawny, flu-ridden devil with the beginnings of a greying stubble on his chin, as if the evident discomfort of the house were not enough, and that damp stain on the floor which looked very much like the result of bad plumbing, the sad tales a doctor could tell about life, if it were not all confidential, On no account must you go out in this state, he added, I'll take care of everything, Doctor, said the Registrar, I'll phone the Central Registry nurse, he'll buy the medicine and come here to give the injections, There aren't many bosses like you left, said the doctor. Senhor José nodded feebly, that was the most he could do, obedient and reliable, yes, he had always been that, and had taken a certain paradoxical pride in it, though without ever being fawning and subservient, he would never, for example, make imbecilic, flattering remarks like, He's the best Registrar there is, There isn't another one like him in the world, They broke the mould when they made him, For him, despite my vertigo, I even climb that wretched ladder. Senhor José is worried and anxious about something else now, he wants his boss to leave, to go before the doctor goes, he trembles to imagine himself alone with him, at the mercy of fatal questions, What's the meaning of that damp stain, What were those record cards on your bedside table, Where did you get them, Where did you hide them, Whose photo was on them. He closed his eyes, adopted an expression of unbearable suffering, Leave me in peace on my bed of pain, he seemed to be begging them, but he suddenly opened his eyes again, when, terrified, he heard the doctor say, Well, I'll be on my way, call me if he gets any worse, though I'm pretty sure he won't, it's definitely not pneumonia, I'll keep you posted, Doctor, said the Registrar while he accompanied him to the door. Senhor José closed his eyes again, heard the door close, Now, he thought. The Registrar's firm steps approached the bed, then stopped, He's probably looking at me now, Senhor José didn't know what to do, he could pretend he'd gone to sleep, that he had fallen gradually asleep the way a weary patient does, but his twitching eyelids betrayed him, he could also, for better or worse, give a pathetic moan, of the kind that pierces the heart, but that was a bit over the top for a mere bout of flu, only a fool would be deceived, certainly not this Registrar, who knows all there is to know about the kingdoms of the visible and the invisible. He opened his eyes and the Registrar was there, a few steps away from the bed, his face expressionless, simply looking at him. Then Senhor José came up with an idea that he thought might save him, he would thank the Central Registry for all their care, he would thank them eloquently, effusively, perhaps that way he would avoid the questions, but just as he was about to open his mouth to utter the familiar phrase, I don't know how to thank you, his boss turned his back, at the same time saying four words, Take care of yourself, that was what he said in a tone that was at once deferential and imperative, only the best bosses can combine contrary feelings in such a harmonious way, which is why their subordinates venerate them. Senhor José tried, at least, to say Thank you, sir, but the Registrar had already left, delicately closing the door behind him, as one should when leaving an invalid's room. Senhor José has a headache, but the headache is almost nothing compared to the tumult going on inside him. Senhor José finds himself in such a state of confusion that his first action, when the Registrar has left, is to slip his hand under the mattress to make sure the record cards are still there. His second action offended even more against common sense, for he got out of bed and went and turned the key in the communicating door twice, like someone desperately barring the door after his house has been burgled. Lying down again was only the fourth action, the third had been when he turned back, thinking, What if the Registrar returns, in that case, it would be more prudent, in order to avoid arousing suspicion, to leave the door on the latch. Senhor José is caught between several devils and the deep blue sea.

It was already dark when the nurse arrived. In fulfilment of the orders he had received from the Registrar, he brought with him the pills and phials that the doctor had prescribed, but, to Senhor José's surprise, he also brought a package which he placed gingerly down on the table and said, I hope it's still hot, I hope I haven't spilled anything, which meant that there was food inside, as the following words confirmed, Eat it while it's hot, but first, I'll give you that injection. Now, Senhor José did not like injections, especially ones into the veins in the arm, when he always had to look away, which was why he was so pleased when the nurse told him that the jab would be in his posterior, he was very polite, this nurse, from another age, he had got used to using the term "posterior" instead of bottom so as not to shock the sensibilities of lady patients, and had almost ended up forgetting the usual term, he used "posterior" even when he was dealing with patients for whom "bottom" was merely a ridiculous euphemism and who preferred the vulgar variant "bum." The unexpected appearance of food and the relief he felt at not being injected in the arm broke down Senhor José's defences, or perhaps he simply forgot, or more simply still, perhaps he hadn't noticed until then that his pyjama trousers were stained with blood at the knees, a consequence of his nocturnal adventures as a climber of school roofs. The nurse, holding the syringe prepared and ready, instead of saying Turn over, asked, What's that, and Senhor José, converted by this lesson from life to the definitive kindness of injections in the arm, replied instinctively, I fell down, You don't have much luck do you, first you fall down, then you get the flu, it's just as well you've got a kind boss, now turn over, then I'll take a look at those knees. Debilitated in body, soul and will, his nerves shattered, Senhor José almost burst into tears like a child when he felt the needle go in and the slow, painful entry of the liquid into the muscle, I'm a wreck, he thought, and it was true, a poor feverish human animal, lying on a poor bed in a poor house, with the dirty clothes worn to carry out the crime hidden away, and a damp stain on the floor that seemed never to dry. Turn over onto your back again, and let's have a look at those knees, said the nurse, and sighing, coughing, Senhor José obeyed, heaving himself around again, and now, bending forwards, he can see the nurse rolling up his pyjama legs above the knee, he can see him removing the dirty plasters, dabbing peroxide on them and very carefully and slowly unsticking them, fortunately he's a real professional, the bag he carries with him is a veritable first-aid kit, he has a cure for almost everything. When he saw the wounds, the look on his face was that of someone unconvinced by Senhor José's explanation, that business about a fall, his experience of grazes and bruises even led him to remark with unconscious perspicacity, Anyone would think you'd been rubbing your knees against a wall, I told you I fell, Did you tell your boss about this, It's nothing to do with work, a person can have a fall without telling his superiors, Unless the nurse they've called in to give you an injection has to do some extra work, Which I didn't ask for, No, that's true you didn't, but if tomorrow you come down with a serious infection because of these wounds, then who's going to get blamed for neglect and lack of professionalism, me, besides, the boss likes to know everything, that's his way of pretending that he doesn't care about anything, All right, I'll tell him tomorrow, I would advise you most strongly to do so, that way the report will be confirmed, What report, Mine, I can't see that a few simple grazes can be significant enough to be mentioned in a report, Even the simplest graze is significant, Once mine have healed they'll leave nothing but a few small scars that will disappear in time, Ah, yes, wounds heal over on the body, but in the report they always stay open, they neither close up nor disappear, I don't understand, How long have you been working at the Central Registry, Going on twenty-six years, How many Registrars have you had up until now, Including this one, three, And you've never noticed anything, Noticed what, You've never twigged, I don't know what you mean, Is it or is it not true that the Registrars have very little to do, It's true, everyone says so, Then it's time you knew that, in the many empty hours they enjoy while their staff are working, their main occupation is collecting information about their subordinates, all kinds of information, they've been doing it for as long as the Central Registry has existed, one after the other, from the very beginning. Senhor José shuddered, which did not pass unnoticed by the nurse, You shuddered, he said, Yes, I did, Just so that you have a clearer idea of what I'm telling you, even that shudder must appear in my report, But it won't, No, it won't, I know why, Tell me, Because then you would have to say that the shudder occurred when you were telling me that the bosses collect information about the staff at the Central Registry and the boss would be bound to want to know why you had that conversation with me and also how a nurse came to know about such a confidential matter, so confidential that in twenty-five years of working in the Central Registry I have never heard anything about it, There's a lot of the confidant in nurses, although rather less so than with doctors, Are you insinuating that the Registrar confides in you, I'm not saying that he does, I'm not even insinuating that he should, I simply take orders, So then you just have to follow them, No, you're wrong, I have to do a great deal more than just follow them, I have to interpret them, Why, Because there's usually a difference between what he tells me to do and what he actually wants, He sent you here so that you could give me an injection, That's how it would appear, And what did you see in this case, apart from what it appears to be, You can't imagine the number of things you can discover by looking at someone's wounds, You only saw them by chance, You can never discount chance, it's a great help, What did you discover in my wounds then, That you grazed them on a wall, I fell, So you said, Information like that, always supposing that it's true, wouldn't be of much help to the Registrar, It doesn't matter to me whether it is or not, I just write the reports, He already knows about the flu, But not about the wounds on your knees, He knows about the damp stain on the floor too, But not about the shudder, If you've nothing further to do here, I'd be grateful if you'd leave, I'm tired, I need to sleep, You must eat first, don't forget, I hope your supper hasn't gone completely cold after all this talking, You don't need much food when you're just lying in bed, But you need some, Was it the Registrar who told you to bring me some food, Do you know anyone else who might have done it, Yes, if she knew where I lived, Who, An elderly lady who lives in a ground-floor apartment, Wounds on the knees, a sudden, unexplained shudder, an old lady in a ground-floor apartment, Yes, ground floor right, This would be the most important report I've ever written in my life, if I wrote it, You're not going to write it though, Yes I am, but only to say that I gave you an injection, Thank you for cleaning my wounds, Of all the things I was taught, that's what I'm best at. After the nurse had left, Senhor José remained lying down for a few more minutes, not moving, recovering his calm and his strength. It had proved a difficult dialogue, with traps and false doors swinging open at every step, the slightest slip could have dragged him into a full and complete confession if his mind had not been attentive to the multiple meanings of the words he carefully pronounced, especially those that appeared to have only one meaning, those are the ones you have to be most careful with. Contrary to what is generally believed, meaning and sense were never the same thing, meaning shows itself at once, direct, literal, explicit, enclosed in itself, univocal, if you like, while sense cannot stay still, it seethes with second, third and fourth senses, radiating out in different directions that divide and subdivide into branches and branchlets, until they disappear from view, the sense of every word is like a star hurling spring tides out into space, cosmic winds, magnetic perturbations, afflictions.

At last, Senhor José got out of bed, put his feet in his slippers and drew on the dressing gown that he also used as an extra blanket on cold nights. Although gripped by hunger, he opened the door and looked out into the Central Registry. He could feel within himself a strange boldness, a feeling of absence, as if many days had passed since the last time he had been there. Nothing had changed though, there was the long counter where they dealt with petitioners and supplicants, beneath them the drawers where they kept the index cards of the living, then the eight tables for the clerks, the four for the senior clerks, the two for the deputies, the large desk belonging to the Registrar with the light above it still on, the huge shelves reaching up as far as the ceiling, the petrified darkness on the side inhabited by the dead. Although there was no one in the Central Registry, Senhor José locked the door, there was no one in the

Central Registry, but still he locked the door. Thanks to the new plasters that the nurse had put on his knees, he could walk more easily, the dressing no longer pulled on his wounds. He sat down at the table, undid the package, there were two pans, one on top of the other, first the soup and below it a dish of meat and potatoes, still warm. He ate the soup eagerly, then, unhurriedly, finished off the meat and potatoes. I'm lucky to have a boss like him, he murmured, remembering the nurse's words, if it weren't for him, I'd be stuck here dying of hunger and neglect, like a lost dog. Yes, I'm lucky, he repeated, as if he needed to convince himself of what he had just said. Feeling restored, he returned to bed, first visiting the cubicle that served as his bathroom. He was just about to fall asleep when he remembered the notebook in which he had set down the first stages of his search. I'll write it tomorrow, he said, but this new urgency was almost as pressing as that of eating, which was why he went to fetch the notebook. Then, sitting on the bed, wearing his dressing gown, his pyjama jacket buttoned up to the neck and bundled up in blankets, he picked up the story where he had left off. The Registrar said to me, If you're not ill, how do you explain the poor work you've been doing recently, I don't know, sir, perhaps it's because I haven't been sleeping well. Assisted by his fever, he continued writing long into the night.

It took not three days but a week for Senhor José's fever to subside and for his cough to get better. The nurse came every day to give him an injection and to bring him some food, the doctor came every other day, but this extraordinary assiduousness, on the doctor's part that is, should not lead us to any hasty conclusions about some imagined standard of efficiency among health officials and home visits, since it was quite simply the consequence of a clear-cut order from the head of the Central Registry, Doctor, treat that man as if you were treating me, he's important. The doctor did not understand the reasons behind this evidently favoured treatment that he was being asked to administer, still less the lack of objectivity of the value judgement expressed, he had occasionally visited the Registrar's own house for professional reasons, and he had seen his comfortable, civilised way of life, an inner world that bore no resemblance whatsoever to the rough hovel of this permanently ill-shaven Senhor José who appeared not even to have a change of sheets. Senhor José did have sheets, he wasn't that poor, but, for reasons known only to him, he rejected out of hand the nurse's offer to air the mattress for him and replace the sheets, for they stank of sweat and fever, It'll only take me five minutes and the bed will be like new, No, I'm fine as I am, don't worry, It's all part of my job you know, Like I said, I'm fine as I am. Senhor José could not reveal to anyone's eyes that he was hiding between the mattress and the base of the bed the school records of an unknown woman and a notebook containing the story of his break-in at the school where she had studied as both a child and a young girl. To put them somewhere else, amid the files he used for his clippings about famous people, for example, would immediately resolve the difficulty, but the sense of defending a secret with his own body was too strong, too thrilling even, for Senhor José to give it up. In order not to have to discuss the matter again with the nurse, or with the doctor, who, although he made no comment, had already cast a critical glance over the crumpled sheets and visibly wrinkled his nose at the smell, Senhor José got up one night and, making a supreme effort, he himself changed the sheets. And so as not to give either the doctor or the nurse the slightest excuse to reopen the matter and, who knows, go and report the clerk's incorrigible lack of hygiene to the Registrar, he went to the bathroom, shaved and washed as best he could, then took an old but clean pair of pyjamas from a drawer and went back to bed. He felt so pleased with himself and so restored that, like someone playing a game with himself, he decided to set down in his notebook an explicit, detailed account of all the hygienic preparations and treatments he had just put himself through. His health was returning, as the doctor was quick to tell the Registrar, The man is cured, in another two days he can go back to work without any danger of a relapse. The Registrar said only, Good, but with a distracted air, as if he were thinking about something else.

Senhor José was cured, but he had lost a lot of weight, despite the bread and victuals brought regularly by the nurse, albeit only once a day, but quite sufficient in quantity to maintain an adult body not subject to any exertions. One has to bear in mind, however, the debilitating effect of fever and prolonged sweating on the adipose tissues, especially when, as in this case, there wasn't much of them to start with. Personal remarks were frowned upon in the Central Registry, especially if in any way connected with people's state of health, which is why Senhor José's frail appearance and extreme thinness were not the object of any comment on the part of colleagues or superiors, that is, of any spoken comments, for the way they looked at him was fairly eloquent in their common expression of a kind of scornful commiseration, which other people, unfamiliar with the customs of the place, would have erroneously interpreted as a discreet and silent reserve. So that people would see how troubled he was to have been absent from work for so many days, Senhor José was first in line at the door of the Central Registry in the morning, awaiting the arrival of the newest deputy, whose job it was to open the door and to close it at the end of the day. The original key, a real work of art by an old Baroque engraver, as well as a physical symbol of authority, of which the deputy's key was merely an austere, inferior copy, was in the possession of the Registrar, though he apparently never used it, either because of the weight and complexity of the design, which made it awkward to carry around, or because, according to some unwritten hierarchical protocol, in effect since the remotest of times, he always had to be the last to enter the building. One of the many mysteries of life in the Central Registry, which really would be worth investigating if the matter of Senhor José and the unknown woman had not absorbed all our attention, was how the staff, despite the traffic jams afflicting the city, always managed to arrive at work in the same order, first the clerks, regardless of length of service, then the deputy who opened the door, then the senior clerks, in order of precedence, then the oldest deputy and, finally, the Registrar, who arrives when he has to arrive and does not have to answer to anyone. Anyway, the fact stands recorded.

The feeling of scornful commiseration which, as we have said, greeted Senhor José's return to work, lasted until the arrival of the Registrar, half an hour after the office had opened, and was instantly replaced by a feeling of envy, understandable in the circumstances, but, fortunately, not manifested in words or deeds. What else could one expect, the human soul being what we know it to be, though we cannot claim to know everything. A rumour had been going around the Central Registry, slipping in through the back door, so to speak, and whispered in corners, that the Registrar had been unusually concerned about Senhor José's bout of flu, even going so far as to have the nurse bring him food, as well as visiting him in his house at least once, and during office hours too, in front of everyone, who knows, he may well have visited him again. It is easy, therefore, to imagine the suppressed outrage, in every rank, when the Registrar, even before going to his own desk, stopped beside Senhor José and asked him if he was now completely recovered from his illness. The outrage was all the greater because this was the second time it had happened, they could all remember that other occasion, not so long ago, when the boss had asked Senhor José if his insomnia had improved, as if Senhor José's insomnia was, as far as the normal running of the Central Registry was concerned, a matter of life or death. Hardly able to credit what they were hearing, the staff witnessed a conversation between equals, utterly absurd however you looked at it, with Senhor José thanking the Registrar for his kindness, even referring openly to the food, which, in the strict atmosphere of the Central Registry, had all the force of a profanity, an obscenity, and the Registrar explaining that he couldn't possibly have abandoned him to the wretched fate of those who live alone, without having anyone to give him a bowl of soup and smooth his sheets. Loneliness, Senhor José, declared the Registrar solemnly, never made for good company, all the great sadnesses, great temptations and great mistakes are almost always the result of being alone in life, without a prudent friend to advise us when we are troubled by something more serious than our normal everyday problems, Well, I don't know that I would say I was actually sad, sir, replied Senhor José, perhaps I am rather melancholy by nature, but that's hardly a defect, and as for temptations, well, I have to say that I am little inclined to them either by my age or my circumstances, I mean, I don't seek them out and they don't seek me, And what about mistakes, Are you referring to mistakes at work, sir, No, I'm referring to mistakes in general, mistakes at work are departmental mistakes which the department ultimately resolves, All I can say is that I've never harmed anyone, at least not knowingly, And what about mistakes committed against yourself, I must have made many of those, perhaps that's why I'm alone, In order to make more mistakes, Only those born of loneliness, sir. Senhor José, who, as was his duty, had got to his feet as the Registrar approached, suddenly felt his legs buckle and a wave of sweat sweep over his body. He went pale, his hands anxiously sought the support of his desk, but that support was not enough, Senhor José had to sit down on his chair, murmuring, Excuse me, sir, excuse me. The Registrar regarded him for some seconds with an impenetrable look on his face and went to his desk. He called over the deputy responsible for Senhor José's section and gave him a muttered order, adding, more audibly, There's no need to go through the official channels, which meant that the instructions the deputy had just received, intended for a clerk, should, against all the rules, customs and traditions, be carried out by himself. The hierarchical chain had been subverted once before, when the Registrar had ordered this same deputy to take Senhor José the pills, but that infraction could be justified by the suspicion that the senior clerk responsible would prove incapable of satisfactorily carrying out the mission which consisted not so much in taking a few anti-flu tablets to a sick man as having a look around the house and reporting back. A senior clerk would find the damp stain on the floor perfectly acceptable, that is, unremarkable and easily explained by the wintry weather they had been having at the time, and would probably not even have noticed the record cards on the bedside table, he would return to the Central Registry in the happy belief that he had done his duty, declaring to the Registrar, Nothing unusual to report, sir. It must be said, however, that the two deputies, and this one in particular, more directly involved in the process by his active participation in it, realised that the Registrar's behaviour was determined by an objective, a strategy, a central idea. They couldn't imagine what that idea or objective might be, but all their experience and knowledge of their boss told them that, in this affair, every word and every deed must inevitably point to one end, and that Senhor José, placed by his own actions or by a chance circumstance on the path towards that end, either was merely an unwittingly useful instrument or was himself its unexpected and entirely surprising cause. Such opposing arguments, such contradictory feelings, meant that the order, from the tone in which it was subsequently communicated to Senhor José, sounded far more like a favour the Registrar had ordered to be asked of him than the clear, categorical instruction that had effectively been issued, Senhor José, said the deputy, the Registrar is of the opinion that, given your fainting fit of a moment ago, your health is not sufficiently recovered for you to come to work, It wasn't a fainting fit, I didn't lose consciousness, it was just a momentary weakness, Well, weakness or fainting fit, momentary or lasting, what the Central Registry wants is for you to make a complete recovery, I'll work sitting down as much as I can, in a few days' time I'll be right as rain, The Registrar thinks it would be best if you took a short holiday, not your whole twenty days, of course, perhaps ten, ten days to rest and regain your strength, take it easy, go for a few strolls round the city, there are gardens to visit, parks, and the weather's glorious just now, a proper period of convalescence, we won't even recognise you when you come back. Senhor José looked at the deputy in amazement, this really wasn't the kind of conversation a deputy had with a mere clerk, there was something almost indecent about it. Obviously the Registrar wanted him to go on holiday, which was, in itself, intriguing, but, as if that were not enough, he was showing an unusual, indeed disproportionate, interest in his health. None of this corresponded to the usual patterns of behaviour in the Central Registry, where holiday plans were always calculated with meticulous precision in order to achieve, by pondering multiple factors, some of which were known only to the Registrar, a fair distribution of the time set aside for annual leisure. It was unheard of for the Registrar to ignore the plans already made for the current year and simply send a clerk home. Senhor José was confused, you could see it in his face. He could sense his colleagues' perplexed eyes on his back, he could feel the deputy's growing impatience with what must seem to him baseless indecision, and he was about to say, Yes, sir, like someone simply obeying an order, when suddenly his face lit up, he had just seen what those ten days of freedom could mean, ten days during which he could carry out his investigations without being tied down to the servitude of work, to a timetable, never mind about parks, gardens or convalescence, God bless whoever invented flu, and so Senhor José smiled when he said, Yes, sir, he should have been more discreet in the way he expressed himself, you never know what a deputy might go and tell the boss, In my opinion, he reacted very strangely, first, he seemed upset, or as if he hadn't quite understood what I'd said, then, it was as if he'd won first prize in the lottery, he didn't seem the same person, Do you have any evidence that he's a gambling man, I don't think so, it was just a manner of speaking, Then there must be some other reason. Senhor José was already saying to the deputy, It would really suit me to have a few days off, I must thank the Registrar, I'll pass your thanks on to him, Perhaps I should do it personally, You know perfectly well that is not the custom, Nevertheless, considering the exceptional nature of the matter, and having said those, bureaucratically speaking, most pertinent of words, Senhor José turned to where the Registrar was sitting, he wasn't expecting him to be looking in his direction, still less that he would have heard the whole conversation, which was what he doubtless intended to indicate with that abrupt gesture of the hand, at once bored and imperious, No ridiculous words of gratitude, please, just fill out the form and leave.

Back at home, Senhor José's prime concern was for the clothes kept in the niche that he used as a wardrobe. They had been dirty before, but now were transformed into pure filth, exuding a sour smell mingled with a whiff of mould, there was even mildew growing in the cuffs of his pants, imagine it, a dank bundle, jacket, shirt, trousers, socks, underwear, all wrapped in a raincoat, which, at the time, had been dripping wet, what condition would you expect to find it in after a whole week. He stuffed the clothes into a large plastic bag, made sure that the record cards and the notebook were still safely tucked away between the mattress and the base of the bed, the notebook at the head, the record cards at the foot, he checked that the communicating door with the Central Registry was locked, and finally, weary, but with his mind at rest, he set off for a nearby laundry of which he was a customer, although hardly one of the most frequent. The woman there could not or did not care to conceal a reproving look when she emptied out the contents of the bag onto the counter, I'm sorry, but anyone would think these clothes had been dragged through the mud, You're not far wrong, since Senhor José had to lie, he decided to do so within the bounds of possibility, Two weeks ago, when I was bringing you these clothes to be cleaned, the bag suddenly burst and all the clothes fell into a big muddy puddle caused by the roadwork they were doing at the time, you remember how much it rained then, And why didn't you bring the clothes in at once, I was confined to bed with the flu, I couldn't risk leaving the house, I could have caught pneumonia, It's going to cost you quite a bit more, it'll have to go in the machine twice, and even then, Never mind, And these trousers, have you seen the state these trousers are in, is it really worth having them cleaned, I mean the knees are all worn, it looks as if you'd been rubbing against a wall in them. Senhor José had not noticed the terrible state in which the climb had left his poor trousers, almost worn through at the knees, with a small tear on one of the legs, a serious matter for a person like him, so ill provided with clothes. Is there nothing you can do about it, he asked, Oh, I can do something about it, but they'll have to be sent to an invisible mender, I don't know of any, Oh, we can deal with that for you, but it's not going to be cheap, these invisible menders charge quite a bit, It'll be better than being without a pair of trousers, Or else we could patch them, If they were patched, I'd only be able to use them at home, I'd never be able to wear them to work, No, of course not, You see I work for the Central Registry, Ah, you work for the Central Registry, said the woman with a new tone of respect in her voice that Senhor José thought it best to ignore, regretting having been so indiscreet as to admit for the first time where he worked, a truly professional burglar would not go around scattering clues like that, what if the woman in the laundry were married to the man in the hardware store where Senhor José went to buy the glass cutter or the butcher's where he bought the lard, and then that night, during one of those banal conversations with which husbands and wives pass the evening, one of them were suddenly to mention these small episodes from daily commercial life, other criminals, convinced that they were above all suspicion, have gone to prison for far less. Anyway, there didn't seem to be much danger there, not unless the woman was concealing some abject, treacherous intention behind the words she was saying to him now, with a kind smile, that this time they'd give him a special price, with the laundry paying for the invisible mender, Seeing that the gentleman works for the Central Registry, she explained. Senhor José thanked her politely but uneffusively and left. He felt unhappy. He was leaving too many trails about the city, talking with too many people, this was not the kind of investigation he had imagined, to tell the truth he hadn't actually imagined anything, the idea had just occurred to him now, the idea of looking for and finding the unknown woman with no one knowing anything about his activities, as if it were a question of one invisible being seeking out another. Instead of that closed secret, that absolute mystery, there were already two people, the wife with the jealous husband and the elderly lady in the ground-floor apartment, who knew what he was up to, and that, in itself, was already a danger, for example, let us suppose that either of them, with the praiseworthy aim of helping him in his search, as befits a good citizen, should appear at the Central Registry during his absence, I'd like to speak to Senhor José, Senhor José isn't here, he's on holiday, Oh, that's a shame, I've got some important information for him about the person he was looking for, What information, what person, Senhor José didn't even want to think about what would follow, the rest of the conversation between the woman with the jealous husband and the senior clerk, I found a journal underneath a loose floorboard in my room, You mean a magazine, No, sir, a journal, a diary, the kind of thing some people like to keep, I used to keep one before I got married, And what's that got to do with us, here at the Central Registry we're only interested in knowing who's born and who dies, Perhaps the diary I found belongs to some relative of the person that Senhor José has been looking for, I didn't know Senhor José was looking for anyone, besides, it's not a matter that affects the Central Registry, the Central Registry does not get involved in the private lives of its staff, It's not private, Senhor José told me he was acting on behalf of the Central Registry, Wait there and I'll call the deputy, but when the deputy came over to the counter, the elderly lady from the ground-floor apartment was already leaving, life had taught her that the best way to protect your own secrets is to respect other people's, When Senhor José gets back from his holidays, would you mind telling him that the old lady from the ground-floor apartment was here, Don't you want to leave your name, It's not necessary, he'll know who I am. Senhor José could breathe easily, the lady in the ground-floor apartment was discretion itself, she would never tell the deputy that she had just received a letter from her goddaughter, The flu has addled my brains, he thought, these are just fantasies, there aren't any diaries hidden beneath floorboards, and, after a silence of so many years, she wouldn't suddenly think to write a letter to her godmother, just as well the old lady had the good sense not to give her name, the Central Registry would only have to get hold of that one loose thread to find out everything, the copying of the record cards, the forging of the letter, it would be as easy for them as putting together a jigsaw puzzle while looking at the picture on the lid of the box. Senhor José went back home, on that first day he preferred not to follow the advice the deputy had given him, to go for walks, go to a garden and feel the good sun on his pale convalescent's face, in a word, to recover the strength that the fever had drained from him. He needed to decide what steps he should take from then on, but he needed above all to quell an anxiety. He had left his small house there at the mercy of the Central Registry, clinging to the monstrous wall as if it were about to be swallowed up by it. There must have been some remnant of fever lingering in his brain for that idea to occur to him, that this was what had happened to the other staff houses, all devoured by the Central Registry so that it could extend its walls. Senhor José quickened his step, if, when he got there, the house had disappeared, and the record cards and the notebook along with it, he didn't even want to imagine such a misfortune, the efforts of weeks all reduced to nothing, the dangers he had gone through all in vain. Curious people would be there asking him if he had lost anything of value in the disaster, and he would say yes, Some papers, and they would ask again, Shares, Bonds, Credits, that's the first thing that would occur to ordinary people, people with no spiritual horizons, their thoughts are all concerned with material interests and gains, he would say yes, mentally giving different meanings to those words, they would be his share in other people's lives, the bonds he had begun to form, the credit he had gained.

The house was there, but it seemed much smaller, unless the Central Registry had grown in size in the last few hours. Senhor José went in, lowering his head, even though it wasn't necessary to do so, the street door was the same height it had always been, and, as far as one could see, those shares, bonds and credits had not made him grow physically in size. He went and listened at the communicating door, not because he expected to hear the sound of voices from the other side, it was the custom at the Central Registry to work in silence, but to assuage the confused feelings of suspicion he had felt ever since the Registrar had ordered him to take some holiday time. Then he went and lifted the mattress on the bed, removed the record cards and set them out in chronological order on the table, from the oldest to the most recent, thirteen small cardboard rectangles, a succession of faces going from small child to larger child, from the beginning of adolescence to near-womanhood. During those years the family had moved three times, but never so far away that she had to change schools. There was no point drawing up complicated plans of action, the only thing that Senhor José could do now was to go to the address on the last card.

He went there the following morning, but he decided not to go up and ask the present occupants of the apartment and the building's other tenants if they had known the girl in the photograph. It was more than likely that they would tell him they hadn't, that they had been living there only a short time, or that they didn't remember, You know how it is, people come and go, I really can't remember anything about the family, it's not worth puzzling your head about, and if someone did say yes and did seem to have a vague recollection, they would probably only go on to add that their relationship had been the usual one among the polite classes, So you never saw them again, Senhor José would ask, No, never, after they moved out, I never saw them again, That's a shame, I've told you everything I know, I'm sorry not to be of more use to the Central Registry. The good fortune of immediately finding the lady in the ground-floor apartment, so well informed, so close to the original sources, could not possibly happen twice, but only much later, when none of what is being related here was of any importance anymore, did Senhor José discover that here too the same good fortune had acted prodigiously in his favour, saving him from the most disastrous of consequences. Unbeknownst to him, by some diabolical coincidence, one of the deputies at the Central Registry lived in that building, you can imagine the terrible scene, our trusting Senhor José knocking at the door, showing the index card, possibly even the forged letter of authority, and the woman who came to the door saying treacherously, Come back later when my husband's at home, he always deals with matters like this, and Senhor José would go back, his heart full of hope, and would come face-to-face with a furious deputy, who would arrest him on the spot, literally not figuratively, for the Central Registry's regulations permit of neither precipitate actions nor improvisation, the worst thing being that we don't even know what all the regulations are. Having resolved this time, as if his guardian angel had been whispering the advice urgently in his ear, to turn his attention to the shops in the area, Senhor José had unwittingly saved himself from the worst disgrace in his long career as a civil servant. He contented himself, then, with looking up at the windows of the apartment where the unknown woman had lived when she was young, and in order to get properly inside the skin of a real investigator, he imagined her leaving for school, carrying her satchel, walking to the bus stop and waiting there, it wasn't worth following her, Senhor José knew perfectly well where she was going, he had the relevant proof hidden between the mattress and the base of his bed. A quarter of an hour later, her father left, he sets off in the opposite direction, that's why he doesn't leave with his daughter when she goes to school, unless it's simply that father and daughter don't like to walk along together and give this as an excuse, or give no excuse at all, but there will be some kind of tacit agreement between the two, so that the neighbours won't notice their mutual indifference. Now Senhor José needs to be patient for a little while longer, until the mother goes out shopping, as usually happens in families, that way he will know where he should make his inquiries, the nearest commercial establishment, three buildings along, is that chemist's shop, but Senhor José immediately doubts that he will obtain any useful information there, the assistant is a young man, young in age and young as an employee, he himself says so, I don't know, I've only been here two years. But Senhor José won't be discouraged by that, he has read more than enough newspapers and magazines, not to mention the lessons life has been teaching him, to know that these investigations, carried out in the old way, take a lot of work, involve a lot of walking, pounding streets and pavements, going up stairs, knocking at doors, coming down stairs, the same questions asked a thousand times, identical replies, almost always in a reserved tone of voice, I don't know, I've never heard of such a person, only very rarely does it happen that from the back room there emerges an older pharmacist who has heard the conversation and is, by nature, extremely inquisitive, Can I help you, he asked, I'm looking for someone, replied Senhor José, at the same time raising his hand to his inside jacket pocket in order to show the letter of authority. He did not complete the movement, a sudden feeling of unease stopped him, this time it wasn't the work of any guardian angel, what made him slowly withdraw his hand was the look in the pharmacist's eye, a look that was more like a dagger, a perforating drill, no one would think it, with his lined face and his white hair, but the effect of that look is to put even the most ingenuous of creatures immediately on guard, which is probably why the pharmacist's curiosity is never satisfied, the more he wants to know the less people tell him. That is what happened with Senhor José. He did not even show him the letter of authority, he did not say that he had come on behalf of the Central Registry, he merely took from his other pocket the girl's most recent school record card, which, fortunately, he had remembered to bring with him, Our school needs to find this lady in order to give her a diploma that she failed to pick up from the secretary's office, Senhor José felt a pang of pleasure, almost enthusiasm, at the exercise of inventive abilities he had never imagined he had, so sure of himself that he remained unperturbed by the pharmacist's question, And you're only looking for her now, all these years later, It's quite possible she won't be interested, he replied, but the school is under an obligation to do all it can to make sure the diploma is delivered, And you've waited all this time for her to appear, To tell you the truth, we didn't even notice, it was a lamentable lack of attention on our part, a bureaucratic error, if you like, but it's never too late to right a wrong, It will definitely be too late if the lady's already dead, We have reason to believe that she's still alive, Why, We began by consulting the records, Senhor José was careful not to mention the words Central Registry, that was what saved him, because, at least at that moment, it meant that the pharmacist did not suddenly recall that a deputy registrar from the said Central Registry was one of his customers and lived three buildings down. For the second time, Senhor José had escaped the ultimate punishment. It's true that the deputy only rarely went into the chemist's, such purchases, and indeed all other purchases, apart from condoms, which the deputy was morally scrupulous enough to go and buy elsewhere, were made by his wife, so it's not that easy to imagine a conversation between the pharmacist and him, although one can't exclude the possibility of another conversation, the pharmacist saying to the deputy's wife, There was some school administrator in here looking for someone who used to live in the building where you live, at one point he mentioned consulting the records, it was only after he'd gone that I thought it strange that he should have said records rather than Central Registry, it seemed to me that he had something to hide, there was even a moment when he raised his hand to his inside jacket pocket as if he were about to show me something, but he had second thoughts and instead took a school record card from his other pocket, I've been racking my brains to think what it could all be about, I think you should talk to your husband, you never know, there are some funny people about, Perhaps it's the same man I noticed the day before yesterday, standing on the pavement looking up at our windows, A middle-aged chap, a bit younger than me, who looked as if he'd only recently recovered from an illness, That's the one, You know I've got an instinct for these things, it never fails, there aren't many people can pull the wool over my eyes, It's a shame he didn't knock at my door, I'd have told him to come back in the afternoon, when my husband was home, then we'd know who he was and what he wanted, I'm going to keep an eye out in case he shows up again, And I'll make a point of mentioning it to my husband. Which she did, but she didn't tell the whole story, she unwittingly left out the most important detail, perhaps the most important of all, she did not say that the man who had been hanging around the building looked as if he had only recently recovered from an illness. Accustomed to making links between causes and effects, since that is essentially what underpins the system of forces which, from the beginning of time, has ruled in the Central Registry, where everything was, is and will continue to be forever linked to everything, what is still alive to what is already dead, what is dying to what is being born, all beings to all other beings, all things to all other things, even when the only thing they seem to have in common, both beings and things, is what at first sight appears to separate them, the wise deputy would immediately have thought of Senhor José, the clerk who, with the inexplicably benevolent compliance of the Registrar, had been behaving very strangely lately. Finding the end of the thread and then untangling the whole skein would be only a step. That will not happen, though, Senhor José will not be seen again in that area. Of the ten different shops he went into to ask questions, including the pharmacy, in only three of them did he find someone who claimed to remember the girl and her parents, the picture on the report card jogged their memories, unless, of course, it merely took the place of their memories, it's quite likely that the people questioned simply wanted to be nice and did not want to disappoint this man who looked as if he had just got over a nasty bout of flu and who spoke to them of a school diploma issued twenty years earlier and never delivered. When Senhor José got home, he felt exhausted and discouraged, this first stage in the new phase of his investigations had indicated no route along which to continue, quite the contrary, it seemed to have placed before him an unscalable wall. The poor man threw himself down on the bed wondering why he didn't do what the pharmacist, with ill-disguised sarcasm, had suggested, If I were you, I would already have solved the problem, How, asked Senhor José, I'd have looked in the phone book, that's the easiest way of finding someone these days, Thanks for the suggestion, but we've already done that, and the lady's name isn't there, replied Senhor José, thinking that would shut the man up, but the pharmacist returned to the charge, Go to the tax office then, they know everything about everyone. Senhor José stood staring at this spoilsport, struggling to disguise his embarrassment, the lady in the ground-floor apartment hadn't thought of that, then he managed to murmur a response, That's a good idea, I'll tell the head teacher. He left the pharmacy feeling furious with himself, as if, at the last moment, he had lacked the presence of mind to respond to an insult, he was all set to go back home without asking any more questions, but then, resigned, he thought, The wine has been poured, I must drink it, he did not, like someone else, say, Take this cup away from me, what you want is to kill me. The second shop was a hardware store, the third a butcher's, the fourth a stationer's, the fifth an electrical goods shop, the sixth a haberdasher's, the usual routine suburban selection, and so on to the tenth shop, fortunately, his luck held, after the pharmacist no one else mentioned the tax office or the telephone directory. Now, lying on his back, with his hands interlaced behind his head, Senhor José looks up at the ceiling and asks, What am I going to do now, and the ceiling replied, Nothing, your knowing her last address, I mean, the last address she lived at during her schooldays, gave you no clue as to how to continue your search, of course, you could go to earlier addresses, but that would be a waste of time, if the most recent shopkeepers couldn't help you, the others certainly won't be able to, So you think I should give up then, You've probably got no option, unless you go to the tax office, it shouldn't be difficult with that letter of authority you've got, besides they're civil servants like you, It's a forgery, Yes, you're right, you'd probably better not use it, I wouldn't like to be in your skin if one day they catch you redhanded, You couldn't be in my skin, you're just a plaster ceiling, I know, but what you're seeing of me is also a skin, besides, the skin is only what we want others to see of us, underneath it not even we know who we are, I'll hide the letter, If I were you, I'd tear it up or burn it, I'll put it with the bishop's papers, where I kept it before, Well, it's up to you, I don't like the tone you said that in, it doesn't augur at all well, The wisdom of ceilings is infinite, If you're such a wise ceiling, then give me an idea, Keep looking at me, sometimes it works.

The idea that the ceiling gave to Senhor José was to cut his holiday short and go back to work, You tell the boss that you're much stronger now and ask him to reserve the other days for another occasion, that is if you ever find a way out of the hole you've got yourself into, with all doors shut and not a single clue to follow, The Registrar is going to find it strange a member of staff going in to work when he's not obliged to and without being called, You've done stranger things than that recently, I lived a peaceful life before this absurd obsession, looking for a woman who doesn't even know I exist, But you know that she exists, that's the problem, I'd better just give up once and for all, Maybe, maybe, anyway just remember that not only the wisdom of ceilings is infinite, life's surprises are too, What do you mean by that tired old cliché, That the days go by and never come again, That's an even tireder cliché, don't tell me that the wisdom of ceilings consists only in clichés like that, said Senhor José scornfully, You know nothing about life if you think there is more than that to know, replied the ceiling and fell silent. Senhor José got off the bed, hid the letter in the wardrobe, among the bishop's papers, then went to fetch his notebook and began describing the frustrating events of the morning, laying particular emphasis on the pharmacist's unpleasant manner and his gimlet eye. At the end of the report he wrote, as if the idea had been his, I think it's best that I go back to work. When he was putting away the notebook underneath the mattress, he remembered that he hadn't had any lunch, his head told him, not his stomach, if, over a period of time, people forget to eat, they get out of the habit of listening to the clock of hunger. If Senhor José were to continue his holiday, he wouldn't in the least mind going back to bed for the rest of the day, skipping lunch and supper, sleeping all night if he could, or taking refuge in the voluntary torpor of someone who has decided to turn his back on the disagreeable facts of life. But he had to feed his body in order to work the following day, he would hate it if weakness made him break out in a cold sweat again and suffer ridiculous dizzy spells that would be greeted with the feigned commiseration of his colleagues and the impatience of his superiors. He beat two eggs, added a few slices of chorizo sausage, a generous pinch of sea salt, put some oil in a frying pan, and waited until it had heated to just the right point, that was his one culinary talent, otherwise he resorted to opening cans. He ate the omelette slowly, in small geometrically precise pieces, making it last as long as possible, not from any gastronomical pleasure, but just to fill the time. Above all, he did not want to think. His imaginary and metaphysical dialogue with the ceiling had served to disguise his complete mental disorientation, the feeling of panic provoked by the idea that he would now have nothing further to do in life, if, as he had reason to fear, the search for the unknown woman was over.

He felt a hard knot in his throat, like when he was told off as a child and he was expected to cry, and he would resist, resist, until at last the tears came, as they came now. He pushed his plate away, rested his head on his folded arms and cried without shame, at least this time there was no one here to laugh at him. On these occasions, ceilings can do nothing to help people in distress, they must merely wait up there until the storm passes, until the soul has unburdened itself, until the body is rested. That is what happened to Senhor José. After a few moments, he felt better, he brusquely wiped away the tears with his shirtsleeve and went to wash his plate and the cutlery. He had the whole afternoon ahead of him and nothing to do. He considered going to visit the lady in the ground-floor apartment, to tell her more or less what had happened, but then he thought that it wasn't worth it, she had told him everything she knew, and perhaps she would finally ask him what the devil the Central Registry was up to going to so much trouble over one person, a woman of no importance, it would be an indecent lie, as well as arrant stupidity, to tell her that we are all equal in the eyes of the Central Registry, just as the sun is there for everyone each time it rises, there are things one should avoid saying to an older person if we don't want them to laugh in our faces. Senhor José went to a corner of the house to get an armful of magazines and old newspapers from which he had already cut out articles and photographs, he might have missed something interesting, or there might be an article about someone who seemed a promising candidate for the rocky road to fame. Senhor José was returning to his collections.

The person who seemed least surprised was the Registrar. Having, as usual, arrived when everyone else was already at their places working, he paused for three seconds beside Senhor José's desk, but he didn't say a word. Senhor José was expecting to be submitted to a thorough interrogation as to the reasons for his early return to work, but the Registrar merely listened to the explanations given by the deputy in charge of that section, whom he later dismissed with an abrupt wave of his right hand, his index finger and middle finger held stiffly together, the others slightly bent, which, according to the gestural code of the Central Registry, meant that he did not care to hear another word on the matter. Caught between an initial expectation that he would be interrogated and relief at being left in peace, Senhor José struggled to clarify his ideas, to concentrate all his senses on the work that the senior clerk had placed on his desk, twenty or so birth certificates the information from each of which had to be transferred onto record cards and then filed away in the card-index system under the counter, in proper alphabetical order. It was a simple task, but a responsible one, which, fortunately for Senhor José, who was still weak in legs and head, could at least be carried out sitting down. The errors of copyists are the least excusable, there's no point in their coming to us and saying, I got distracted, on the contrary, recognising that one was distracted is the same as confessing that one was thinking about something else instead of giving full attention to the names and dates whose supreme importance lies in the fact that, in the present instance, it is those names and dates that give legal existence to the reality of existence. Especially the name of the person who was born. A simple error of transcription, a change in the initial letter of a surname, for example, would mean that the index card would be put in the wrong place, possibly far from where it should be, as would inevitably happen in this Central Registry, where there are so many names, indeed where all the names are. If the clerk who in times past had copied Senhor José's name onto the card, had written Xosé instead, his mind confused by a similarity in pronunciation that verges on coincidence, there would be no end of work involved in trying to find the lost record card in order to write on it any of the three most commonly occurring notes, marriage, divorce, death, two more or less avoidable, the other not. That is why Senhor José copies with the greatest of care, letter by letter, these proofs of the existence of these new beings which have been entrusted to him, he has already transcribed sixteen birth certificates, now he is drawing the seventeenth towards him, he's preparing the record card, when his hand suddenly trembles, his eyes swim, beads of sweat appear on his forehead. The name before him, of a person of the female sex, is, in almost every detail, identical to that of the unknown woman, only the last name is different, and even then, the first letter is the same. It is highly likely that this card, bearing the name that it does, will have to be filed immediately after the other one, which is why Senhor José, like someone unable to control his impatience as the moment of a long-awaited encounter approaches, got up from his chair as soon as he had finished the transcription, ran to the appropriate drawer in the card index, nervously riffled through the cards, looked for and found the place. The unknown woman's card was not there. The fatal words immediately flashed up in Senhor José's head, the fulminating words, She's dead. Because Senhor José knows that the absence of a card from the card-index system inevitably means the death of the person whose name is on the card, he has lost count of the cards which he himself, in his twenty-five years as a civil servant, has removed from there and carried to the archive of the dead, but now he is refusing to accept the evidence that this could be the reason for the disappearance, some careless, incompetent colleague must have misfiled the card, perhaps it's a little further on, a little further back, Senhor José, out of desperation, wants to deceive himself, never, in all the centuries of the Central Registry's existence, has a card in this index system been misplaced, there is only one possibility, only one, that the woman might still be alive, and that is if her card is temporarily in the possession of one of the other clerks because some new piece of information is to be added to it, Perhaps she's got married again, thought Senhor José, and, for an instant, his un-expected irritation at the idea mitigated his disquiet. Then, barely noticing what he was doing, he placed the card onto which he had copied the details from the birth certificate in the place of the one that had disappeared, and, his legs trembling, he returned to his desk. He could not ask his colleagues if, by any chance, they had the woman's card, he could not walk around all their desks trying to get a glimpse of the papers they were working on, all he could do was watch the drawer in the card-index system to see if someone replaced the small card-board rectangle taken from there by mistake or for a less routine reason than death. The hours passed, morning gave way to afternoon, Senhor José barely managed to eat a thing at lunchtime, he must have something wrong with his throat to be so easily afflicted by these knots, these tightnesses, these anxieties. During the whole day not one colleague went to open that drawer, not one lost card found its way back, the unknown woman was dead.

That night, Senhor José returned to the Central Registry. He took with him the flashlight and a hundred-yard roll of strong string. He had put a new battery in his flashlight that would suffice for several hours of continual use, but, more than chastened by the difficulties he had been obliged to confront during the dangerous break-in and theft at the school, Senhor José had learned that in life you can never be too careful, especially when you abandon the straight paths of honest behaviour and wander off down the tortuous shortcuts of crime. What if the little bulb were to blow, what if the lens that protects and intensifies the light were to come loose from the casing, what if the flashlight, with the battery lens and bulb intact, were to fall down a hole so that he couldn't reach it with his arm or even with a hook, then, not daring to use the real Ariadne's thread, despite the fact that the drawer in the Registrar's Office where it was kept, along with a powerful flashlight, was never locked, Senhor José will instead use an ordinary, rustic ball of string bought at the hardware store, and that string will lead back to the world of the living the person who, at this very moment, is preparing to enter the kingdom of the dead. As a member of the Central Registry, Senhor José has legitimate access to any documents in the civil register, which are, need we repeat, the very substance of his work, so some may think it strange that, when he found the card missing, he did not simply say to the senior clerk he worked under, I'm going to look for the card of a woman who died. For it would not be enough just to say that, he would have to give a reason that was both administratively sound and bureaucratically logical, the senior clerk would be bound to ask, What do you want it for, and Senhor José could hardly reply, To be quite sure that she's really dead, what would happen to the Central Registry if everyone started satisfying the same or similar curiosities, which were not only morbid but unproductive too. The worst that could come of Senhor José's nocturnal expedition would be that he would be unable to find the unknown woman's papers in the chaos that is the archive of the dead. Of course, at first, since we're dealing with a recent death, the papers should be at what was commonly termed the entrance, which is immediately problematic because of the impossibility of knowing exactly where the entrance to the archive of the dead is. It would be too simple to say, as do some stubborn optimists, that the space designated for the dead obviously begins where the space for the living ends, and vice versa, perhaps adding that, in the outside world, things are arranged in a similar fashion, given that, apart from exceptional events, albeit not that exceptional, such as natural disasters or wars, you don't normally see the dead mingling in the street with the living. Now, for both structural and non-structural reasons, this can in fact happen in the Central Registry. It can and it does. As we have already explained, from time to time, when the congestion caused by the continual and irresistible accumulation of the dead begins to block the path of staff along the corridors and, consequently, to obstruct any documentary research, they have no option but to demolish the wall at the rear and rebuild it a few yards farther back. However, through an involuntary oversight on our part, we failed to mention the two perverse effects of this congestion. First, while the wall is being built, it is inevitable that, for lack of a space of their own at the back of the building, the cards and files of the recently dead come dangerously close to, and, on the near side, even touch the files of the living, which are to be found on the far end of their respective shelves, giving rise to an embarrassing fringe of confusion between those who are still living and those who are now dead. Second, once the wall has been built and the roof extended, and the filing away of the dead can at last return to normality, that same border conflict, as it were, will prevent, or, at the very least, prove extremely prejudicial to, the transport into the outer darkness of the dead intruders, if you'll pardon the expression. Added to these far from minor inconveniences is the fact that, without the knowledge of the Registrar or their colleagues, the two youngest clerks have no qualms, either because they have not been properly trained or because of a grave deficiency in their personal ethics, about simply sticking a dead person anywhere, without going to the trouble of seeing if there might be space inside the archive of the dead. If luck were not on Senhor José's side this time, if chance did not favour him, the adventure of breaking into the school, however risky, will have been child's play compared to what awaits him here.

One might ask why Senhor José needs a hundred-yard-long piece of string if the length of the Central Registry, despite successive extensions, is no more than eighty. That is the question of a person who imagines that one can do everything in life simply by following a straight line, that it is always possible to proceed from one place to another by the shortest route, perhaps some people in the outside world believe that they have done so, but here, where the living and the dead share the same space, sometimes, in order to find one of them, you have to make a lot of twists and turns, you have to skirt round mountains of bundles, columns of files, piles of cards, thickets of ancient remains, you have to walk down dark gulleys, between walls of grubby paper which, up above, actually touch, yards and yards of string will have to be unravelled, left behind, like a sinuous, subtle trail traced in the dust, there is no other way of knowing where you have to go next, there is no other way of finding your way back. Senhor José tied one end of the string to the leg of the Registrar's desk, not out of any lack of respect, but merely to gain a few yards, then tied the other end to his ankle, and, placing on the floor the ball of string, which unravelled with each step he took, he set off along one of the central corridors filled by the files of the living. His plan is to start his search at the far end, where the unknown woman's file and card should be, even though, for reasons already explained, it is highly unlikely that they will have been filed away correctly. As Senhor José is a civil servant from another age, trained in the old methods and disciplines, his strict character would be repelled by any collusion with the irresponsible habits of the new generation, by beginning the search in a place where a dead person would have been deposited only by a deliberate and scandalous infraction of basic archivistic rules. He knows that the main difficulty he is going to have to do battle with is the lack of light. Apart from the Registrar's desk, above which hangs the inevitable lamp giving off its usual dull light, the whole of the Central Registry is plunged in darkness, in dense shadows. Turning on other lights in the building, however dim they might be, would be too risky, a keen policeman doing his rounds of the area, or a good citizen, the sort who is concerned about the safety of the community, might spot the diffuse light through the high windows and immediately sound the alarm. Senhor José will, therefore, have only the feeble circle of light, which wavers before him in time to the rhythm of his steps, but also because the hand holding the flashlight is trembling. There is an enormous difference between visiting the archive of the dead in normal working hours, with the presence behind you of your colleagues, who, although not particularly supportive, as we have seen, would always come running if there were any real danger or if your nerve suddenly, irresistibly failed, especially if the Registrar said, Go and see what's happened to him, between that and venturing alone, in the middle of a black night, into the heart of those catacombs of humanity, surrounded by names, hearing the whisper of the papers, or a murmur of voices, for those who have ears to hear.

Senhor José has gone as far as the end of the shelves of the living, he is now looking for a passage along which he can reach the far end of the Central Registry, in theory, and in accordance with the way the space was laid out, it should follow the bissecting longitudinal line on the plan, the imaginary line that divides the rectangular design of the building into two equal parts, but the avalanches of files, which are always happening however firmly the masses of paper are held in place, have made something that was intended to provide direct, rapid access into a complex network of passages and paths, where you are constantly confronted by obstacles and cul-de-sacs. During the day and with all the lights on, it is still relatively easy for the researcher to keep a straight course, you just have to pay attention, be vigilant, take care to follow the least dusty roads, a sign that they are the most frequented, and up until now, apart from a few scares and some worrying delays, there has not been a single instance of a staff member failing to return from an expedition. But the light from a pocket flashlight does not fill one with confidence, it seems to create its own shadows, what Senhor José should have done, since he did not dare to use the Registrar's flashlight, was to have bought one of those really powerful modern ones, the sort that can light everything to the farthest ends of the earth. It's true that the fear of getting lost doesn't trouble him too much, to a certain extent the constant tension of the string tied round his ankle comforts him, but if he starts wandering about, going in circles, getting caught up in the cocoon, he will eventually be unable to take another step, and will have to go back and start again. He has already had to do so for another reason, when

142

the fine string, too fine really, got caught up among the bundles of paper and snagged on the corners, and then there could be no going backwards or forwards. Given all these problems and entanglements, it is understandable that any progress will be slow, and that Senhor José's knowledge of the topography of the place will be of little use to him, especially since a huge pile of files, the height of a man, has just blocked what had every appearance of being a straight path, throwing up a thick cloud of dust, in the midst of which fluttered terrified moths, almost transparent in the beam of the flashlight. Senhor José hates these creatures, which, at first sight, one would have said had been placed in the world as ornaments, just as he hates the silverfish that proliferate here too, they are all voracious eaters, blamed for the destruction of so many memories, for so many parentless children, for so many legacies fallen into the eager hands of the State owing to lack of legal proof, however vehemently one swears that the relevant document was eaten, sullied, chewed up and devoured by the beasts that infest the Central Registry, and which, as a matter of common humanity, should be taken into account, no one, alas, can convince the lawyer working for the widows and orphans, who should be on their side but isn't, Either the paper turns up, or there's no legacy. As for the mice, one need hardly mention how destructive they are. Nevertheless, despite the extensive damage they cause, these rodents also have their positive side, if they didn't exist the Central Registry would have burst at the seams, or would be twice the length it is. An unwary observer might be surprised that the colonies of mice have not increased so in numbers that they have devoured every single one of the files, especially considering the obvious impossibility of a hundred-percent-efficient deinfestation programme. The explanation, although there are those who harbour certain doubts as to its real relevance, must lie in the lack of water or the insufficient moisture in the atmosphere, in the dry diet of the creatures who find themselves trapped in the place where they have chosen to live or where ill luck has brought them, which would have resulted in a marked atrophy of the genital musculature with extremely negative consequences for their copulatory performance. Others disagree with this attempt at an explanation and insist that muscles have nothing to do with it, and so the controversy rages on.

Meanwhile, covered in dust, with the heavy tatters of spiders' webs clinging to his hair and shoulders, Senhor José finally reached a clearing between the most recent papers to be filed away and the wall at the back, still separated by about three yards and forming an irregular corridor, narrower with each day that passed, that joins the two side walls. The darkness here is absolute. The feeble daylight that manages to penetrate the layer of filth covering the windows inside and out, especially the last windows on either side, which are nearest to him, does not reach this far because of the soaring piles of bundled documents that almost touch the ceiling. As for the rear wall, it is entirely and inexplicably blank, that is, there isn't even a simple bull's-eye window to aid the frail beam from the flashlight. No one has ever been able to understand why the board of architects, resorting to a rather unconvincing aesthetic excuse, have stubbornly refused to modify the historic plan and authorise the creation of windows in the wall when it proves necessary to move it back yet again, despite the fact that from a layman's point of view, it would simply be satisfying a practical need. They should be here now, muttered Senhor José, then they'd know how difficult it is. The piles of paper on either side of the central passage are of different heights, the file and card of the unknown woman could be in either of them, although it's more likely to be in one of the lower piles, if the law of least effort was that preferred by the clerk charged with filing them away. Unfortunately, in our disoriented society, there is no shortage of twisted minds, and it would come as no surprise if the clerk who came to put away the unknown woman's file and card, if indeed it was here that he came, had had the mischievous idea, born of sheer malice, of placing the enormous stepladder used for this purpose next to the highest pile of papers and climbing up it to place file and card right on the top. That is how things are in this world.

In a methodical, unhurried way, almost as if he were remembering the gestures and movements of the night he had spent in the school attic, when the unknown woman was probably still alive, Senhor José began his search. There was far less dust covering the papers here, which is easy enough to understand when you bear in mind that not a day passes without the files and cards of the deceased being brought here, which, imaginatively speaking, but in evident bad taste, would be the same as saying that in the depths of the Central Registry the dead are always clean. Only up high, where, as we have already said, the papers almost touch the ceiling, the dust sieved by time settles tranquilly on the dust already sieved by time, so much so that with the files you find up there, you have to clap the covers together to remove the dust, if you want to know who they belong to. If Senhor José fails to find what he's looking for on the lower levels, he will again have to sacrifice himself and climb the stepladder, but this time he will only have to be perched up there for a minute, he won't even have time to get dizzy, the flashlight beam will show him, at a glance, if a file was placed there recently. If the death of the unknown woman could be placed with a considerable degree of probability within the extremely short period of time corresponding, give or take a day, according to Senhor José, to one of the two periods in which he was absent from work, the week when he had flu and during his briefest of holidays, checking the documents in each of the piles can be done quite quickly, and even if the woman had died before, immediately after the memorable day on which the card fell into Senhor José's hands, not so much time had elapsed that the documents would now be filed away beneath an excessive number of other files. This repeated examination of situations as they arise, these persistent reflections, these meticulous ponderings on the light and the dark, on the straight and the labyrinthine, on the clean and the dirty, are all going on, just as we describe them, in Senhor José's head. But the apparently exaggerated amount of time it takes to explain them, or, strictly speaking, to reproduce them, is the inevitable consequence not only of the complexity, in both form and content, of the above-mentioned factors, but also of the very special nature of the mental circuitry of our particular clerk, who is now about to be tested to the limit. Advancing step by step along the narrow corridor formed, as we said, by the piles of documents and by the back wall, Senhor José has gradually been moving closer to one of the side walls. In principle, and speaking purely abstractly, no one would think of describing such a corridor, with its comfortable width of almost three yards, as narrow, but if you consider it in relation to the actual length of the corridor, which, we repeat, stretches from wall to wall, then we should really ask how it is that Senhor José, whom we know to be subject to serious perturbations of a psychological nature, for example, vertigo and insomnia, has not until now suffered a violent attack of claustrophobia in this enclosed and suffocating space. The explanation can perhaps be found precisely in the fact that the darkness does not allow him to perceive the limits of this space, which could be here or there, and that all he can see before him is the familiar, calming mass of papers. Senhor José has never spent so much time here, usually you just go there, file away the documents of a finished life and return to the safety of your desk, and if it's true that, on this occasion, from the moment he set off into the archive of the dead, he has been unable to shrug off a disquieting feeling of a presence surrounding him, he has attributed it to the diffuse terror of the hidden and the unknown to which even the most courageous of people have an all too human right. Senhor José had not felt fear, what you could really call fear, until he reached the end of the corridor and came face-to-face with the wall. He bent down to examine some papers fallen on the floor and that could well have been those of the unknown woman scattered here at random by the indifferent clerk, and suddenly, before he even had time to examine them, he stopped being Senhor José, clerk at the Central Registry, he stopped being fifty years old, now he is a very young José who has just started going to school, he is the child who hated going to sleep because every night he had the same obsessive nightmare, a massive stone wall, a blind wall, a prison, and over there, at the far end of the corridor, hidden in the darkness, there is just a small stone. A small stone that was slowly growing, that he could not see now with his eyes, but which the memory of the dreams he had dreamed told him was there, a stone that was increasing in size and moving as if it were alive, a stone that was expanding sideways and upwards, that was climbing the walls, and dragging itself towards him, curled in upon itself, as if it were not stone but mud, as if it were not mud but thick blood. The child emerged screaming from the nightmare when the filthy mass was touching his feet, when the tightening garrote of fear was almost strangling him, but poor Senhor José cannot wake from a dream which is no longer his. Cowering against the wall like a frightened dog, he points the flashlight with tremulous hand towards the other end of the corridor, but the beam doesn't reach that far, it stops halfway, more or less where the path to the archive of the living is to be found. He thinks that if he runs fast he'll be able to escape the advancing stone, but fear tells him, Be careful, how do you know it isn't there waiting for you, you'll walk straight into the lion's den. In the dream, the advance of the stone was accompanied by a strange music that seemed to be born out of the air, but here the silence is absolute, total, so dense that it swallows up

Senhor José's breathing, just as the darkness swallows the beam from the flashlight, and which it has just swallowed completely. It was as if the darkness had suddenly advanced and covered Senhor José's face like a sucker. The child's nightmare was over though. For the child, ah, who can understand the human heart, the fact that he could not see the walls of the prison, both near and far, was tantamount to their having ceased to be there, it was as if the space around him had suddenly grown larger, freer, stretching out to infinity, as if the stones were just the inert mineral of which they are made, as if water were simply the basic ingredient of mud, as if blood flowed only in his veins, not outside them. Now it is not a childhood nightmare that is frightening Senhor José, what paralyses him with fear is once more the thought that he might die in this place, just as, all that time ago, he imagined that he might fall from that other ladder and lie dead here, undocumented in the midst of all the documents of the dead, crushed by the darkness, by the avalanche that would soon unleash itself from above, and that tomorrow they would come and find him, Senhor José hasn't come in to work, I wonder where he is, He'll turn up, and when a colleague came to transfer other files and other cards, he would find him there, exposed to the light of a far superior flashlight than this one which had served him so badly when he needed it most. The minutes passed that had to pass before Senhor José could gradually begin to hear inside himself a voice saying, Look, apart from being afraid, nothing really bad has happened to you yet, you're sitting here quite unharmed, it's true the flashlight went out on you, but what do you need a flashlight for, you've got the string tied round your ankle, with the other end tied to the leg of the Registrar's desk, you're safe, like an unborn child attached by the umbilical cord to its mother's womb, not that the Registrar is your mother, or your father, but relationships between people here are complicated, what you must remember is that childhood nightmares never come true, far less dreams, that business with the stone really was pretty horrible, but it's probably got a scientific explanation, like when you used to dream you were flying over houses and gardens, rising, falling, hovering with your arms outstretched, do you remember, it was a sign that you were growing, probably the stone had a function too, if you have to experience terror, then rather sooner than later, besides, you should know better than anyone that the dead people here aren't really dead, it's a macabre exaggeration to call this the archive of the dead, if the papers you have in your hand are those of the unknown woman, they are just paper, not bones, they're paper, not putrefying flesh, that was the miracle worked by your Central Registry, transforming life and death into mere paper, it's true that you wanted to find that woman, but you didn't manage it in time, you couldn't even do that, or, rather, you wanted it and didn't want it, you hesitated between desire and fear, it happens to lots of people, you probably should have just gone to the tax office after all, as someone told you to, it's over, it's best just to leave it, her time has run out and the end of your time isn't far off either.

Pressed right up against the unstable wall formed by the files, Senhor José got to his feet, very slowly and carefully so that none of the files would fall on top of him. The voice that had addressed that speech to him was now saying things like this, Don't be afraid, the darkness you're in is no greater than the darkness inside your own body, they are two darknesses separated by a skin, I bet you've never thought of that, you carry a darkness about with you all the time and that doesn't frighten you, a little while ago, you nearly started screaming just because you imagined some danger, just because you remembered the nightmare you used to have when you were little, my dear chap, you have to learn to live with the darkness outside just as you learned to live with the darkness inside, now, please, get up and put the flashlight back in your pocket, it's useless now, and, since you're determined to take them with you, slip the papers in between your jacket and your shirt, or to be safer, between your shirt and your skin, take a firm hold of the piece of string, wind it up as you go along so that you don't get it tangled round your feet, and off you go, you don't want to be that worst of all things, a coward. Lightly brushing the wall of paper with his shoulder, Senhor José took two timid steps. The darkness opened like black water and closed behind him, another step and another, he had already lifted five yards of string from the floor and wound them up, Senhor José could have done with a third hand to feel the air in front of him, but there's a simple enough remedy, he merely has to raise his two hands to face height, one hand rolling, the other being rolled, the bobbin principle. Senhor José is nearly out of the corridor, a few steps more and he'll be safe from any new attack by the nightmare stone, the string tightens a little, but that's a good sign, it means that it's got caught, at floor level, on the corner of the passage leading to the archive of the living. Oddly enough, during that whole walk, right to the end, just as if someone were throwing them down from above, papers and more papers kept raining down on Senhor José's head, slowly, first one, then another and another, like a farewell. And when, at last, he reached the Registrar's desk, when, even before he untied the string, he took out from inside his shirt the file he had picked up from the floor, and when he opened it and saw that it was the unknown woman's file, his excitement was such that he did not hear the door of the Central Registry closing, as if someone had just left the building.

The fact that psychological time is not the same as mathematical time was something that Senhor José had learned in exactly the same way as, over a lifetime, he had acquired other types of useful knowledge, drawing first of all, of course, on his own experiences, for, despite never having risen higher than the post of clerk, he does not merely follow where others go, but drawing too on the formative influence of a few books and magazines of a scientific nature in which one can put one's trust or faith, depending on the feeling of the moment, and also, why not, a number of popular works of fiction of an introspective type, which also tackled the subject, though employing different methods and with an added dash of imagination. However, on no other occasion had he had a real objective sense, as physical as a sudden muscular contraction, of the effective impossibility of measuring the time that we might call the time of the soul, as when, back in his house again, looking once more at the unknown woman's date of death, he struggled, vaguely, to place it in the time that had passed since he first set out to find her. To the question, What were you doing on that day, he could give an almost immediate response, he would just have to go and look at the calendar and, thinking simply as plain Senhor José, the Central Registry clerk who had been away from work sick, he would say, That day I was in bed with flu, I didn't go to work, but if they went on to ask him,

Now relate it to your activities as a researcher and tell me when it was, then he would have to go and consult the notebook that he kept beneath the mattress, It was two days after I broke into the school, he would reply. Assuming the date of death written on the card was correct, the unknown woman had indeed died two days after the deplorable episode that had transformed a hitherto honest Senhor José into a criminal, but these intersecting statements, that of the clerk cutting across that of the researcher, that of the researcher cutting across that of the clerk, apparently more than enough to match the psychological time of one with the mathematical time of the other, did not remove from either statement a feeling of dizzying disorientation. Senhor José is not standing on the top rungs of a very high ladder, looking down and seeing how the rungs grow ever narrower until they become one point touching the ground, but it is as if his body, instead of seeing itself as an integral unit existing in each passing moment, found itself fragmented during those last few days, during that period not of real or mathematical time, but of psychological or subjective time, as if it were contracting and dilating along with time itself. I am utterly absurd, Senhor José told himself sternly, the day already contained twenty-four hours when it was determined how many hours it should have, an hour has and always has had sixty minutes, the sixty seconds of the minute have been there since eternity, if a clock starts to go fast or slow it is a defect in the machine not in time, Perhaps one of my springs has gone. The idea brought a faint smile to his lips, Since, as far as I know, the fault does not lie in the mechanism of real time, but in the psychological mechanism that measures it, what I should do is look for a psychologist who could repair my escape wheel. He smiled again, then grew serious, The matter can be resolved more easily than that, besides, nature has already done so, the woman is dead, there's nothing more to do, I'll keep the file and the card in case I want to have some palpable souvenir of this adventure, for the Central Registry it will be as if that person had never been born, I doubt that anyone will ever need these papers, otherwise I could just leave them in some part of the archive of the dead, at the entrance, along with the oldest ones, here or there it doesn't matter, they all share the same history, they were born, they died, who now is going to be interested in who she was, her parents, if they loved her, will weep for her for a time, then they will weep less, then they will stop weeping, that's how it usually is, it will make no difference to the man she divorced, it's true she might have some current romantic relationship, she might be living with someone, or about to marry again, but that will be the history of a future that cannot now be lived, there is no one else in the world interested in the strange case of the unknown woman. He had before him the file and the card, he also had the thirteen school reports, the same name repeated thirteen times, twelve different images of the same face, one of them repeated, but each and every one of them dead in the past, already dead before the woman they later became had died, old photographs are very deceiving, they give us the illusion that we are alive in them, and it's not true, the person we are looking at no longer exists, and if that person could see us, he or she would not recognise him- or herself in us, Who's that looking at me so sadly, he or she would say. Then, suddenly, Senhor José remembered that there was another picture, the one the lady in the ground-floor apartment had given him. He had unexpectedly just found the answer to the question of who else would be interested in the strange case of the unknown woman.

Senhor José did not wait until Saturday. The following day when the office closed, he went to the laundry to pick up the clothes he had left there to be cleaned. He listened abstractedly to the conscientious assistant saying to him, Now just have a look at this darning, look, run your fingers over it and tell me if you can notice any difference, you wouldn't even know there was anything there, that is how people who content themselves with mere appearances speak. Senhor José paid her, put the package under his arm and went home to change his clothes. He was going to visit the lady in the ground-floor apartment and he wanted to look clean and presentable, to take advantage not only of the perfect, truly praiseworthy work done by the invisible mender, but also of the rigorous crease in his trousers, the gleaming starch in his shirt, the miraculous recovery of his tie. He was just about to leave when a morbid thought went through his mind, which is, as far as one knows, the only thinking organ at the service of the body, What if the lady in the ground-floor apartment has died too, she wasn't exactly brimming with health, besides, in order to die you need only be alive, especially at her age, he imagined himself ringing the bell again and again, and, after a long time, hearing the door of the ground-floor apartment opposite opening and a woman appearing, irritated by all the noise, and saying, There's no point ringing, no one's there, Has she gone out, She's dead, Dead, Exactly, When did it happen, A fortnight ago, and who might you be, I'm from the Central Registry, Well, it doesn't look like you do your work very well over there, you say you're from the Central Registry, but you didn't even know she'd died. Senhor José told himself he was being obsessive, but he preferred to sort things out right there and then, so as not to have to put up with the rudeness of the woman in the other ground-floor apartment. He would go in to the Central Registry and in less than a minute he would have checked the old lady's card, by now, the two cleaning ladies must have finished their work, not that it takes them long, they just empty the wastepaper bins, sweep and lightly mop the floor as far as the shelf just behind the Registrar's desk, it's impossible to persuade them, with kind words or cruel, to go any farther, they're afraid, they wouldn't be caught dead in there, they say, they too are of the kind who content themselves with appearances, that's just the way they are. After looking at the unknown woman's card to check the name of the lady in the ground-floor apartment, her godmother, Senhor José very gingerly opened the door and peered out. As he had foreseen, the cleaning ladies were no longer there. He entered, walked quickly over to the card index and looked for her name, She's here, he said, and gave a sigh of relief. He went back home, finished dressing and went out. In order to get the bus that would drop him near where the lady lived, he had to go to the square opposite the Central Registry, that was where the stop was. Although the evening was quite advanced, much of the daylight lingering in the sky still hovered over the city, it would be at least twenty minutes before the street lamps came on. Senhor José was waiting for the bus with a few other people, he probably wouldn't manage to get on the first bus to come along. And indeed that is what happened. But a second bus appeared soon afterwards, and this one wasn't full. Senhor José got on in time to get a place by the window. He looked out, noticing how, due to some unusual optical effect, the diffusion of light in the atmosphere lit the façades of the buildings with a reddish tone, as if the sun were about to rise at that very moment for each and every one of them. There was the Central Registry, with its ancient door and the three black stone steps that led up to it, and the five narrow windows on the front, the whole building had the air of a ruin fixed in time, as if it had been mummified rather than restored when the dilapidated state of its materials demanded it. Some hold-up in the traffic was preventing the bus from proceeding. Senhor José felt nervous, he didn't want to arrive too late to call on the lady in the ground-floor apartment. Despite the full and frank conversation they had had, despite certain confidences exchanged, some of which were unexpected in people who had only just met, they hadn't become so close that he could go knocking on her door at any hour of the day or night. Senhor José looked again at the square. The light had changed, the façade of the Central Registry had grown suddenly grey, but it was nevertheless a luminous grey that seemed to vibrate, to tremble, and it was then, just as the bus was pulling away, slowly moving out into the traffic lane, that a tall, well-built man walked up the steps of the Central Registry, opened the door and went in. The Registrar, murmured Senhor José, what's he doing at the Central Registry at this hour. Impelled by a sudden, inexplicable panic, he got up suddenly from his seat, made as if to get off, provoking a look of surprise and irritation in the passenger beside him, then sat down again, puzzled by his own behaviour. He realised that his impulse was to rush home, as if to protect it from some danger, which was, of course, absurdly illogical. A thief, always supposing, now really, yet another absurd illogicality, that the boss was a thief, wouldn't go in through the front door of the Central Registry in order to reach Senhor José's front door. But then it was bordering on the absurd for the Registrar to want to go back there after the office was closed, for, as we stated earlier, there would be no work waiting for him, Senhor José could stake his life on that. Imagining the head of the Central Registry doing overtime was rather like trying to imagine a square circle. The bus had already left the square, and Senhor José was still trying to work out the deep reasons that had driven him to behave in that disoriented fashion. He decided in the end that the reason must lie in the fact that, after a good few years as sole resident, he had grown used to being the only nocturnal tenant of the group of edifices formed by the Central Registry and his house, if the latter deserves the name of edifice, doubtless appropriate from a rigorously linguistic point of view, since an edifice can be any kind of building, but obviously inappropriate when compared with the architectural dignity that seems to emanate from the word itself, especially when spoken. Seeing his boss go into the Central Registry had had the same impact on him, he thought, as if, when he went back home, he were to find him sitting in his chair. The relative calm that this idea brought Senhor José, that is, not taking into account pertinent and morally embarrassing considerations, the physical and material impossibility of the Registrar entering the private rooms of his subordinate and even using his chair, immediately melted away when he remembered the unknown woman's school record cards and wondered if he had put them back under the mattress or carelessly left them out on the table. Even if his house were as safe as a bank vault, with special combination locks and reinforced floors, walls and ceiling, those record cards should never but never have been left out. The fact that there was no one there to see them did not excuse the grave imprudence committed, how are we, being ignorant, to know how far the advances of science might go, just as radio waves, which no one can see, carry sounds and images through the air and the wind, leaping over mountains and rivers, crossing oceans and deserts, it would not be so very extraordinary if scanner waves and photographic waves had not already been discovered or invented, or were to be discovered tomorrow, waves capable of penetrating walls and recording and transmitting to the outside world the deeds, mysteries and humiliations of our life that we had thought safe from indiscretions. Hiding them, those deeds, mysteries and humiliations under a mattress, still continues to be the safest way of hiding things, especially when we bear in mind that it is increasingly difficult for the customs of today to understand the customs of yesterday. However expert that scanner wave or photographic wave might be, it would never think of sticking its nose between a mattress and a bed base.

As everyone knows, our thoughts, both anxious and happy thoughts, and others which are neither one thing nor the other, sooner or later grow weary and bored with themselves, it's just a question of letting time do its work, it's just a matter of leaving them to the lazy daydreaming that comes naturally to them, adding no new irritating or polemical reflection to the bonfire, above all taking supreme care not to intervene whenever an attractive bifurcation, branch line, or turning appears before a thought which is already ripe for distraction. Or, rather, you can intervene, but only to give it a gentle shove from behind, especially if it's a troubling thought, as if we were saying, Go on, off you go, you're fine. This was what Senhor José did when that mad, providential fantasy of the photographic wave and the scanner wave came to him, he at once abandoned himself to his imagination, let it show him those invasive waves scouring the whole room in search of those records, which he had not, in fact, left on the table, perplexed and ashamed because they could not carry out the orders they had received, Remember, either you find those records, read them and photograph them, or we go back to the old-style espionage. Senhor José still thought about the Registrar, but it was a purely residual thought, one that helped him find an acceptable explanation for his return to the Central Registry outside of normal hours, He must have forgotten something he needed, what other reason could there be. Without realising, he repeated out loud the final part of the phrase, What other reason could there be, again provoking the distrust of the passenger travelling next to him, whose thoughts immediately became clear and explicit when he changed his seat, The guy is mad, we're sure that he used these or similar words to think it. Senhor José did not notice the withdrawal of the man next to him on the seat, he moved seamlessly on to thoughts of the lady in the ground-floor apartment, she was there before him at the door, Do you remember me, I'm from the Central Registry, Of course I do, I've come here about that matter we discussed the other day, You've found my goddaughter, No, I haven't, or rather, yes, that is, I mean, I'd like to have a little chat with you, if you wouldn't mind, if you've got a moment, Come in, I've got something to tell you too. That, more or less, was what Senhor José and the lady in the ground-floor apartment said when she opened the door and saw him there, Ah, it's you, she exclaimed, so he had no need to ask, Do you remember me, I'm Senhor José from the Central Registry, but despite this, he couldn't resist asking the question, so constant, so imperious, so demanding it would seem is our need to go about the world declaring who we are, even when we've just heard someone else say, Ah, it's you, as if just because they've recognised us, they know us and need to know nothing more about us, or as if the little that remained unknown wasn't worth the effort of formulating another question.

Nothing had changed in the small living room, the chair where Senhor José had sat the first time was in the same place, at the same distance from the table, the curtains hung as they had before, in the same folds, the woman made the same gesture when she folded her hands in her lap, right over left, only the light from the ceiling seemed slightly paler, as if the bulb were burning out. Senhor José asked, How have you been since my last visit, and then he reproached himself for his lack of sensitivity, worse still, for the utter crassness he was revealing, he should know that you don't always have to follow the rules of elementary politeness to the letter, you must take into account the circumstances, you have to weigh each case, let's imagine that the woman responds now with a broad smile, I'm very well, thank you, my health is excellent, I'm in good spirits, I haven't felt this fit for ages, and then he blurts out, Well, I'm sorry to tell you this, but your goddaughter has died, what do you make of that. But the woman didn't reply to his question, she merely shrugged indifferently, then she said, Do you know, for some days I've been thinking of phoning you at the Central Registry, then I decided not to, I thought that sooner or later you would come and visit me, It's just as well you didn't phone, the Registrar doesn't like us getting phone calls, he says it gets in the way of work, Of course, but that needn't have been a problem, I just had to give him the information I had, he wouldn't have had to call you over. Beads of sweat broke out on Senhor José's forehead. He had just discovered that, for weeks, ignorant of the danger, unconscious of the threat hanging over him, he had been living on the brink of absolute disaster, the public exposure of irregularities in his professional conduct, the continual and wilful affront he was in the process of committing against the venerable deontological laws of the Central Registry, whose chapters, articles, paragraphs and clauses, however complex, due to the extreme archaism of the language, had finally been reduced down by the experience of two centuries to nine practical words, Don't stick your nose in where it isn't wanted. For a moment, Senhor José hated and detested the woman before him, he insulted her mentally, he called her a feeble old woman, cretin, nincompoop, and like someone who can find no better way of overcoming some sudden, violent shock, he was almost on the point of saying to her, Well, try this on for size, your goddaughter, the one in the picture, has kicked the bucket. The woman asked, Are you feeling ill, Senhor José, would you like a glass of water, No, I'm fine, don't worry, he replied, ashamed of that wicked impulse, I'm going to make you some tea, There's no need, really, I don't want to be any bother, at that moment, Senhor José was feeling as base and humble as the dust in the street, the woman had left the room, he heard her rattling cups in the kitchen, a few minutes passed, first you have to boil the water, Senhor José remembers having read somewhere, probably in one of the magazines where he gets his clippings of famous people, tea should be made with water that has just boiled but is not actually boiling, he would have been quite happy with a glass of cold water, but the tea would do him far more good, everyone knows that there's nothing like a nice cup of tea for lifting the spirits, all the manuals say so, both in the East and the West. The lady of the house appeared with a tray, she had also brought a plate of biscuits, as well as the teapot, cups and the

sugar bowl. I didn't even ask if you liked tea, it only just occurred to me that perhaps you would prefer coffee, she said,
No, I like tea, I really do, Do you take sugar, No, I don't, suddenly he went pale and started sweating, he thought he should
explain, It must be the remains of the flu I caught, So if I'd
phoned, you probably wouldn't even have been there, and I
really would have had to tell your boss what had happened.
This time the sweat only dampened Senhor José's palms, but
even so it was lucky that his cup was on the table, had he been
holding it at that moment it would have fallen to the floor, or
spilled scalding tea all over the wretched clerk's legs, with inevitable consequences, first the burn, then the return of his
trousers to the laundry. Senhor José took a biscuit from the
plate, nibbled at it slowly, listlessly and, disguising with chewing the difficulty he was having in formulating any words, he
managed to ask the long-delayed question, And what was this
information you had to give me. The woman took a sip of tea,
reached a hesitant hand out to the plate of biscuits, but did not
complete the gesture. She said, You remember that I suggested
to you, at the end of your visit, just when you were leaving,
that you should look up my goddaughter's name in the phone
book, Yes I do, but I decided not to follow your advice, Why, It's
rather difficult to explain, Well, you probably had your reasons,
It's easy enough to give reasons for what we do or don't do,
when we see that we haven't got a reason or not enough of a
reason, then we try to invent one, in the case of your goddaughter, for example, I could now say that I preferred to take
the longest, most complicated route, And is that one of the real
reasons or one of the invented ones, Let's just say there's as
much truth in it as there is falsehood, And which bit is the falsehood, Me pretending that the reason I gave to you should be
taken as the whole truth, And it isn't, No, because I've left out
the reason why I preferred that route and not another more direct one, You're bored with the routine of your job, That could

be another reason, How are your investigations going, Tell me first what happened, let's pretend that I was at the Central Registry when you first thought of phoning me and that the boss doesn't mind us getting phone calls. The woman raised the cup to her lips again, replaced it on the saucer without making the slightest noise and said, as her hands returned to her lap, again her right hand covering her left, I did what I told you to do, You phoned her, Yes, You spoke to her, Yes, When was that, A few days after you came here, I couldn't cope with all the memories, I couldn't sleep, And what happened, We talked, She must have been surprised, She didn't seem to be, But that would be the normal reaction after so many years of separation and silence, You obviously don't know much about women, especially when they're unhappy, So she was unhappy, It didn't take long before we were both crying, as if we were bound to each other by a thread of tears, What happened next, What do you mean, Did she tell you anything about her life, Very little, just that she'd been married, but was now divorced, We know that already, it's on her card, We left it that she would come and visit me as soon as she had time, Did she come, No, not as yet, What do you mean, Just that she hasn't come, And she hasn't phoned either, No, she hasn't, How long ago was this, About two weeks, More or less, Less I think, yes, less, And what did you do, At first, I thought she'd changed her mind, that she didn't want to renew old friendships, that she didn't want us to get close, those tears must have been a moment of weakness and nothing more, it happens often enough, there are times in our lives when we just let go, when we're capable of telling the first stranger we meet about our pain and sorrow, do you remember, when you were here, Of course I remember, and I never thanked you properly for the trust you placed in me, It wasn't a question of trust, it was despair, Whatever it was, I promise you will never regret it, you can trust me, I'm very discreet, Yes, I'm sure I won't regret it, Thank you, But the reason

I know I won't regret it is because nothing really matters to me anymore, Ah. It wasn't easy passing from a disconsolate interjection like that to a direct question of the type, So, then what did you do, it required time and tact, so Senhor José fell silent, waiting for what would happen next. As if she were aware of that too, the woman asked, Would you like some more tea, he accepted, Yes, please, and held out his cup. Then the woman said, A few days ago I telephoned her house, And what happened, No one answered, I got the answering machine, You only phoned once, On the first day, yes, but the following days I tried several times and at different hours, I phoned in the morning, I phoned in the afternoon, I phoned after supper, I even phoned at midnight, And nothing, Nothing, I thought perhaps she'd gone away, Did she tell you where she worked, No. The conversation could not continue to roll around the black hole hiding the truth, the moment was approaching when Senhor José would say Your goddaughter is dead, in fact, he should have told her as soon as he arrived, that's what the woman will say to him shortly, Why didn't you tell me straightaway, why did you ask all those questions if you knew she was already dead, and he will be unable to lie alleging that he remained silent because he didn't want to spring the painful news on her, without preparation, without due respect, in truth, the only reason for this long, slow dialogue had been the words she had said at the start, I've got something to tell you too, at that point, Senhor José lost the resigned serenity that would have made him reject the temptation of knowing about that tiny, useless thing, whatever it was, he lacked the serene resignation necessary to say, It doesn't matter, she's dead. It was as if what the lady in the ground-floor apartment had to tell him might still, who knows how, make time run backwards and, at the very last moment, steal the unknown woman back from death. Weary, with no other desire now than to delay the inevitable for a few more seconds, Senhor José asked, You didn't consider going to her house, asking the neighbours if they'd seen her, Of course I did, but I didn't go, Why, Because it would look as if I was interfering, she might not like that, But you phoned, That's different. There was a silence, then the expression on the woman's face began to change, it became interrogative, and Senhor José realised that she was going to ask, at last, what questions relating to the matter of her goddaughter had brought him there today, had he managed to speak to her and when, was the problem with the Central Registry resolved and how, I regret to tell you that your goddaughter is dead, said Senhor José. The woman opened her eyes very wide, raised her hands from her lap and covered her mouth, What, Your goddaughter has died, How do you know, asked the woman without thinking, That's what the Central Registry is there for, said Senhor José, and he shrugged his shoulders slightly, as if to say, It's not my fault, When did she die, I've got the card here, if you want to see it. The woman reached out her hand, held the card close to her eyes then moved it farther off, mumbling, My glasses, but she didn't go and look for them, she knew they wouldn't help, even if she wanted to she wouldn't be able to read what was written there, her tears were blurring the words. Senhor José said, I'm very sorry. The woman left the room and was gone for a few brief moments, when she came back she was drying her eyes with a handkerchief. She sat down, poured herself some more tea, then asked, Did you come here just to tell me that my goddaughter had died, Yes, That was very kind of you, I thought it was my duty really, Why, Because I felt I was in your debt, Why, Because of the nice way you received me and helped me, the way you answered my questions, Now that force of circumstances has brought the job they gave you to an end, you won't have to wear yourself out any more looking for my poor goddaughter, No, I won't, Perhaps the Central Registry has already instructed you to start looking for another person, No, no, cases like this are very rare, That's the good thing about death, it brings everything to a close, It's not always like that, that's when the battles begin between heirs, the ferocious dividing up of the spoils, then there's inheritance tax to be paid, For the person who's died I meant, As for that, yes, you're right, everything ends, It's odd, you never explained to me why the Central Registry was looking for my goddaughter, why they were so interested in her, As you said, death resolves all problems, So there was a problem, Yes, What, It's not worth talking about it, the matter is of no importance now, What matter, Please don't insist, it's confidential, said Senhor José desperately. The woman angrily put down her cup and saucer and, looking straight at him, said, All the time that you and I have been together here, both the other day and today, right from the start, one of us has always told the truth and the other has always lied, But I didn't lie then and I'm not lying now, You'll admit that I always talked to you frankly, clearly, openly, that it would never even have occurred to you that there might be a single lie in anything I said, Absolutely, Then if there's a liar in this room, as I know there is, it's certainly not me, I'm not a liar, No, I'm sure you're not a liar by nature, but you lied when you first came here, and you've been lying ever since, You wouldn't understand, I understand enough not to believe that the Central Registry sent you here looking for my goddaughter, You're wrong, they did send me, Then if you've nothing more to say to me, if that is your final word, please leave my house this instant, now, she almost shouted that last word, and then she began to cry. Senhor José got up, took a step towards the door, then sat down again, Forgive me, he said, don't cry, I'll tell you everything.

When I'd finished talking, she asked me, And what do you think you'll do now, Nothing, I said, Are you going to go back to your collections of famous people, I don't know, possibly, I'll have to fill my time somehow, I fell silent, thinking, and then said, No, I don't think I will, Why, Well, when you think about it, their lives are always the same, they never change, they appear, they talk, they show themselves off, they smile for the photographers, they're always arriving or departing, Just like us, Not like me, Like you and me and everyone, we all show ourselves off in various places, we talk, we leave our homes and come back, sometimes we even smile, the difference is that no one takes any notice of us, We can't all be famous, Just as well, imagine if your collection were as big as the Central Registry, It would have to be even bigger, the Central Registry only wants to know when we're born and when we die, and that's about it, Whether we marry, get divorced, widowed or remarried, the Central Registry has absolutely no interest in finding out if we were happy or unhappy while all that was going on, Happiness and unhappiness are just like famous people, they come and they go, the worst thing about the Central Registry is that they're not interested in what we're like, for them we're just a piece of paper with a few names and dates on it, Like my goddaughter's card, Or yours, or mine, What would you have done if you'd actually met her, I don't know, perhaps

I'd have spoken to her, perhaps not, I never really thought about it, And did it occur to you that, at the moment when she was actually there before you, you would know as much about her as you did on the day you first decided to look for her, that is, nothing, and that if you wanted to know who she was, you would have to begin looking again and that, from then on, it would be much more difficult, if, unlike famous people, who like showing themselves off, she preferred not to be found, You're right, But, since she's dead, you can go on looking for her, she won't mind now, I don't understand, Up until now, despite all your efforts, the only thing you've found out is that she went to a school, in fact, the very one I told you about, I've got photographs, Photographs are just bits of paper too, We could share them, And we would imagine that we were sharing her out between us, one bit for you, one bit for me, There's nothing more to be done, that's what I said at the time, assuming that she considered the matter closed, but she asked me, Why don't you go and talk to her parents, to her ex-husband, What for, To try and learn something more about her, how she lived, what she did, Her husband probably wouldn't want to talk about her, it's all water under the bridge, But her parents are bound to, parents never let slip a chance to talk about their children, even if they're dead, at least that's been my experience, I didn't go and see them before and I'm certainly not going to now, before, I could have said that I'd been sent by the Central Registry, What did my goddaughter die of, I don't know, How is that possible, her death must be registered at the Central Registry, On the card we just put the date of death, not the cause, But there must be a certificate, doctors are obliged by law to certify a death, when she died, they wouldn't just write She's dead, The death certificate wasn't with the papers I found in the archive of the dead, Why, I don't know, they must have dropped it when they were taking her file to be put away, or else I dropped it, anyway, it's lost, it would be like looking for a needle in a haystack, you can't imagine what it's like in there, From what you've told me I can, You can't, it's impossible, you'd have to actually be there, In that case you've got a perfect reason to go and talk to her parents, tell them that, unfortunately, her death certificate has got lost in the Central Registry, that you have to complete the file otherwise your boss will punish you, show them how humble and anxious you are, ask the name of the doctor who came, where she died, and what of, if it happened at home or in the hospital, ask everything, you've still got your letter of authority, I suppose, Yes, but don't forget it's a false one, It fooled me, it'll probably fool them too, no life is without its lies, perhaps there's some deceit involved in this death as well, If you worked at the Central Registry, you'd know that there is no deceiving death. She must have thought the remark didn't merit a response, and she was perfectly right, because what I'd said was just for effect really, one of those essentially empty expressions that appear to be deep but have nothing inside. We were silent for about two minutes, she was looking at me reproachfully, as if I had made her a solemn promise which I had broken at the last moment. I didn't know where to put myself, I just wanted to say goodnight and leave, but that would have been both stupid and rude, a lack of consideration which the poor lady certainly didn't deserve, it's just not in my nature to do something like that, that's the way I was brought up, it's true I can't remember ever having gone to tea at someone's house when I was small, but it comes to the same thing. I was thinking that it would be best to take up her idea and begin searching again, only from the opposite direction this time, that is, from death into life, when she said, Take no notice, I get these ridiculous ideas now and then, when you're old and realise that time is running out, you start imagining that you have the cure for all the ills of the world in your hand, and get frustrated because no one pays you any attention, I've never had ideas like that, You will, in time, you're still very young, Me, young, I'm nearly fifty-one, You're in the prime of life, Don't make fun of me, You only become wise after seventy, and then it's no use to you anyway, not to you or anyone else. Since I still have a long way to go before I reach that age, I didn't know whether to agree or not, so I thought it best to say nothing. It was time I said goodbye, so I said, I won't trouble you any more, thank you for all your patience and kindness, and forgive me, it was that mad idea of mine that got me into this, it's all absolutely absurd, there you were, sitting contentedly in your home, and along I come with my lies, my deceitful stories, I blush to think of some of the questions I asked you, Contrary to what you've just said, I wasn't sitting here contentedly, I was lonely, being able to tell you some of the sad things that have happened in my life was like getting rid of a great weight, Well, if that's how you feel, then I'm glad, It is and I don't want you to leave without asking you something, Ask anything you like, as long as it's within my power to help, You're the only person who can help, what I have to ask you is very simple, come and see me now and then, when you remember or feel like visiting, even if it's not to talk about my goddaughter, Why I'd be delighted to come and visit you, There'll always be a cup of coffee or tea waiting for you, That would be reason enough to come, but there are plenty of others, Thank you and, look, don't take any notice of that idea of mine, it's as mad as yours was, I'll think about it. I kissed her hand as I had on the first occasion, but then something unexpected happened, she kept hold of my hand and raised it to her lips. No woman had ever done that to me, I felt something like a shock in my soul, a tremor in my heart, and even now, now that it's morning, and many hours have passed, while I finish writing up the events of the day in my notebook, I look at my right hand and it seems different to me, although I can't quite say how, it must be an internal rather than an external matter. Senhor José stopped writing, put down his pen, put the unknown woman's school record cards carefully away in the notebook, he had, in fact, left them on top of the table, and went and hid them away again between the mattress and the base of the bed. Then he heated up the stew left over from lunch and sat down to eat. There was an almost absolute silence, you could scarcely hear the noise made by the few cars still out and about in the city. What you could hear most clearly was a muffled sound that rose and fell, like a distant bellows, but Senhor José was used to that, it was the Central Registry breathing. Senhor José went to bed, but he wasn't sleepy. He remembered the events of the day, the unpleasant surprise of seeing his boss go into the Central Registry out of hours, and his troubling conversation with the lady in the ground-floor apartment, which he had set down in his notebook, faithful as to the meaning, less so as regards form, which is both understandable and forgivable, since memory, which is very sensitive and hates to be found lacking, tends to fill in any gaps with its own spurious creations of reality, but more or less in line with the facts of which it has only a vague recollection, like what remains after the passing of a shadow. It seemed to Senhor José that he had still not reached a logical conclusion about what had happened, that he still had to make a decision, otherwise his last words to the lady in the ground-floor apartment, I'll think about it, would be no more than a vain promise, of the sort that is always cropping up in conversation and that no one expects will be kept. Senhor José was desperate to get to sleep when, suddenly, from unknown depths, the longed-for solution welled up within him, like the end of a new Ariadne's thread, On Saturday, I'll go to the cemetery, he said out loud. The excitement made him sit up in bed, but the calm voice of good sense stepped in with some advice, Now that you've decided what you're going to do, lie down and go to sleep, don't be such a child, you don't really want to go there at this time of night, do you, and jump over the cemetery wall, although that's just a manner of speaking, of course. Obediently, Senhor José slipped down between the sheets, pulled them up to his nose and lay for a minute, his eyes open, thinking, I'm not going to be able to get to sleep. A minute later he was sleeping.

He woke late, shortly before the Central Registry was due to open, he didn't even have time to shave, he pulled on some clothes and left the house at a crazy gallop quite inappropriate to his age and his condition. All the other staff, from the eight clerks to the two deputies, were sitting down, their eyes fixed on the wall clock, waiting until the minute hand was resting exactly on the number twelve. Senhor José addressed the senior clerk in charge of his section, to whom he was expected to offer his first excuse, and he apologised for being late, I slept badly, he said, even though he knew, from long years of experience, that such an explanation was pointless, Sit down, came the abrupt reply. When, immediately after that, the minute hand slipped forward to indicate the transition from waiting time to work time, Senhor José, tripping over his shoelaces, which he had forgotten to tie, still had not reached his desk, a fact coldly observed by the senior clerk, who noted down this remarkable fact in the day's diary. More than an hour passed before the Registrar arrived. He looked rather withdrawn, almost sombre, and this filled the staff with fear, at first sight, anyone would say that he had slept badly too, but he was his usual composed self, perfectly shaven, without a crease in his suit or a hair out of place. He paused for a moment by Senhor José's desk and looked at him severely, though without saying a word. Embarrassed, Senhor José began a gesture that seems instinctive in men, that of raising his hand to rub his cheek to see if his beard had grown, but he stopped halfway, as if, by doing so, he might disguise what was obvious to everyone else, his unforgivably scruffy appearance. Everyone thought that a reprimand would not be long in coming. The Registrar went over to his own desk, sat down and called over the two deputies. The general feeling was that things were looking very bad for Senhor José, if not, the boss would not have summoned both of his immediate inferiors, he must have wanted to hear their opinion of the heavy sanction he intended to impose, His patience has run out, the other clerks thought gleefully, for they had been scandalised by the recent unmerited favouritism shown to Senhor José by the boss, About time too, they said to themselves sententiously. They soon realised, however, that this was not the case. While one of the two deputies gave orders for everyone, senior clerks and clerks, to turn and face the Registrar, the other went around the counter and closed the entrance door, having first affixed a notice outside saying Closed temporarily for official business. What on earth's going on, wondered the staff, including the deputies, who knew as much as the others, or perhaps slightly more, only that the Registrar had told them that he was going to speak. The first thing he said was Sit down. The order passed from the deputies to the senior clerks, from the senior clerks to the clerks, there was the inevitable noise produced by the scuffing of chairs, placed with their backs to their respective desks, but all this was done quickly, in less than a minute the silence in the Central Registry was absolute. You couldn't hear a fly, although everyone knew they were there, some perched in safe places, others dying in the filthy spiders' webs hanging from the ceiling. The Registrar rose slowly to his feet, equally slowly he surveyed the staff, one by one, as if he were seeing them for the first time, or as if he were trying to recognise them after a long absence, oddly enough, his expression was no longer sombre, or, rather, it was, but in a different sense, as if he were tormented by some moral pain. Then he spoke, Gentlemen, in my role as head of the Central Registry, the latest in a long line of Registrars begun when the oldest of the documents existing in our archives was first collected, in fulfilment of the responsibilities bestowed on me and following the example of my predecessors, I have been scrupulous in obeying and in making others obey the written laws that regulate our work, never forgetting, indeed, at every moment, always mindful of tradition. I am aware that times have changed, I am aware of society's need for a continuous updating of working methods and processes, but I understand, as did those who were in charge of the Central Registry before me, that the preservation of the spirit, of the spirit of what I will call continuity and organic identity, must prevail over any other consideration, for if we fail to proceed along that path, we will witness the collapse of the moral edifice which, as the first and last depositories of life and death, we continue here to represent. There will doubtless be those who protest because there is not a single typewriter to be seen in the Central Registry, still less other far more modern equipment, because the cabinets and shelves are made of wood, or because the staff still have to dip their pens in inkwells and use blotters, there will be those who consider us to be ridiculously frozen in time, who demand of the government the rapid introduction into our work of advanced technologies, but while it is true that laws and regulations can be altered and substituted at any moment, the same cannot be said of traditions, which is, as such, both in form and sense, immutable. No one is going to travel back in time in order to change a tradition that was born in time and that was fed and sustained by time. No one is going to tell us that what exists did not exist, no one would ever dare, like a child, to want what has happened not to have happened. And if they did, they would be wasting their time. These are the foundations of our reason and our strength, this is the wall behind which we have, until today, been able to defend both our identity and our autonomy. Thus we have continued and thus we would continue if new thoughts had not surfaced indicating to us the need for new paths.

So far there had been nothing new in the Registrar's speech, although it was true that this was the first time that anyone in the Central Registry had heard something resembling a solemn declaration of principles. The uniform mentality of the staff had been based on providing a service, which was regulated in the early days by rigour and precision, but, due perhaps to a certain degree of historical institutional weariness, had allowed among more recent generations the grave and continuing acts of neglect mentioned before and which were worthy of censure even from the most benevolent of viewpoints. Their dulled consciences touched, the staff assumed that this would be the main subject of the unexpected lecture, but they were soon undeceived. Besides, if they had paid a little more attention to the expression on the Registrar's face, they would have realised at once that his objective was not of a disciplinary nature, it wasn't a general reprimand, in which case his words would have sounded like sharp blows and his whole face would have been filled with a look of scornful indifference. None of these signs was apparent in the attitudes the Registrar struck, merely a feeling as of someone who, having been accustomed always to winning, finds himself for the first time in his life confronted by a force greater than his. And the few, in particular the deputies and the odd senior clerk, who thought they had deduced from the Registrar's last words that he was about to announce the immediate introduction of modernisations which were already current coinage beyond the walls of the Central Registry, were soon forced to recognise, much to their amazement, that they had been wrong. The Registrar continued to speak, Do not imagine, however, that the thoughts to which I refer are merely such thoughts as would lead us to open our doors to modern inventions, that would not even require any thought, we would simply call in the appropriate technician and within twenty-four hours we would have the place full of machinery of every kind. Much as it pains me to say this and however scandalous it may seem to you, the matter that my thoughts called into question, much to my surprise, was one of the fundamental aspects of Central Registry tradition, that is, the spatial distribution of the living and the dead, their obligatory separation, not only into different archives, but in different areas of the building. There was a faint whispering, as if the common thought of the astonished workers had become audible, there can be no other explanation, since none of them would have dared to utter a word. I realise that this troubles you, continued the Registrar, because, when I first thought it, I too felt almost as if I had committed a heresy, worse still, I felt guilty of offending against the memory of those who held this position of authority before me, and against those who worked at the desks now occupied by you, but the irresistible pressure of evidence forced me to confront the weight of tradition, a tradition which, all my life, I had considered immovable. Becoming aware of these facts was no chance occurrence nor the fruit of a sudden revelation. On two occasions since I have been head of the Central Registry, I have received two premonitory warnings, to which, at the time, I attributed no particular importance, except that I reacted to them in a way which I myself can only describe as primitive, but which I now realise paved the way for me to welcome with an open heart a third and more recent warning, about which I will not speak on this occasion, for reasons which I believe should remain secret. The first occasion, which you will all doubtless remember, was when one of my deputies here present proposed that the archive of the dead should be arranged the other way around, that is, with the oldest farthest off and the most recent nearest. Because of the amount of work involved in such a change and bearing in mind the small staff we have at our disposal, the suggestion was manifestly impracticable, and I conveyed those feelings to the proposer of the idea, however, I did so in terms that I would prefer now to forget and that I would like him to forget too. The deputy referred to blushed with satisfaction and turned around to show himself, before turning back to face his superior, nodding slightly, as if he were thinking, You see, if you paid a little more attention to what other people told you. The Registrar went on, I did not realise then that behind an apparently absurd idea, which, from the operational point of view, was indeed absurd, lay an intuition of something absolutely revolutionary, an unwitting, unconscious intuition it's true, but no less effective for that. Of course, one could expect no more from the brain of a mere deputy, but as Registrar, I was obliged, both by the duties imposed on me by my post and by reason of experience, to understand immediately what the seeming futility of the idea concealed. This time the deputy did not turn around, and if he blushed with hurt pride no one saw it because he kept his head bowed. The Registrar paused to give a deep sigh and then went on, The second occasion was when the researcher went missing in the archive of the dead and was only discovered a week later, almost at death's door, when we had nearly lost hope of finding him alive. Since it was, in a sense, such a common occurrence, for I cannot believe that anyone here has not, at least once in his life, got lost in there, I merely took the necessary precautions, issuing an order imposing the obligatory use of Ariadne's thread, a classical, and if I may say, ironic description, of the length of string that I keep in the drawer. The fact that since then nothing similar has occurred is proof that it worked. In light of the direction my talk is taking, one might ask what conclusions I should have drawn from the affair of the lost genealogist, and I would say, with all humility, that but for certain other recent events and the thoughts which those events aroused in me, I would never have come to understand the double absurdity of separating the dead from the living. It is absurd in the first place from the archivistic point of view, when one considers that the easiest way of finding the dead would be to look for them among the living, since the latter, because they are alive, are always there before us, but it is equally absurd from the mnemonic point of view, for if the dead are not kept in the midst of the living, sooner or later they will be forgotten and then, if you'll forgive the rather vulgar expression, it's the Devil's own job to find them when we need them, which, again, sooner or later, we always do. For all those listening to me, without regard to rank or personal circumstance, it will be clear that I have been talking only about the Central Registry, not the outside world, where, in order to protect the physical hygiene and mental health of the living, we usually bury the dead. But I would go so far as to say that an identical need for physical hygiene and mental health should ensure that we of the Central Registry, we who write and manipulate the papers of life and death, should reunite the dead and the living in one single archive which we will call the historic archive, and where they will be inseparable, a circumstance which, beyond these walls, law, custom and fear do not allow. I will issue an order that will specify, firstly, that from this date on, the dead will remain in the same place that they occupied in the archive while alive, secondly, that gradually, file by file, document by document, from the most recent to the most ancient, we will move towards the reintegration of the past dead into the archive which will then become everyone's present. I know that the second part of the operation will take several decades to carry out, that we will no longer be alive, nor, probably, will the subsequent generation, when the papers of the last dead person, torn, worm-eaten, darkened by the dust of ages, return to the world from which, by one last, unnecessary act of violence, they were removed. Just as definitive death is the ultimate fruit of the will to forget, so the will to remember will perpetuate our lives. Were I expecting you to express an opinion, you would perhaps argue, with what you fondly imagine to be subtlety, that such a perpetuity will be of no use to those who have died. That would be the argument of one who sees no further than the end of his own nose. In that case, and always assuming I took the trouble to respond, I would have to explain to you that I have been talking only about life here, not death, and if you failed to realise that before, that is because you will never be capable of understanding anything at all.

The reverential silence in which the final part of his speech had been heard was rudely shaken by the sarcasm of those last words. The Registrar had gone back to being the boss they had always known, arrogant and ironic, implacable in his judgements, rigorous as regards discipline, as he immediately went on to demonstrate, Purely in your interests, not in mine, I must make it clear to you that you would be making the biggest mistake of your lives if you were to consider the fact that I have spoken to you with an open heart and mind a sign of personal weakness or a diminution of official authority. The reason I did not simply issue an order for the reintegration or unification of the two archives to take place, without further explanation, as I would have been perfectly entitled to do, was that I wanted you to understand the deeper reasons behind the decision, it was because I wanted the work awaiting you to be carried out in the spirit of one who feels he is engaged in building something and not with the sense of bureaucratic alienation of one who has simply been ordered to put one set of papers together with another. Discipline in the Central Registry will continue to be what it has always been, no distractions, no daydreaming, no word not directly concerned with work, no unpunctuality, no negligence in matters of personal behaviour, in either manners or appearance. Senhor José thought, He must mean me, because I haven't shaved, but this didn't worry him, the reference was probably intended to be a general one, but, just in case, he lowered his head very slowly, like a student who has not learned his lesson and wants to avoid being called to the blackboard. It seemed that the speech had reached its end, but no one moved, they had to await the order to go back to work, which is why they all jumped when the Registrar said in a loud, sharp tone, Senhor José. Senhor José got swiftly to his feet, What can he want of me, he no longer thought that the reason for that abrupt call could be his unshaven beard, something far more serious than a simple reprimand was about to take place, or so he judged from the severe expression on the Registrar's face, at least that was what a terrible fear was beginning to scream at him inside his head when he saw the Registrar advancing in his direction, stopping in front of him, Senhor José can barely breathe, he awaits the first word as a condemned man waits for the blade to fall, for the rope to tighten or for the firing squad to shoot, then the Registrar said, That beard. He then turned on his heel and signalled to his deputies for work to recommence. There was a certain look of placid calm on his face now, an air of strange peace, as if he too had come to the end of a day's work. No one will share these impressions with Senhor José, in the first place, so as not to fill his head with even more fantasies, secondly, because the order is clear, No word not directly concerned with work.

One enters the cemetery via an old building with a façade which is the twin sister of the Central Registry façade. There are the same three black stone steps, the same ancient door in the middle, the same five narrow windows above. Apart from the great two-leaved door alongside the façade, the only observable difference would be the sign above the entrance, in the same enamelled lettering, that says General Cemetery. The large door was closed many years ago, when it was clear that access through there had become impracticable, that it had ceased satisfactorily to fulfil the end for which it had been intended, that is, to allow easy passage not only for the dead and their companions, but also for those who would visit the dead afterwards. Like all cemeteries in this or any other world, it was tiny when it started, a small patch of land on the outskirts of what was still the embryo of a city, turned to face the open air of the fields, but later, alas, with the passing of time, the inevitable happened, it kept growing and growing and growing, until it became the immense necropolis that it is today. At first, it was surrounded by a wall and, for generations, whenever the pressure inside began to hinder both the orderly accommodation of the dead and the free circulation of the living, they did the same as in the Central Registry, they would demolish the walls and rebuild them a little farther on. One day, it must be close to four centuries ago, the then keeper of the cemetery had the idea of leaving it open on all sides, apart from the area facing onto the street, alleging that this was the only way to rekindle the sentimental relationship between those inside and those outside, much diminished at the time, as anyone could see just by looking at the neglected state of the graves, especially the oldest ones. He believed that, although walls served the positive aims of hygiene and decorum, ultimately, they had the perverse effect of aiding forgetfulness, which is hardly surprising, given the popular wisdom which has declared, since time began, that what the eye doesn't see the heart doesn't grieve over. We have many reasons to think that the motives behind the Registrar's decision to break with tradition and routine and to unify the archives of the dead and of the living, thus reintegrating human society in the specific documentary area under his jurisdiction, were purely internal. It is, therefore, all the more difficult for us to understand why no one immediately applied the earlier lesson provided by a humble, primitive cemetery keeper, who, as was only natural in his line of work and bearing in mind the times he lived in, was doubtless not particularly well educated, but was, nevertheless, a man of revolutionary instincts, and who, sad to say, has not even been given a decent gravestone to point out the fact to future generations. On the contrary, for four centuries now, curses, insults, calumnies and humiliations have been heaped upon the memory of the unfortunate innovator, for he is held to be the person historically responsible for the present state of the necropolis, which is described as disastrous and chaotic, mostly because not only does the General Cemetery still have no walls about it but it could never possibly be walled in again. Allow us to explain. We said earlier that the cemetery grew, not, of course, because of some intrinsic reproductive powers of its own, as though, if you will permit us a somewhat macabre example, the dead had engendered more dead, but simply because the city's population grew and so therefore did its size. Even when the General Cemetery was still surrounded by walls, something occurred which, in the language of municipal bureaucracy, is called an urban demographic explosion, and this happened more than once and in successive ages. Little by little, people came to live in the wide fields behind the cemetery, small groups of houses appeared, villages, hamlets, second homes, which grew in turn, occasionally contiguous, but still leaving between them large empty spaces, which were used as farmland or woods or pasture or areas of scrub. Those were the areas into which the General Cemetery advanced when its walls were demolished. Like floodwaters that begin by encroaching on the low-lying land, snaking along valleys and then, slowly, creeping up hillsides, so the graves gained ground, often to the detriment of agriculture, for the besieged owners had no alternative but to sell off strips of land, at other times, the graves skirted orchards, wheat fields, threshing floors and cattle pens, always within sight of the houses, and, often, if you like, right next door. Seen from the air, the General Cemetery looks like an enormous felled tree, with a short, fat trunk, made up of the nucleus of original graves, from which four stout branches reach out, all from the same growing point, but which, later, in successive bifurcations, extend as far as you can see, forming, in the words of an inspired poet, a leafy crown in which life and death are mingled, just as in real trees birds and foliage mingle. That is why the main door of the General Cemetery ceased to serve as a passageway for funeral processions. It is opened only very infrequently, when a researcher into old stones, having studied one of the very early funerary markers in the place, asks permission to make a mould of it, with the consequent deployment of raw materials, such as plaster, tow and wires, and, a not unusual complement, delicate, precise photographs, the sort that require spotlights, reflectors, batteries, light meters, umbrellas and other artifacts, none of which are allowed through the small door that leads from the building into the cemetery because it would disturb the administrative work carried on inside.

Despite this exhaustive accumulation of details, which some may consider insignificant, a case, to resort to botanical comparisons again, of not being able to see the forest for the trees, it is quite possible that some vigilant, attentive listener to this story, someone who has not lost a sense of standards inherited from mental processes determined, above all, by the logic acquired from knowledge, it is quite possible that such a listener might declare himself radically opposed to the existence, and still more to the spread, of such wild, anarchic cemeteries as this, which has grown to the point where it is almost cheek by jowl with the places that the living had intended for their exclusive use, that is, houses, streets, squares, gardens and other public amenities, theatres and cinemas, cafés and restaurants, hospitals, insane asylums, police stations, playgrounds, sports fields, fairgrounds and exhibition areas, car parks, large department stores, small shops, side streets, alleyways, avenues. For, while aware of the General Cemetery's irresistible need for growth, in symbiotic union with the development of the city and its increased population, they consider that the area intended for one's final rest should nevertheless keep within strict bounds and obey strict rules. An ordinary quadrilateral of high walls, with no decoration or fantastic architectural excrescences, would be more than sufficient, instead of this vast octopus, more octopus really than tree, however much that may pain poetic imaginations, reaching out with its eight, sixteen, thirty-two, sixty-four tentacles, as if to embrace the whole world. In civilised countries, the correct practice, with advantages proven by experience, is for bodies to remain beneath the earth for a few years, five usually, at the end of which, apart from the odd case of miraculous incorruptibility, what little is left after the corrosive work of quicklime and the digestive work of worms is dug up to make room for the new occupants.

In civilised countries, they do not have this absurd practice of plots in perpetuity, this idea of considering any grave forever untouchable, as if, since life could not be made definitive, death can be. This has obvious consequences, the blocked-off door, the anarchic internal traffic system, the ever longer route that funerals have to make around the General Cemetery before they reach their destination at the far end of one of the octopus's sixty-four tentacles which they would never find if they did not have a guide with them. Like the Central Registry, although, by some deplorable lapse of memory, this information was not given at the appropriate moment, the General Cemetery's unwritten motto is All the Names, although it should be said that, in fact, these three words fit the Central Registry like a glove, because it is there that all the names are to be found, both those of the dead and those of the living, while the cemetery, given its role as ultimate destination and ultimate depository, has to content itself only with the names of the dead. This mathematical evidence, however, is not enough to silence the keepers of the General Cemetery who, confronted by what they call their apparent numerical inferiority, usually shrug their shoulders and argue, With time and patience everyone ends up here, the Central Registry, from this point of view, is merely a tributary of the General Cemetery. Needless to say, it is an insult to the Central Registry to call it a tributary. Despite these rivalries, this professional competitiveness, relations between those who work in the Central Registry and those in the Cemetery are openly friendly and full of mutual respect, because, at bottom, apart from the inevitable institutional collaboration between them, given the formal similarity and objective contiguity of their respective statutes, they know that they are digging at either end of the same vine, the vine called life and which is situated between two voids.

This is not the first time that Senhor José has been to the General Cemetery. The bureaucratic need to check certain data, clarify discrepancies, compare facts, clear up differences, means that the people working in the Central Registry have to go to the cemetery with relative frequency, a task that nearly always falls to the clerks, hardly ever to the senior clerks, and never, need it be said, to the deputies or the Registrar. Sometimes, for similar reasons, the clerks and, on rare occasions, the officials from the General Cemetery go to the Central Registry, where they are received with the same cordiality with which Senhor José will be greeted here. Like the façade, the interior of the building is a perfect copy of the Central Registry, although, of course, one must point out that the people working in the General Cemetery usually say that the Central Registry is a perfect copy of the cemetery building, indeed an incomplete copy, since they lack the great door, to which those at the Central Registry reply that a fat lot of good the door is anyway, since it's always closed. Nevertheless, here we find the same long counter stretching the whole length of the enormous room, the same towering shelves, the same arrangement of staff, in a triangle, with the eight clerks in the first row, the four senior clerks behind them, then the two deputy keepers, for that is what they are called here, not deputy registrars, just as the keeper, at the apex, is not a registrar, but a keeper. However, there are other members of staff at the cemetery apart from the clerks. Sitting on two continuous benches, on either side of the entrance door, opposite the counter, are the guides. Some people continue bluntly to call them gravediggers, as in the old days, but their professional title, in the city's official gazette, is cemetery guide, which, contrary to what one might expect or imagine, is not just a well-intentioned euphemism intended to disguise the painful brutality of a spade digging a rectangular hole in the earth, rather, it is a correct description of a role which is not merely a question of lowering the dead into the depths, but of leading them over the surface too. These men, who work in pairs, wait there in silence for the funeral cortèges to arrive and then, armed with the respective pass, filled in by the clerk chosen to deal with the matter, they get into one of the cars waiting in the parking lot, the ones that have a luminous sign at the rear that flicks on and off and says Follow me, like the cars used at airports, at least the keeper of the General Cemetery is quite right in that regard, when he says that they are more advanced in matters of modern technology than they are at the Central Registry, where tradition still dictates that the clerks use old-fashioned pens and inkwells. The fact is that when you see the funeral car and those in it obediently following the guides along the well-tended streets of the city and along the rough roads of the suburbs, with the light flashing on and off all the way to the grave, Follow me, Follow me, Follow me, it is impossible not to agree that not all changes in the world are for the worst. And although the detail may not be of any real importance for a global understanding of the story, it may be of interest to explain that a marked personality trait among these guides is a belief that the universe is in fact ruled by a superior thought process which is permanently alert to human needs, because if that were not so, they argue, cars would not have been invented at precisely the moment when they became most necessary, that is, when the General Cemetery had become so vast that it would be a real calvary to bear the deceased to his or her particular Golgotha by the traditional methods, whether using stick and rope or a two-wheeled cart. When someone sensibly remarks to them that they should be more careful in their use of words, since Golgotha and calvary originally mean one and the same thing, and that it makes no sense to use terms denoting pain and sorrow with regard to the transportation of someone who will never suffer again, you can guarantee that they will respond, rudely, that each man knows himself, but only God knows all men.

Senhor José went in and went straight up to the counter, casting a cold eye over the seated guides, whom he disliked because their existence tilted the numerical balance of staff in the cemetery's favour. Since he was known to the people there, he did not need to show the identity card proving that he was a member of staff at the Central Registry, and as for the famous letter of authority, it hadn't even occurred to him to bring it, besides, even the least experienced of the clerks would have seen at a glance that it was false from beginning to end. Of the eight clerks lined up behind the counter, Senhor José chose one of the men with whom he got on best, a man a little older than himself, who had the absorbed air of one who no longer expects anything more from life. Like all the other clerks, he always seemed to be there whatever day it was. At first, Senhor José had thought that the people who worked at the cemetery never got a day off or took a holiday, that they worked every day of the year, until someone told him that this was not the case, that there was a group of casual workers contracted to work on Sundays, we are no longer in the days of slavery, Senhor José. Needless to say, the clerks at the General Cemetery have long hoped that the aforesaid casual workers might take over on Saturday afternoons too, but, for alleged reasons of budgets and finances, that demand has not yet been met, and in vain did the cemetery staff invoke the example of the Central Registry staff, who only worked on Saturday mornings, for, according to the sibylline communiqué issued from above refusing their request, The living can wait, the dead cannot. Anyway, it was unheard of for a member of staff from the Central Registry to appear there for work reasons on a Saturday afternoon, when everyone assumed he would be enjoying his weekly leisure time with his family, going on a trip into the country, or occupied with domestic tasks that have to wait until there's a bit of free time, or merely lazing about, or even wondering what is the point of having leisure time if we don't know what to do with it. In order to avoid any awkward questions, which could easily become embarrassing, Senhor José adroitly pre-empted the other person's curiosity, giving the excuse he had already prepared, It's a special case, very urgent, my deputy needs this information first thing on Monday morning, that's why he asked me to come to the General Cemetery today, in my free time, I see, you'd better tell me what it's about then, It's very simple, we just want to know when this woman was buried. The man took the card that Senhor José held out to him, copied the name and date of death onto a piece of paper, and went to consult the relevant senior clerk. Senhor José couldn't catch what they said, here, as in the Central Registry, you can speak only in a low voice, and they were some way away from him too, but he saw the senior clerk nod and, judging by his lips, he was sure that he had said, Fine, go ahead. The man went to look in the card index under the counter, where all the cards of those who died in the last fifty years were to be found, the others filled the high shelves that stretched into the interior of the building, he opened one of the drawers, found the woman's card, copied down the relevant date and came back to where Senhor José was standing, Here it is, he said, and added, as if he thought the information might be useful, She's in the section for suicides. Senhor José felt a sudden contraction in the pit of his stomach which, according to an article he had read once in a popular magazine about science, is the approximate location of a kind of many-pointed star of nerves, a radiating junction called the solar plexus, however, he managed to hide his surprise behind an automatic mask of indifference, the cause of death would, of course, be on the lost death certificate, which he had never seen, but as a clerk in the Central Registry, especially coming to the cemetery, as he was, on business, he could not let on that he did not know. Very carefully he folded up the piece of paper and put it in his wallet and thanked the clerk, not forgetting to add, as one official to another, although that is purely a manner of speaking, since both were mere clerks, that he was always at his disposal should he need anything at the Central Registry and always assuming that it was within his power to grant it. When he had taken two steps towards the door, he turned around, I've just had an idea, since I'm here, I think I'll spend part of the afternoon taking a little stroll around the cemetery, if you could let me through here, I wouldn't have to go the long way around, Hang on, I'll go and ask, said the clerk. He took the request to the senior clerk to whom he had spoken before, but instead of replying, the latter got up and went over to the deputy keeper in charge of his work. Although he was even farther away this time, Senhor José could see by the nod the deputy gave and by the movement of his lips that he was going to be allowed to use the inner door. The clerk did not return to the counter immediately, he first opened a cabinet from which he took a large card which he then placed beneath the lid of a machine with little coloured lights on it. He pressed a button, there was a mechanical noise, more lights came on, and then a smaller piece of paper emerged from a slit in the side. The clerk put the card back in the cabinet and then came back to the counter, You'd better take a map with you, there have been cases of people getting lost, and it's incredibly difficult to find them again, the guides have to go out looking for them in the cars and that gums up the works, you get funerals backed up outside, People panic easily, all they have to do is go in a straight line in the same direction, they're bound to reach somewhere, now in the archive of the dead in the Central Registry it really is complicated, because there are no straight lines, In theory, you're right, but the straight lines here are like the straight lines in a labyrinth of corridors, they're constantly breaking off, changing direction, you walk around a grave and suddenly you don't know where you are, In the Central Registry, we use Ariadne's thread, it never fails, There was a time when we used it too, but it didn't last long, the thread was found cut on several occasions and no one ever found out who the culprit was or why they'd done it, It certainly wasn't the dead, that's for sure, Who knows, The people who got lost were people with no initiative, they could have oriented themselves by the sun, Some probably would have if they hadn't been unlucky enough to get lost on a cloudy day, We haven't got one of those machines in the Central Registry, We've found them really useful. The conversation could not go on any longer, the senior clerk had already looked at them twice, and the second time he was frowning, it was Senhor José who remarked in a low voice, That senior clerk has already looked over here twice, I don't want you to get into any trouble on my account, I'll just show you where the woman is buried, see the end of this path, the wavy line here is a stream which, for the moment, still serves as a boundary line, the grave is in that corner there, you can identify it by the number, And by the name, Yes, if someone's put one there, but it's the numbers that count, the names wouldn't fit on the map, you'd need a map the size of the world, Scale one to one, Yes, scale one to one, and even then, the names would have to be superimposed on each other, Is it up-to-date, We update it every day, Now tell me, what made you think I'd want to see the woman's grave, No reason, perhaps because, in your place, I'd have done the same, Why, Just to be certain, That she's dead, No, to be certain that she'd been alive. The senior clerk looked at them for a third time, made a movement as if he were about to get up, but did not complete it, Senhor José bade a hasty farewell to the clerk, Thank you, thank you, he said, at the same time nodding slightly in the direction of the keeper, a person to whom one should always bow, just as one gives thanks to heaven, even when it's cloudy, with the important difference that then you don't lower your head, you raise it.

The oldest part of the General Cemetery, which was a few dozen yards behind the administrative building, was the one preferred by archaeologists for their investigations. These ancient stones, some so worn by time that you could only make out a few barely visible marks that could as easily be the remains of letters as the result of scratches made by an unskilled chisel, continued to be the object of intense debate and polemic in which, with no hope, in the majority of cases, of ever knowing who had been buried beneath them, archaeologists merely discussed, as if it were a matter of vital import, the probable date of the tombs. Such insignificant differences as a few hundred years here or there were the motive for long, long controversies, both public and academic, which almost always resulted in the violent breakup of personal relationships and even in mortal enmities. Things got still worse, if that were possible, when historians and art critics decided to stick their oar in, for while it was relatively easy, in the circumstances, for the board of archaeologists to reach agreement over a broad concept of antiquity acceptable to all, leaving aside actual dates, the matter of truth and beauty created a veritable tug-of-war among the men and women of aesthetics and history, each pulling for their own side, and it was a not uncommon sight to see a critic suddenly changing his opinion simply because the changed opinion of another critic meant that they both now agreed. Throughout the centuries, the ineffable peace of the General Cemetery, with its banks of spontaneous vegetation, its flowers, its creepers, its dense bushes, its festoons and garlands, its nettles and its thistles, the powerful trees whose roots often dislodged tombstones and forced up into the sunlight a few startled bones, had been both the target of and a witness to fierce wars of words and to one or two physical acts of violence. Whenever incidents of this nature occurred, the keeper would begin by ordering the available guides to go and separate the illustrious contenders, and when some particularly difficult situation arose, he would go there in person to remind the fighters ironically that there was no point tearing their hair out over such minor matters during their lifetime, since, sooner or later, they would all end up together in the cemetery bald as coots. Just like the Registrar, the keeper of the General Cemetery made brilliant use of sarcasm, which confirms the general assumption that this character trait had proved indispensable in their rise to their respective high ranks, together, of course, with a competent knowledge, both practical and theoretical, of archivistic technique. On one matter, however, historians, art critics and archaeologists are in agreement, the obvious fact that the General Cemetery is a perfect catalogue, a showcase, a summary of all styles, especially architectural, sculptural and decorative, and therefore an inventory of every possible way of seeing, being and living that has existed up until now, from the first elementary drawing of the outline of the human body, subsequently carved and chiselled out of bare stone, to the chromium-plated steel, reflecting panels, synthetic fibres and mirrored glass which are used willy-nilly in the current age.

The first funerary monuments were made of dolmens, cromlechs and menhirs, then there appeared, like a great blank page in relief, niches, altars, tabernacles, granite bowls, marble urns, tombstones, smooth and carved, columns, Doric, Ionic, Corinthian and Composite, caryatids, friezes, acanthuses, entablatures and pediments, false vaults, real vaults, as well as stretches of brick wall, the gables of Cyclopean walls, lancet windows, rose windows, gargoyles, oriel windows, tympanums, pinnacles, paving stones, flying buttresses, pillars, pilasters, recumbent statues representing men in helmet, sword and armour, capitals with and without ornamentation, pomegranates, lilies, immortelles, campaniles, cupolas, recumbent statues representing women with small hard breasts, paintings, arches, faithful dogs lying down, swaddled infants, the bearers of gifts, mourners with their heads covered, needles, mouldings, stained-glass windows, daises, pulpits, balconies, more pinnacles, more tympanums, more capitals, more arches, angels with wings spread, angels with wings folded, tondos, empty urns, or urns filled with false stone flames or with a piece of languid crepe draped about them, griefs, tears, majestic men, magnificent women, delightful children cut down in the flower of life, old men and old women who could have expected no more, whole crosses and broken crosses, steps, nails, crowns of thorns, lances, enigmatic triangles, the occasional unusual marble dove, flocks of real doves wheeling above the cemetery. And silence. A silence interrupted only from time to time by the steps of the occasional sighing lover of solitude drawn here by a sudden bout of sadness from the rustling outskirts where someone can still be heard weeping at a graveside on which they have placed bunches of fresh flowers, still damp with sap, piercing, one might say, the very heart of time, these three thousand years of graves of every shape, meaning and appearance, united by the same neglect, by the same solitude, for the sadness they once gave rise to is now too old for there to be any surviving heirs. Orienting himself with the map, although occasionally wishing he had a compass, Senhor José walks towards the area set aside for suicides, where the woman on the card is buried, but his step is slower now, less determined, from time to time he stops to study a sculptural detail stained by lichen or discoloured by the rain, a few mourners caught in mid-lament, a few solemn depositions, a few hieratic folds, or else he struggles to decipher an inscription whose lettering attracted him in passing, it's understandable that even the very first line takes him a long time to decipher, for, despite having occasionally had to examine parchments more or less contemporary with these in the Central Registry, this clerk is not versed in ancient forms of writing, which is why he has never got beyond being a clerk. On top of a small rounded hillock, in the shadow of an obelisk that was once a geodesic marker, Senhor José looks around him as far as he can see, and he finds nothing but graves rising and falling with the curves of the land, graves poised on the edge of the occasional precipitous slope and spreading out over the plains, There are millions of them, he murmurs, then he thinks of the vast amount of space they would have saved if the dead had been buried standing up, side by side, in serried ranks, like soldiers at attention, and at their head, as the only sign of their presence there, a stone cube on which would be written, on the five visible sides, the principal facts about the life of the deceased, five stone squares like five pages, the summary of a whole book that had proved impossible to write. Almost as far as the horizon, far, far into the distance, Senhor José can see slowly moving lights, like yellow lightning, flicking on and off at constant intervals, they are the guides' cars calling to the people behind them, Follow me, Follow me, one of them suddenly stops, the light disappears, that means it's reached its destination. Senhor José looked up at the sun, then at his watch, it's getting late, he'll have to walk fast if he wants to reach the unknown woman before dusk. He consulted the map, ran his index finger over it to reconstruct, approximately, the route he had followed from the administrative building to the place where he now finds himself, compared it with the distance he still has to walk, and almost lost courage. In a straight line, according to the scale, it would be about three miles, but, as we have already said, in the General Cemetery, the straight continuous line never lasts for long, to those three miles as the crow flies, you will have to add another two, or possibly three, travelling overland. Senhor José calculated the amount of time left and the strength still remaining in his legs, he heard a prudent voice telling him to leave it for another day, when he had more time to visit the grave of the unknown woman, because, now he knows where she is, any taxi or bus could drop him off nearer to the actual place, skirting around the cemetery, as families do when they come to weep over their loved ones and place new flowers in the jars or refresh the water, especially in summer. Senhor José was still weighing this perplexing problem when he remembered his adventure at the school, the grim, rainy night, the steep, slippery mountain slope of the porch roof, and then, soaked from head to toe, his grazed knee rubbing painfully against his trousers, his anxious search inside the building, and how, by dint of tenacity and intelligence, he had managed to conquer his own fears and overcome the thousand difficulties that blocked his path until he discovered and finally entered the mysterious attic, confronting a darkness even more frightening than that in the archive of the dead. Anyone brave enough to do all that had no right to feel discouraged by the thought of a walk, however long it might be, especially when doing so in the frank brilliance of the bright sun which, as we all know, is the friend of heroes. If the shades of dusk caught up with him before he had reached the unknown woman's grave, if night came to cut off all paths back, sowing them with invisible terrors and preventing him from going any farther, he could lie down on one of these mossy stones, with a sad stone angel to watch over his sleep, and wait for the birth of the new day. Or else he could shelter beneath a flying buttress like that one over there, thought Senhor José, but then it occurred to him that, farther on, he wouldn't find any flying buttresses. Thanks to the generations yet to come and to the consequent development of civil engineering, it won't be long before they invent less expensive means of holding up a wall, indeed it is in the General Cemetery that the results of progress are set out before the eyes of the studious or the merely curious, there are even those who say that a cemetery like this is a kind of library which contains not books but buried people, it really doesn't matter, you can learn as much from people as from books. Senhor José looked back, from where he was he could see only the roof ridge of the administrative building above the taller funerary monuments, I had no idea I'd come so far, he murmured, and having said that, as if, in order to make a decision, he had needed only to hear the sound of his own voice, he once more continued on his way.

When he at last reached the section of the suicides, with the sky already sifting the still-white ashes of the dusk, he thought that he must have gone the wrong way or that there was something wrong with the map. Before him was a great expanse of field, with numerous trees, almost a wood, where the graves, apart from the barely visible gravestones, seemed more like tufts of natural vegetation. You could not see the stream from there, but you could hear the lightest of murmurs slipping over the stones, and in the atmosphere, which was like green glass, there hovered a coolness which was not just the usual coolness of the first hour of dusk. Being so recent, only a matter of a few days ago, the grave of the unknown woman must be on the outer limit of the area, the question was in which direction. Senhor José thought that the best thing, in order not to get lost, would be to walk over to the small stream and then go along the bank until he found the latest graves. The shadow of the trees covered him immediately, as if night had suddenly fallen. I should be afraid, murmured Senhor José, in the midst of this silence, among these tombs, with these trees surrounding me, instead I feel as calm as if I were in my own house, except that my legs ache from having walked so much, here's the stream, if I was afraid, I could leave here this minute, all I'd have to do is cross the stream, I'd just have to take my shoes and socks off and roll up my trouser legs, hang my shoes around my neck and wade across, the water wouldn't even reach my knees, I'd soon be back in the land of the living again, with those lights over there that have just gone on. Half an hour later, Senhor José reached the end of the field, when the moon, almost full, almost completely round, was just coming up over the horizon. There the graves did not as yet have carved headstones to cover them nor any sculptural adornments, they could only be identified by the white numbers painted on the black labels stuck in at the head of the grave, like hovering butterflies. The moonlight gradually spread over the field, slipped slowly through the trees like a habitual, benevolent ghost. In a clearing, Senhor José found what he was looking for. He didn't take from his pocket the piece of paper the cemetery clerk had given him, he had made no particular effort to remember the number, but he knew it when he needed to, and now it was there before him, brilliantly lit, as if written in phosphorescent paint. Here she is, he said.

Senhor José got cold during the night. After having uttered those redundant, useless words, Here she is, he wasn't sure what else he should do. It was true that, after long and arduous labours, he had managed, at last, to find the unknown woman, or rather, the place where she lay, a good six feet beneath an earth that still sustained him, but, he thought to himself, the normal response would be to feel afraid, fearful of the place, the hour, the rustling trees, the mysterious moonlight, and, in particular, of the strange cemetery surrounding him, an assembly of suicides, a gathering of silences that, from one moment to the next, might begin to scream, We came before our time was due, our own will brought us here, but what he felt inside him seemed more like indecision, doubt, as if, just when he thought he had reached the end of everything, he realised that his search was not yet finished, as if having come here were merely another point on the journey, of no more importance than the ground-floor apartment belonging to the elderly lady, or the school, or the chemist's where he had gone to ask questions, or the archive in the Central Registry where they kept the papers of the dead. He was so overcome by this feeling that he even muttered, as if trying to convince himself, She's dead, there's nothing more I can do, there's nothing anyone can do about death. For long hours he had walked through the General Cemetery, he had passed through epochs, eras, dynasties, through kingdoms, empires and republics, through wars and epidemics, through infinite numbers of disparate deaths, beginning with the first sorrow felt by humanity and ending with this woman who had committed suicide only a few days ago, Senhor José, therefore, knows all too well that there is nothing anyone can do about death. On that walk made up of so many dead, not one of them got up when they heard him pass, not one begged him to help them reunite the scattered dust of their flesh with the bones fallen from their sockets, not one asked him, Come and breathe into my eyes the breath of life, they know all too well that there is nothing anyone can do about death, they know it, we all know it, but, in that case, where does it come from, this feeling of angst that grips Senhor José's throat, this unease of mind, as if he had cravenly abandoned a half-completed task and now did not know how to return to it with any dignity. On the other side of the stream, not far off, one can see a few houses with the windows lit, the moribund lights of the street lamps in the suburbs, the fleeting beam of a car passing on the road. And immediately ahead, only thirty paces away, as sooner or later had to happen, a small bridge joins the two banks of the stream, so Senhor José won't have to take off his shoes and roll up his trouser legs when he wants to cross to the other side. In normal circumstances he would have done so a long time ago, especially since we know he is not a person of great courage, courage he is going to need if he is to survive a whole night in a cemetery unscathed, with a dead person lying beneath his feet and a moonlight capable of making shadows walk. The circumstances, however, are these and no others, here it is not a question of courage or cowardice, here it is a matter of life and death, which is why Senhor José, despite knowing that he will often feel afraid during the night, despite knowing that the sighing of the wind will terrify him, that at dawn, the cold fallen from the sky will join forces with the cold rising from the earth, Senhor José is going to sit down beneath a tree, huddled up in the shelter of a providential hollow trunk. He turns up his jacket collar, makes himself as small as possible in order to retain the warmth of his body, folds his arms so that his hands are in his armpits, and prepares to wait for day. He can feel his stomach asking him for food, but he takes no notice, no one ever died from going for a while without eating between meals, except when the second meal was so long in being served that it did not appear in time to be served at all. Senhor José wants to know if it really is all over, or if, on the contrary, there is still something he has forgotten to do, or, more important, something that he had never even considered before and that might turn out to be, after all, the essence of the strange adventure into which chance had plunged him. He had looked for the unknown woman everywhere, and had found her here, beneath that little mound of earth which will soon be overgrown by weeds, if the stonemason doesn't come first to level it out and place on it the marble stone with the usual inscription of dates, the first and the last, and the name, though the family might be the sort who prefer a simple rectangular frame, in the middle of which they will later sow a decorative lawn, a solution that offers the double advantage of being less expensive and providing a home for the insects that live above ground. The woman is there then, all the roads in the world have closed for her, she walked that part of the road she had to walk and stopped where she wanted to, end of story, but Senhor José cannot rid himself of an obsessive thought, that he is the only person who can move the final piece on the board, the definitive piece, the one which, if moved in the right direction, will give real meaning to the game, at the risk, if he does not do so, of leaving the game at stalemate for all eternity. He has no idea what magical move that will be, but his decision to spend the night here was not made in the hope that the silence would come and whisper it in his ear or that the moonlight would kindly sketch it out for him among the shadows of the trees, he is simply like someone who, having climbed a mountain to reach the landscapes beyond, resists going back down into the valley until his astonished eyes have taken their fill of vast horizons.

The tree in which Senhor José has taken shelter is an ancient olive tree, whose fruits the local people still come and pick despite the fact that the olive grove has now become a cemetery. Over the many years of its life, the tree's trunk has gradually split open down one side, from top to bottom, like a cradle stood on its end so as to take up less space, and it is there that Senhor José manages to doze off now and then, it is there that he jerks awake, startled by the wind buffeting his face or when the silence and stillness of the air grew so profound that his drowsing spirit began to dream about the cries of a world sliding into the void. At one point, like someone determined to cure a dog bite with a hair of the dog that bit him, Senhor José decided to make use of his imagination in order to re-create mentally all the classic horrors appropriate to the place in which he found himself, the processions of lost souls swathed in white sheets, the *danses macabres* of skeletons rattling their bones in time to the music, the ominous figure of death skimming the ground with a bloody scythe to make sure that the dead resign themselves to remaining dead, but, because none of this was actually happening in reality, because it was just the work of his imagination, Senhor José gradually began to drift towards an enormous inner peace, only occasionally disturbed by the irresponsible flutterings of will-o'-the-wisps, enough to strain most people's nerves to breaking point, however tough they might be or however much they might know about the elementary principles of organic chemistry. Indeed, our fearful Senhor José is displaying a courage which the many upsets and afflictions through which we saw him pass earlier would not have led us to expect, which, once again, just goes to show that it is in moments of extreme duress that the spirit gives the true measure of its greatness. Towards dawn, now almost indifferent to fear, lulled by the gentle warmth of the tree embracing him, Senhor José dropped off to sleep with remarkable calm, while the world about him slowly re-emerged from the malevolent shadows of the night and from the ambiguous brilliance of a now departing moon. When Senhor José opened his eyes, it was already broad daylight. He was chilled to the bone, the tree's friendly vegetable embrace must have been just another deceiving dream, unless the tree, considering that it had fulfilled the duty of hospitality to which all olive trees, by their very nature, are obliged, had released him too soon and abandoned him, helpless, to the cold of a low, delicate mist that hovered over the cemetery. Senhor José struggled to his feet, feeling every joint in his body creak, and stumbled towards the sun, at the same time beating his arms vigorously about him in order to warm himself. Beside the grave of the unknown woman, nibbling the damp grass, was a white sheep. All around, here and there, there were other sheep grazing. And an old man, with a crook in his hand, was coming towards Senhor José. He was accompanied by an ordinary dog, neither large nor small, which, while it gave no sign of aggression, looked very much as if it were only awaiting a word from its master to attack. The man stopped on the other side of the grave with the inquisitive air of one who, without asking for any explanation, clearly believes he is owed one, and Senhor José said, Good morning, to which the other man replied, Good morning, It's a lovely day, Not bad, I fell asleep, Senhor José said, Ah, you fell asleep, said the man in a doubtful tone, I came here to visit the grave of a friend of mine, I sat down to rest under that olive tree and I went to sleep, You spent the night here, Yes, It's the first time I've ever met anyone here at this hour, which is when I bring the sheep to graze, You're not here during the rest of the day, then, asked Senhor José, It would look bad, it would show a lack of respect, with the sheep getting in the way of the funerals or leaving their droppings when the people who come here to remember their loved ones are walking about praying and crying, besides, the guides don't want us to get in the way when they're digging graves, so I have no option but to bring them a bit of cheese now and then so that they don't go complaining to the keeper, Since the General Cemetery is open on all sides, anyone can come in, and that includes animals, in fact, I'm surprised that I didn't see a single cat or dog when I walked up here from the office, There's no shortage of stray cats and dogs, Well, I didn't see any, You mean you walked all the way, Yes, You could have caught a bus, or a taxi, or come in your car, if you've got one, I didn't know where the grave was, that's why I had to go and ask first at the office, and then it was such a lovely day, I decided to walk, It's odd that they didn't tell you to go around, they usually do, I asked them to let me in and they did, Are you an archaeologist, No, A historian, No, An art critic, Certainly not, A genealogist, Please, Then I don't understand why you would want to make that great long trek, nor how you managed to sleep among all these tombs, I'm pretty used to the place, but I wouldn't stay here a minute after the sun's gone down, Well, that's what happened, I sat down and I went to sleep, You're a brave man, No, I'm not that either, Did you find the person you were looking for, It's that one there, right beside you, Is it a man or a woman, A woman, She still hasn't got a name, I imagine the family will be deciding on a headstone now, I've noticed that the families of suicides are more likely to neglect that elementary duty than others, perhaps they're filled with remorse, they probably think they're to blame, It's possible, Considering that we don't know each other, how come you're answering all my questions, most people would tell me to mind my own business, It's just the way I am, I always answer what I'm asked, You're a subaltern, a subordinate, a dependant, a manservant, an errand boy, I'm a clerk at the Central Registry, Then you're just the person to be told the truth about the land of suicides, but first, you must swear solemnly that you'll never reveal the secret to anyone, I swear by all that I hold most sacred, And what exactly do you hold most sacred, I don't know, Everything, Or nothing, It's a bit of a vague oath, don't you think, I can't come up with a better one, Swear on your honour, that used to be the surest oath, All right then, I'll swear on my honour, but, you know, the head of the Central Registry would die laughing if he heard one of his clerks swearing on his honour, Between a shepherd and a clerk it's a serious enough oath, not laughable at all, so we'll stick with that, So what is the truth about the land of suicides, asked Senhor José, Not everything here is what it seems, It's a cemetery, it's the General Cemetery, It's a labyrinth, You can see when something's a labyrinth, Not always, This is the invisible kind, I don't understand, For example, the person lying here, said the shepherd, touching the mound of earth with the end of his crook, is not the person you think. Suddenly, the ground began to shake beneath Senhor José's feet, the one remaining piece on the board, his final certainty, the unknown woman who had at last been found, had just disappeared. Do you mean that this number is wrong, he asked, trembling, A number is a number, a number is never wrong, replied the shepherd, if you took this one from here and put it somewhere else, even if it was at the very ends of the earth, it would still continue to be the number it is, I don't understand, You will, Please, I'm all confused, None of the bodies buried here corresponds to the names you see on the marble stones, I don't believe it, Well, it's true, And what about the numbers, They've all been swapped around, Why, Because someone changes them before the stones with the names on them are brought and put in place, Who, Me, But that's a crime, protested Senhor José indignantly, There's no law against it, I'm going to report you right now to the cemetery officials, You swore on your honour, I withdraw the oath, this situation invalidates it, You can replace a bad word with a good word, but neither one nor the other can be withdrawn, your word is your word, an oath is an oath, Death is sacred, It's life that's sacred, Mr. Clerk, at least so they say, But in the name of decency, you should have a minimum of respect for the person who died, people come here to remember their relatives and friends, to meditate or pray, to place flowers or to weep before a beloved name, and now it seems, because of one mischievous shepherd, the person lying there has another name entirely, these venerable mortal remains don't belong to the person they were thought to belong to, that way, you make death a farce, Personally, I don't believe one can show greater respect than to weep for a stranger, But death, What, Death should be respected, And what in your opinion does respecting death involve, Not profaning it for a start, Death itself cannot be profaned, You know very well that it's the dead I'm talking about, not death itself, And can you see the slightest sign of profanation here, Swapping the names around is hardly a minor profanation, Well, I can understand a clerk in the Central Registry having ideas like that about names. The shepherd stopped, made a sign to the dog to go and fetch a sheep that had wandered off, then went on, I haven't yet told you the reason why I began changing the numbers on the graves, I doubt it's of any interest to me, I'm sure it will be, Go on then, If, as I believe, it's true that people who commit suicide do so because they don't want to be found, these people here, thanks to what you called a mischievous shepherd, are now free forever from importunate visitors, in truth, not even I, even if I wanted to, would be able to remember where the numbers should be, all I know is what I think when I pass by these marble stones complete with the person's name and the correct dates of birth and death, What do you think, That it's possible not to see a lie even when it's right in front of us. The mist had vanished a long time ago, you could now see how large the flock of sheep was. The shepherd made a movement above his head with the crook, it was an order for the dog to gather the sheep together. The shepherd said, It's time for me to take the sheep away, the guides might find me here, I can already see the lights of two cars, but they're not coming this way, I'm going to stay for a while longer, said Senhor José, Are you really going to report me, asked the shepherd, I'm a man of my word, what is sworn is sworn, They'd probably tell you to keep your mouth shut anyway, Why, Imagine the work involved in disinterring all these people and identifying them, many of them are nothing more than dust now anyway. The sheep were all gathered together, apart from the occasional straggler which came leaping nimbly over the graves to escape the dog and join its sisters. The shepherd asked, Were you a friend or a relative of the person you came to visit, I didn't even know her, And despite that you came looking for her, It was precisely because I didn't know her that I came looking for her, You see I was right when I said that one can show no greater respect than to weep for a stranger, Goodbye, We might see each other again sometime, I doubt it, You never know, Who are you, I'm the shepherd of these sheep, And that's all, That's all. A light flickered in the distance, That one's coming over here, said Senhor José, It looks like it, said the shepherd. With the dog at their head, the flock began to move towards the bridge. Before disappearing behind the trees on the other side, the shepherd turned around and waved. Senhor José waved back. He could see the intermittent light on the guides' car more clearly now. It disappeared occasionally into a hollow or was momentarily concealed from view by one of the motley structures in the cemetery, the towers, the obelisks, the pyramids, then it reappeared, brighter, nearer, and it was coming fast, a clear sign that there were not many people accompanying it. When he had said to the shepherd, I'm going to stay for a while longer, Senhor José's intention had been merely to remain alone for a few minutes before setting off again. He just wanted to ponder his own feelings a little, to judge the real depths of his disappointment, to accept it, to put his spirit to rest, to say once more, It's over, but now he had another idea. He went across to one of the graves and adopted the pose of someone meditating deeply on the irremediable precariousness of existence, on the vacuity of all dreams and all hopes, on the absolute fragility of worldly and divine glories. He was so deep in thought that he didn't even appear to notice the arrival of the guides and the half dozen or so people, slightly more, accompanying the coffin. He did not move during the whole time that it took to open the grave, lower the coffin, fill in the hole, make the usual mound with the surplus earth. He did not move when one of the guides placed at the head of the mound the black metal tag marked in white with the number of the grave. He did not move when the guides' car and the hearse moved off, he did not move during the bare two minutes that the people lingered by the grave uttering useless words and wiping away the odd tear, he did not move when the two cars they had arrived in drove off across the bridge, he did not move until he was alone again. He took the number corresponding to the unknown woman and placed it on the new grave. Then he took the number from that one and placed it on the other grave. The exchange was made, the truth had become a lie. Besides, it might well be that the shepherd, finding a new grave there tomorrow, would unwittingly move the false number on it back to the unknown woman's grave, an ironic possibility in which the lie, apparently repeating itself, would become true again. The workings of chance are infinite. Senhor José headed for home. On the way, he went into a café, where he ordered coffee and toast. He couldn't stave off hunger a moment longer.

Determined to catch up on his lost sleep, Senhor José got into bed as soon as he arrived home, but only two hours later, he was awake again. He had had a strange, enigmatic dream in which he saw himself in the middle of the cemetery, amid a multitude of sheep so numerous that he could barely see the mounds of the graves, and each sheep had a number on its head that kept changing continually, but, because the sheep were all the same, you couldn't tell if it was the sheep that were changing numbers or if the numbers were changing sheep. He heard a voice shouting, I'm here, I'm here, it couldn't come from the sheep because they stopped talking a long time ago, nor could it be the graves because there is no record of a grave ever having spoken, and yet the voice kept calling insistently, I'm here, I'm here, Senhor José looked in that direction and saw only the raised snouts of the animals, then the same words rang out behind him, or to the right, or to the left, I'm here, I'm here, and he would turn swiftly, but he couldn't tell where it was coming from. Senhor José began to grow desperate, he wanted to wake up and he couldn't, the dream was continuing, now the shepherd was there with his dog, and Senhor José thought, There's nothing this shepherd doesn't know, he'll tell me whose voice it is, but the shepherd didn't speak, he just made a gesture with his crook above his head, the dog went to round up the sheep, herding them towards a bridge which was crossed by silent cars with signs made of lightbulbs that flickered on and off, saying Follow me, Follow me, Follow me, in a moment the flock disappeared, the dog disappeared, the shepherd disappeared, all that remained was the cemetery floor strewn with numbers, the ones that before had been on the heads of the sheep, but, because they were now all together, all attached end to end in an uninterrupted spiral of which he himself was the centre, he couldn't tell where one began and the other finished. Anxious, drenched in sweat, Senhor José woke up saying, I'm here. His eyes were closed, he was half-conscious, but he said, I'm here, I'm here, twice out loud, then opened his eyes to the mean little space where he had lived for so many years, he saw the low ceiling, the cracked plaster, the floor with its warped floorboards, the table and the two chairs in the middle of the living room, if such a term has meaning in a place like this, the cupboard where he kept the clippings and photos of his celebrities, the corner beyond which lay the kitchen, the narrow recess that served as a bathroom, that was when he said, I must find a way of freeing myself from this madness, he meant, obviously, the woman who would now forever be unknown, the house, poor thing, was not to blame, it was just a sad house. Fearful that the dream would return, Senhor José did not attempt to fall asleep again. He was lying on his back, looking up at the ceiling, waiting for it to ask him, Why are you looking at me, but the ceiling ignored him, it merely observed him, expressionless. Senhor José gave up any hope of help coming from there, he would have to resolve the problem on his own, and the best way would still be to persuade himself that there was no problem, When the beast dies, the poison dies with it, was the rather disrespectful proverb that came to his lips, calling the unknown woman a poisonous beast, forgetting for a moment there are poisons so slow-acting that they produce an effect only when we have long since forgotten their origin. Then the penny dropped, he muttered,

Careful, death is often a slow poison, then he wondered, When and why did she begin to die. It was at that point that the ceiling, without there being any apparent connection, direct or indirect, with what it had just heard, emerged from its indifference to remind him, There are at least three people you haven't spoken to yet, Who, asked Senhor José, Her parents and her ex-husband, It wouldn't be a bad idea to go and talk to her parents, I thought of doing that earlier on, but I decided to leave it for another occasion, If you don't do it now, you never will, meanwhile you can divert yourself by going a little farther down this road, before you finally bump your nose against the wall, If you weren't a ceiling, stuck up there all the time, you would know that it has not been a diverting experience, But it has been a diversion, What's the difference, Go and look it up in the dictionary, that's what they're there for, I was just asking, everyone knows that a diversion is not the same as something being diverting, What about the other one, What other one, The ex-husband, he would probably be the person who could tell you most about your unknown woman, I imagine that married life, a life lived in common, must be like a sort of magnifying glass, I can't imagine any reserve or secret that could resist the microscope of continual observation, On the other hand, there are those who say that the more you look the less you see, but whatever the truth of the matter, I don't think it's worth going to talk to him, You're afraid he'll start talking about the reasons for the divorce, you don't want to hear anything bad about her, People on the whole are rarely fair, not to themselves or to other people, and he would more than likely tell me the story so that it looked as if he had been in the right all along, An intelligent analysis, I'm not stupid, No, you're not, it's just that you take a long time to understand things, especially simple things, For example, That there was no reason why you should go looking for this woman, unless, Unless what, Unless you were doing it out of love, Only a ceiling would come up with such an absurd idea, I believe I've told you on another occasion that the ceilings of houses are the multiple eye of God, I don't remember, I may not have said it in those precise words, but I'm saying it now, Tell me then how I could possibly love a woman I didn't even know and whom I'd never even seen, That's a good question, there's no doubt about it, but only you can answer it, The idea doesn't have a leg to stand on, It doesn't matter whether it's got legs or not, I'm talking about quite another part of the anatomy, the heart, the thing that people say is the engine and seat of affections, I repeat that I could not possibly love a woman I didn't know, whom I never saw, except in some old photos, You wanted to see her, you wanted to know her, and that, whether you like it or not, is love, These are the imaginings of a ceiling, They're your imaginings, a man's imaginings, not mine, You're so arrogant, you think you know everything about me, I don't know everything, but I must have learned a thing or two after all these years of living together, I bet you've never considered that you and I live together, the great difference between us is that you only notice me when you need advice and cast your eyes upwards, while I spend all my time looking at you, The eye of God, You can take my metaphors seriously if you like, but don't repeat them as if they were yours. After this, the ceiling decided to remain silent, it had realised that Senhor José's thoughts were already turned to the visit he was going to make to the unknown woman's parents, the last step before bumping his nose against the wall, an equally metaphorical expression which means, You've reached the end.

Senhor José got out of bed, cleaned himself up as best he could, prepared something to eat and, having thus recovered his physical vigour, he summoned up his moral vigour in order to telephone, with suitable bureaucratic coolness, the unknown woman's parents, in the first place, to find out if they were home, in the second place, to ask if they would mind receiving a visit today from a member of staff from the Central Registry who needed to talk with them about a matter concerning their dead daughter. Had it been any other kind of call, Senhor José would have gone out to use the public phone box on the other side of the street, however, in this case, there was a danger that, when they picked up the phone, they would hear the sound of coins dropping into the machine, and even the least suspicious of people would be bound to want to know why a member of staff from the Central Registry was phoning from a public call box, especially on a Sunday, about matters relating to his work. The solution to that difficulty was, it seemed, not far away, all he had to do was to creep once more into the Central Registry and use the telephone on the Registrar's desk, but it was just as risky doing that, because the detailed list of telephone calls, sent every month by the exchange and checked, number by number, by the Registrar himself, would inevitably register the clandestine call, What call is this, made on a Sunday, the Registrar would ask his deputies, and then, without waiting for a reply, he would say, Set up an inquiry into this at once. Resolving the mystery of the secret phone call would be the easiest thing in the world, he would just have to dial the suspect number and be told, Yes, sir, someone from the Central Registry did phone us on that day, and he didn't just phone, he came here in person, he wanted to know why our daughter had committed suicide, he said it was for your statistics, Statistics, Yes, statistics, at least that's what he said, Fine, now listen very carefully, Go on, In order to clear this matter up completely, I must be able to rely on your and your husband's collaboration with the Central Registry, What do we have to do, Come to the Central Registry and identify the member of staff who came to visit you, We'll be there, A car will come and pick you up. Senhor José's imagination did not stop at creating this troubling dialogue, once it was over, he went on to enact in his mind what would happen afterwards, the unknown woman's parents coming into the Central Registry and pointing, That's the man, or else, still in the car that had been sent to fetch them, seeing the members of staff going in and suddenly pointing, That's the man. Senhor José murmured, I'm lost, there's no way out. Yes there was, one that was simple and definitive, he could either give up the idea of going to see the unknown woman's parents, or he could go there without warning and simply knock on the door and say, Good afternoon, I work for the Central Registry, I'm sorry to bother you on a Sunday, but work has piled up so much lately at the Central Registry, with so many people being born and dying, that we've had to adopt a system of permanent overtime. That, without a doubt, would be the most intelligent way of going about it, affording Senhor José the maximum number of guarantees as regards his future safety, but it seemed that the last few hours he had lived through, the enormous cemetery with its outstretched octopus tentacles, the night of dull moonlight and shifting shadows, the convulsive dance of the will-o'-the-wisps, the old shepherd and his sheep, the dog, as silent as if it had had its vocal cords removed, the graves with the numbers changed, it seemed that all this had scrambled his mind, in general sufficiently clear and lucid for him to cope with life, otherwise, how can one understand why he continued to cling stubbornly to the idea of phoning, still less when he tries to justify it to himself with the puerile argument that a phone call would make it easier for him to gather information. He even thinks he has a formula that will immediately dispel any distrust, he will say, as indeed he is already saying, sitting in the Registrar's chair, I'm speaking on behalf of the special branch of the Central Registry, those words special branch, he thinks, are the skeleton key that will open all doors to him, and it seems that he was right, at the other end a voice is saying, Certainly, sir, come whenever you like, we'll be in all day. A last vestige of common sense prompted the fleeting thought that he had probably just tied the knot in the rope that would hang him, but his madness calmed him, it told him that the exchange would not submit the list of telephone calls for some weeks, and, who knows, the Registrar might be on holiday then, or he might be ill at home, or he might merely ask one of his deputies to confirm the numbers, it wouldn't be the first time, which would mean that the crime would almost certainly go undiscovered, bearing in mind that none of the deputies liked the task, so, before the lash falls again, the prisoner's back can rest, murmured Senhor José in conclusion, resigned to whatever fate might bring him. He replaced the telephone book in its precise place, aligning it carefully with the corner of the desk, he wiped the receiver with his handkerchief to remove any fingerprints and went back into his house. He began by polishing his shoes, then he brushed down his suit, put on a clean shirt, his best tie, and he was just about to open the door when he remembered his letter of authority. Going to the house of the unknown woman's parents and simply saying, I'm the person who phoned from the Central Registry, would certainly not have as much force of conviction and authority as slipping under their noses a piece of paper stamped, sealed and signed, giving the bearer full rights and powers in the exercise of his functions and for the proper fulfilment of the mission with which he had been charged. He opened the cabinet, took out the bishop's file and removed the letter, however, when he glanced over it, he realised that it wouldn't do. In the first place, because it was dated before the suicide, and in the second place, because of the actual terms in which it was written, for example, that he was ordered and charged to find out and clarify everything about the past, present and future life of the unknown woman, I don't even know where she is now, thought Senhor José, and as for a future life, at that moment, he remembered a popular verse that went, What lies beyond death, no one has seen nor ever will, of all those who climbed that hill, never a one came back. He was just about to return the letter to its place, when, at the last moment, he again felt obliged to obey the state of mind forcing him to concentrate in an obsessive manner on one idea and to see it through to the end. Now that he had thought of the letter, he would have to take one with him. He went straight back into the Central Registry to the cabinet containing the forms, but he had forgotten that, ever since the inquiry, the cabinet was always locked. For the first time in his tranquil life, he felt a rush of anger, he even considered smashing the glass and to hell with the consequences. Fortunately, he remembered just in time that the deputy charged with keeping an eye on the number of forms used, kept the key to the cabinet in a drawer in his desk, and, as was the strict rule in the Central Registry, deputies could not keep their desk drawers locked, The only one here who has a right to secrets is me, the Registrar had said, and his word was law, which, at least this time, did not apply to officials and clerks for the simple reason that they, as we have seen, worked at plain desks, with no drawers. Senhor José wrapped his right hand in his handkerchief in order not to leave the slightest trace of fingerprints that might betray him, picked up the key and opened the cabinet. He removed a piece of paper bearing the Central Registry stamp, locked the cabinet and replaced the key in the deputy's desk drawer, at that moment, the lock on the outer door of the building creaked, he heard the bolt slide back once, for a second, Senhor José remained paralysed, but then, as he had in those ancient childhood dreams, in which he flew weightlessly above gardens and rooftops, he crept lightly away on tiptoe, and by the time the bolt was drawn completely back, Senhor José was safe in his house again, breathing hard, his heart in his mouth. A long minute passed until, on the other side of the door, he heard someone cough, It's the Registrar, thought Senhor José, feeling his legs go weak, I just escaped, by the skin of my teeth. Then he heard the cough again, louder this time, perhaps nearer, but this time it seemed deliberate, intentional, as if the person who had come into the Central Registry were announcing his presence. Terrified, Senhor José stared at the lock on the flimsy door separating him from the Central Registry. He hadn't had time to turn the key, the door was only on the latch, If he comes in, if he turns the handle, if he comes in here, a voice was screaming inside Senhor José's head, he'll catch you in flagrante with that piece of paper in your hand and the letter of authority on the table, that was all the voice said, for it felt sorry for the clerk and did not speak to him of the consequences. Senhor José walked slowly over to the table, picked up the letter and went and hid it among his still-rumpled bedclothes, along with the piece of paper stolen from the cabinet. Then he sat down and waited. If he had been asked what he was waiting for, he would not have known what to reply. An hour passed and Senhor José began to grow impatient. There were no further sounds from the other side of the door. The unknown woman's parents would be wondering what was keeping the man from the Central Registry, given that urgency is one of the principal characteristics of matters being dealt with by a special branch, whatever its nature, water, gas, electricity or suicide. Senhor José waited another quarter of an hour without moving from his chair. After that time had passed, he realised that he had made a decision, and it wasn't just his usual decision to follow up an obsession, it really was a decision, although he couldn't have explained how he came to make it. He said almost out loud, What has to happen, will happen, fear doesn't solve anything. With a serenity which no longer surprised him, he fetched the letter of authority and the blank piece of paper, sat down at the table, placed the inkwell before him and, copying, abbreviating and adapting, devised a new document, As Registrar of the Central Registry, I make it known to all those, civil or military, private or public, who see, read or peruse this document, that X is under direct orders from me to find out and ascertain all the facts surrounding the suicide of Y, in particular its causes, both immediate and remote, the ensuing text went on the same way, right down to the resounding final imperative, So be it. Unfortunately, the paper would not bear the correct seal, since that had become inaccessible with the arrival of the Registrar, but the important thing was the authority evident in every word. Senhor José put away the first letter among the bishop's clippings, put the one he had just written in his inside jacket pocket and looked defiantly at the communicating door. The silence on the other side continued. Then Senhor José murmured, I don't care if you're in there or not. He went over to the door and locked it, briskly, with two sharp turns of the wrist, click, clack.

A taxi carried him to the house of the unknown woman's parents. He rang the bell, it was answered by a woman who looked about sixty or so, younger than the woman in the ground-floor apartment, with whom her husband had deceived her thirty years before, I'm the person who phoned from the Central Registry, said Senhor José, Come in, we were expecting you, I'm sorry I couldn't come at once, but I had to handle another very urgent matter, That's all right, come this way. The house had a sombre air, there were curtains covering the windows and the doors, the furniture was heavy, the walls were hung with ominous paintings of landscapes that had probably never existed. The lady of the house ushered Senhor José into what appeared to be a study, where a man, quite a bit older than she, was waiting, It's the gentleman from the Central Registry, said the woman, Sit down, said the man, pointing to a chair. Senhor José took the letter from his pocket, holding it in his hand as he said, I'm terribly sorry to bother you at this sad time, but that's what my job demands, this document will tell you the exact nature of my mission. He handed the piece of paper to the man, who read it, holding it very close to his eyes, saying when he had done so, Your mission must be extremely important to justify a document written in these terms, It's the usual Central Registry style, even when it's a simple thing like this, an investigation into the causes of a suicide, That's hardly unimportant, No, don't misunderstand me, what I meant was that whatever mission they charge us with and for which a letter of authority is deemed necessary, it's always written in the same style, The rhetoric of authority, You could call it that. The woman intervened to ask, And what does the Central Registry want to know, First, the immediate cause of the suicide, And second, asked the man, The antecedents, the circumstances, the signs, anything that can help us towards a better understanding of what happened, Isn't it enough for the Central Registry to know that my daughter killed herself, When I said I needed to talk to you about a statistical question, I was simplifying matters, Now's your chance to explain, It's no longer enough for us to be content with numbers, what we're trying to do now is to find out as much as possible about the psychological background against which the suicidal process takes place, Why, asked the woman, that won't bring my daughter back to life, The idea is to set up parameters for intervention, I don't understand, said the man, Senhor José was sweating, it was proving far more complicated than he had thought, It's terribly hot, isn't it, he said, Would you like a glass of water, asked the woman, If it's not too much trouble, Of course not, the woman got up and went out, in a minute she was back. While he was drinking the water, Senhor José decided to change tactics. He placed the glass on the tray the woman was holding and said, Imagine that your daughter had not yet committed suicide, imagine that the investigation which the Central Registry is currently undertaking had managed to draw up certain guidelines and recommendations, capable eventually, if applied in time, of halting what I earlier referred to as the suicidal process, That was what you meant by parameters for intervention, asked the man, Exactly, said Senhor José, and without leaving room for any further remarks, he delivered the first thrust, We may not have been able to stop your daughter from commit- ting suicide, but perhaps we can, with your collaboration and with that of other people in the same situation, avoid a great deal of grief and many tears. The woman was crying, mur- muring, My dear daughter, while the man was roughly wiping away his tears with the back of his hand. Senhor José hoped he would not be forced to resort to his final expedient, which would, he thought, be a reading of the letter of authority in a loud, severe voice, word by word, like doors being closed one after the other, until they left only one possible way out for the person listening, to do as they were asked and to speak. If this failed, he would have no option but to come up with some ex- cuse to withdraw as gracefully as possible. And just pray that it would not occur to the unknown woman's stubborn father to phone the Central Registry demanding an explanation for that visit by a member of their staff called Senhor José something or other, I can't remember the rest of his name. It wasn't nec- essary. The man folded up the letter and gave it back. Then he said, What can we do for you. Senhor José gave a sigh of relief, the way was now open for him to get down to business, Did your daughter leave a letter, No letter, no word, Do you mean she committed suicide just like that, It wouldn't have happened just like that, she obviously had her reasons, but we don't know what they were, My daughter was unhappy, said the woman, No one happy commits suicide, said her impatient husband, And why was she unhappy, asked Senhor José, I don't know, she was sad even as a little girl, I used to ask her what was wrong and she would always say the same thing, I'm fine, Mom, So the cause of the suicide wasn't her divorce, On the contrary, the only time I saw my daughter happy was when she sepa- rated from her husband, They didn't get on well, then, They didn't get on well or badly really, it was just a rather average marriage, Who asked for the divorce, She did, Was there some concrete reason, Not that we know of, no, it was as if they'd both reached the end of the road, What's he like, Fairly ordinary, a decent man, he never gave us any reason for complaint, And he loved her, Yes, I think so, And what about her, did she love him, Yes, she did, I believe, And despite that they weren't happy, They never were, How strange, Life is strange, said the man. There was a silence, the woman got up and went out. Senhor José stopped, he didn't know whether it would be better to wait for her to return or to continue the conversation. He was afraid that the interruption might have set the interrogation on the wrong track, you could almost feel the tension in the room. Senhor José wondered if the man's words, Life is strange, were not an echo of his former relationship with the lady in the ground-floor apartment and if his wife's sudden exit were not the reply of someone who, at that moment, could give no other. Senhor José picked up the glass, drank a little water to gain time, then asked a random question, Did your daughter work, Yes, she taught mathematics, Where, In the same school where she studied before going to university. Senhor José again picked up the glass, almost dropping it in his haste, he stammered ridiculously, S-s-sorry, and suddenly his voice failed him, while Senhor José drank, the man was looking at him with an expression of scornful curiosity, it seemed to him that the Central Registry was pretty ill served by its staff, at least judging by this example, there was no point turning up armed with a letter of authority like that and then behaving like an imbecile. The woman came in at the point where her husband was asking ironically, Would you like me to give you the name of the school, it might be of some use to you for the success of your mission, That would be most kind of you. The man bent over the desk, wrote down the name and address of the school on a piece of paper and handed it brusquely to Senhor José, but the man who was sitting before him now was not the same man of a few moments ago, Senhor José had regained sufficent control of himself to remember that he knew a secret about this family, an old secret that neither of them could possibly imagine he knew. This thought lay behind his next question, Do you know if your daughter kept a diary, I don't think so, at least we didn't find anything like that, said the mother, But there must be papers, notes, jottings, there always are, if you could perhaps give me permission to glance over them, I might find something of interest, We haven't removed anything from her apartment yet, said the father, and I've no idea when we'll get around to it, Your daughter's apartment was rented, No, she owned it, I see. There was a pause, Senhor José slowly unfolded the letter of authority, he looked at it from top to bottom as if he were checking to see if there were any powers he had left undeployed, then he said, Would you allow me to go to the apartment, in your presence, of course, No, the reply was sharp, cutting, My letter of authority, began Senhor José, Your letter of authority will have to make do for now with the information you've got, said the man, adding, We can, if you like, continue our conversation tomorrow at the Central Registry, now, if you'll forgive me, I have other matters to resolve, There's no need to go to the Central Registry, what you've told me about the situation before the suicide seems quite adequate, said Senhor José, but I still have three questions to ask, Go on, How did your daughter die, She took an overdose of sleeping tablets, Was she alone in the house, Yes, And have you already arranged for a gravestone, We're dealing with that now, why do you ask, Oh nothing, just simple curiosity. Senhor José stood up. I'll show you out, said the woman. When they reached the corridor, she raised a finger to her lips and indicated to him to wait. She noiselessly removed a small bunch of keys from the drawer of a small table placed against the wall. Then, as she was opening the door, she pressed them into Senhor José's hand. They're hers, she whispered, one of these days I'll stop by the Central Registry to pick them up, and coming closer still, almost in a whisper, she told him the address.

Senhor José slept like a log. After returning from his dangerous but successful visit to the unknown woman's parents, he wanted to set down the weekend's extraordinary events in his notebook, but he was so tired that he didn't get any further than his conversation with the clerk at the General Cemetery. He went to bed without any supper, fell asleep in less than two minutes and when he opened his eyes, at the first light of dawn, he discovered that, without knowing how or when, he had made the decision not to go in to work. It was Monday, the very worst day to miss work, especially if you were a clerk. Whatever the alleged reason, and however convincing it might have been on any other occasion, it was always suspected of being merely an excuse, a way of justifying prolonging the indolence of Sunday into a day that was legally and customarily devoted to work. After the repeated and increasingly serious irregularities in his behaviour since he had started looking for the unknown woman, Senhor José is aware that not going to work could be the last straw as far as his boss's patience was concerned. This frightening prospect, however, was not enough to shake the firmness of his decision. There are two important reasons why Senhor José cannot postpone what he has to do until he has an afternoon off. The first of these is that, one day, the mother of the unknown woman will come to the Central Registry in order to recover the keys, the second is that the school, as Senhor José knows all too well, from harsh experience, is closed on the weekend.

Despite his decision not to go to work, Senhor José got up very early. He wanted to be as far away as possible before the Central Registry opened, he didn't want his immediate superior to come knocking at the door to find out if he was ill again. While he was shaving, he wondered whether it would be best to begin by going to the unknown woman's apartment, or to the school, but he opted for the school, he is one of the many who always leave the most important till last. He also wondered if he should take the letter of authority with him, or if, on the contrary, it would be dangerous to show it, bearing in mind that a headmaster, given his job, was likely to be a knowledgable, well-read, educated person, what if the terms in which the document was written struck him as unusual, extravagant, hyperbolic, he might demand to know why there was no official stamp, prudence tells Senhor José to leave both letters of authority behind with the innocent clippings about the bishop, My identity card proving that I work for the Central Registry should be more than enough, concluded Senhor José, after all, I'm only going to confirm something concrete, objective, factual, that a woman who committed suicide was a teacher of mathematics at the school. It was still very early when he left the house, the shops were closed, with no lights on and the shutters down, there were scarcely any cars, probably even the earliest risers among the Central Registry staff would only just be getting out of bed. In order not to be seen in the vicinity, Senhor José went and hid in a park two blocks away from the main avenue, along which the bus had taken him to visit the lady in the ground-floor apartment, late one afternoon when he saw his boss going into the Central Registry. Unless you actually knew he was there, he was invisible among the bushes and the low branches of the trees. The benches were all wet with the night dew, so Senhor José did not sit down, instead, he passed the time walking along the garden paths, enjoying himself looking at the flowers and wondering what their names were, it's not surprising that he knows so little about botanical matters, since he's spent his whole life between four walls, breathing the pungent smell of old papers, still more pungent when the air is filled by that smell of chrysanthemums and roses mentioned on the very first page of this story. When the clock marked the opening time for the Central Registry to the public, Senhor José, now safe from any possible unfortunate encounters, set off for the school. He was in no hurry, today was his, which is why he decided to go on foot. As he left the garden, he was doubtful which direction to take, if he had bought a map of the city, as he had intended, he would not now have to be asking a policeman the way, but the fact is that the situation, the law giving advice to the criminal, gave him a certain subversive pleasure. The affair of the unknown woman had reached its end, all that was needed now was the inquiry at the school, then the inspection of the apartment, and, if he had time, he would drop in on the lady in the ground-floor apartment to tell her about the latest developments, and then nothing. He wondered how he would live his life from then on, if he would go back to his collections of famous people, for a few brief seconds he imagined himself sitting at the table in the evening, with a pile of newspapers and magazines beside him, cutting out articles and photographs and trying to guess whether a celebrity was on the rise or, alternatively, on the wane, occasionally in the past he had foreseen the fate of certain people who later became important, occasionally he had been the first to suspect that the laurels of this man or that woman were beginning to fade, to wrinkle, to crumble into dust, It all ends up in the rubbish bin, said Senhor José, without quite knowing, at that precise moment, if he meant lost reputations or his clippings collection.

With the sun beating down on the façade, the trees in the playground looking green and leafy and the flower beds blooming, there was nothing about the appearance of the school that recalled the gloomy edifice into which Senhor José had entered one rainy night, by scaling its walls and breaking in. Now he was going in through the main door, he was saying to a member of the staff, I need to talk to the headmaster, no, I'm not a parent and I'm not a supplier of school materials, I work for the Central Registry, it's an official matter. The woman rang an internal number, she told someone about the visitor's arrival, then she said, Please go up, the headmaster's in the secretary's office on the second floor, Thank you, said Senhor José, and began going calmly up the stairs, he already knew that the secretary's office was on the second floor. The headmaster was talking to a woman who presumably was in charge, he was saying to her, I need that chart tomorrow without fail, and she was saying, I'll make sure you get it, Senhor José had stopped in the doorway, waiting for them to notice him. The headmaster finished his conversation and looked at him, only then did Senhor José say, Good morning, headmaster, then, with his identity card in his hand, he took three steps forward, As you can see, I work for the Central Registry, I've come on an official matter. The headmaster made as if to brush aside the identity card, then asked, What's it about, It's about one of your teachers, And what has the Central Registry got to do with the teachers at this school, Not as teachers, but as the people they are or were, Could you explain what you mean, We're carrying out an investigation into the phenomenon of suicide, both its psychological aspects and its sociological implications, and I've been put in charge of the case of a lady who taught mathematics at this school and who recently committed suicide. The headmaster put on a sorrowful face, Poor woman, he said, it's a very sad story that I don't think any of us has as yet really understood, My first action, said Senhor José, using the most official language he could, would be to compare the identifying data that we have in the archives in the Central Registry with the lady's professional registration, I suppose you mean the staff list, I do, sir. The headmaster turned to the woman in charge of the secretary's office, Find me her record card, will you, We still haven't taken it out of the drawer, the woman said in an apologetic tone, at the same time running her fingers across the cards in a drawer, Here it is, she said. Senhor José felt a sharp contraction in the pit of his stomach, a feeling of dizziness swept through his brain, but, fortunately, it came to nothing more, this man's nervous system really is in a terrible state, not that we can blame him in the circumstances, we have only to remember that the card being shown to him now was within his grasp that night, it would have been just a matter of opening that drawer, the one with the label that says Teachers, but how could he have imagined that the young girl he was looking for would be teaching mathematics in the very school she had studied at. Disguising his agitation, but not the tremor in his hands, Senhor José pretended to compare the card from the school with the copy of the card from the Central Registry, then he said, It's the same person. The headmaster looked at him with interest, Don't you feel well, he asked, and he replied simply, It's just that I'm not as young as I used to be, Right, I imagine you'll want to ask me a few questions, I will, Come with me then, we'll go to my study. Senhor José smiled to himself as he followed the headmaster, I didn't know that her card was right there in that drawer, and you don't know that I spent the night on your sofa. They went into the study, the headmaster said, I haven't got much time, but I'll do all I can to help you, do sit down, and he indicated the sofa that had served as a bed to the visitor, I'd like to know, said Senhor José, if anyone noticed any change in her normal state of mind in the days before the suicide, None, she was always a very private person, very quiet, Was she a good teacher, One of the best the school has had, Was she friends with any particular colleague, Friends in what sense, Just friends, She was friendly, polite to everyone, but I don't think anyone here could say that they were friends with her, And did her students respect her, Very much, Was she in good health, As far as I can judge, yes, It's strange, What's strange, I've already spoken to her parents, and everything they said and everything I'm hearing now seems to point to there being no explanation for this suicide, I wonder, said the headmaster, if suicide can be explained, Do you mean this particular suicide, I mean suicide in general, Sometimes people leave letters, That's true, but I'm not sure you could describe the contents of those letters as an explanation, there's no shortage of things to explain in life, That's true, For example, what explanation could there be for what happened here a few days before the suicide, What was that, The school was burgled, Yes, How do you know, I'm sorry, my yes was intended to be interrogative, perhaps I didn't give it the right intonation, but, anyway, burglaries are usually fairly easy to explain, Except when the burglar climbs up onto the roof, breaks a window and then climbs in, wanders all over the place, sleeps on my sofa, eats what there is in the fridge, uses the first-aid box and then leaves without taking anything, What makes you think he slept on your sofa, Because on the floor was the blanket I usually cover my knees with so as not to get cold, as you said of yourself, I'm not as young as I used to be, Did you report it to the police, What for, since nothing had been stolen, it didn't seem worth it, the police would tell me that they were there in order to investigate crimes, not to explain mysteries, It's certainly strange, there's no doubt about it, We checked everywhere, all the equipment was there, the safe was intact, everything was in its proper place, Except the blanket, Yes, except the blanket, now what explanation can you find for that, You'd have to ask the burglar, he must know, having said those words, Senhor José got up, I won't rob you of any more of your time, I'm very grateful for your help in the unfortunate matter that brought me here, I don't know that I've been of much help, You were probably right when you said that perhaps no suicide can be explained, Rationally explained, you understand, It was as if she had just opened a door and gone out, Or gone in, Yes, or gone in, depending on your point of view, Well, there you have an excellent explanation, It was a metaphor, Metaphors have always been the best way of explaining things, Goodbye, sir, and my heartfelt thanks, Goodbye, it was a pleasure talking to you, I don't mean the sad matter in hand, of course, I mean you yourself, Naturally, it was just a manner of speaking, I'll go with you to the stairs. When Senhor José was going down the second flight of stairs, the headmaster suddenly remembered that he hadn't asked him his name, No matter, he thought, that particular story's over.

The same could not be said of Senhor José, he still had to take the final step, to seek out and find in the unknown woman's apartment a letter, a diary, a simple piece of paper on which she might have set down her feelings, the scream, the I-can't-go-on that every suicide is under strict obligation to leave behind before departing through that door, so that those left on this side can soothe the fears of their own consciences saying, Poor thing, she had her reasons. The human spirit, though, how often do we need to say it, is the favourite home of contradictions, indeed they do not seem to prosper or even find viable living conditions outside it, and that must be why Senhor José wanders the city, from one side to the other, up and down, as if lost without a map or a guide, for he knows perfectly well what he has to do on this last day, he knows that tomorrow will be a different time, or that he will be the one who will be different in a time exactly like this one, and the proof that he knows this to be so is the fact that he thought, Who will I be tomorrow when this is all over, what kind of clerk is the Central Registry going to have. Twice he passed by the unknown woman's apartment building, twice he did not stop, he was afraid, don't ask why, this is the most common of contradictions, Senhor José both wants and doesn't want, he both de-

sires and fears what he desires, that is what his whole life has
been like. Now, to gain time, to postpone what he knows to be
inevitable, he has decided that first, he will have to have lunch,
in a cheap restaurant, as his modest pocket dictates, but above
all somewhere far from here, he doesn't want some curious
neighbour to suspect the intentions of a man who has already
passed by twice. Although there's nothing about his appearance to distinguish him from other supposedly honest people,
the truth is that there are never any solid guarantees about what
you see, appearances are very deceptive, that's why they're called
appearances, although in the case in point, taking into account
his age and fragile physical constitution, no one would think,
for example, that Senhor José made his living breaking into
houses at night. He took as long as he could over the frugal
lunch, got up from the table long after three o'clock and, unhurriedly, as if he were dragging his feet, he went back to the
street where the unknown woman had lived. Before turning
the last corner, he stopped and took a deep breath, I'm not a
coward, he thought to give himself courage, but as so often
happens with so many brave people, he was valiant about
some things, cowardly about others, the fact that he spent a
night in the cemetery won't stop his legs shaking now. He put
his hand into his jacket pocket, felt the keys, one, small and narrow, was for the postbox, and so was naturally excluded, the remaining two were almost the same, but one was the street
door, the other the door to the apartment, he hoped he got it
right the first time, if the building has a concierge and she's the
sort who pokes her nose out at the slightest noise, what explanation would he give, he could say he was there with the
authorisation of the parents of the woman who committed
suicide, that he's come to make an inventory of her posses-
sions, I work for the Central Registry, madam, here's my card,
and as you see, they've given me the keys to the apartment.
Senhor José chose the right key on the first try, the guardian of

the door, if the building had one, did not appear and ask him, Excuse me, where are you going, there's a lot of truth in the saying that fear of the guard is the best guard against theft, so he tells himself to begin by conquering his fear, then see if the guard appears. It's an old building but it has a lift, which is just as well, because Senhor José's legs are so heavy now that he would never have made it to the sixth floor, where the mathematics teacher lived. The door creaked as it opened, startling the visitor, who suddenly doubted the efficacy of the excuse he had thought he would give to the concierge should she intervene. He slipped quickly into the apartment, very carefully closed the door, and found himself in the midst of a dense, almost pitch-black darkness. He felt the wall next to the door frame, found a switch, but prudently didn't turn it on, it might be dangerous to put on the lights. Gradually, Senhor José's eyes became used to the shadows, you might say that in a similar situation the same would happen with anyone, but it is not generally known that, after a certain time, the clerks in the Central Registry, given their obligatory regular visits to the archive of the dead, acquire a remarkable talent for optical adaptation. They would all have cat's eyes if they didn't reach retirement age first.

Although the floor was carpeted, Senhor José thought it best to take off his shoes to avoid any shock or vibration that might betray his presence to the tenants on the floor below. With enormous care he slid back the bolts on the inner shutters of one of the windows that opened onto the street, but only enough to let in a little light. He was in a bedroom. There was a dressing table, a wardrobe, a bedside table. A narrow bed, a single, as they are called. The furniture had light, simple lines, the opposite of the dull, heavy furniture in her parents' house. Senhor José walked through the other rooms in the apartment, which comprised a living room furnished with the usual sofas and a bookshelf that took up the whole of one wall, a much smaller room that served as a study, a tiny kitchen and a minimal bathroom. Here lived a woman who committed suicide for unknown reasons, who had been married and got divorced, who could have gone to live with her parents after the divorce, but had preferred to live alone, a woman who, like all women, was once a child and a girl, but who even then, in a certain indefinable way, was already the woman she was going to be, a mathematics teacher whose name while she was alive was in the Central Registry, along with the names of all the people alive in this city, a woman whose dead name returned to the living world because Senhor José went to rescue her from the dead world, just her name, not her, a clerk can only do so much. With the inner doors all open, there is enough light from outside to be able to see the whole apartment, but Senhor José will have to get his search under way quickly if he doesn't want to have to leave it half done. He opened a drawer in a desk, glanced at its contents, they seemed to be math problems for school, calculations, equations, nothing that could explain the reasons for the life and death of the woman who used to sit in this chair, who used to switch on this lamp, who used to hold this pencil and write with it. Senhor José slowly closed the drawer, he even started to open another but did not complete the movement, he stopped to think for a long minute, or perhaps it was only a few seconds that seemed like hours, then he firmly pushed the drawer shut, left the study and went and sat on one of the small sofas in the living room, where he remained. He looked at his old darned socks, the trousers that had lost their crease and had ridden up a little, his bony white shins with a few sparse hairs on them. He felt his body sinking into the soft concavity left by another body in the upholstery and the springs, She'll never sit here again, he murmured. The silence, which had seemed to him absolute, was interrupted now by noises from the street, especially, from time to time, by the passing of a car, but in the air too there was a slow breathing, a slow pulse, perhaps it was the way houses breathe when they are left alone, this one has probably not even realised yet that there is someone here now. Senhor José tells himself that there are still drawers to go through, the ones in the dresser, where people usually keep their more intimate garments, the ones in the bedside table, where intimate things of a different nature are generally stored, the wardrobe, he thinks that if he went to open the wardrobe he would be unable to resist the desire to run his fingers over the clothes hanging there, like that, as if he were stroking the keys of a silent piano, he thinks that he would lift up the skirt of one of those dresses to breathe in the aroma, the perfume, the smell. And then there are the drawers in the desk that he hasn't even looked in yet, and the small cupboards in the bookcase, what he is looking for, the letter, the diary, the word of farewell, the trace of the last tear, must be hidden somewhere. Why, he asked, supposing such a piece of paper does exist, supposing I find it, read it, just because I read it doesn't mean that her dresses will cease to be empty, from now on all those math problems will remain unsolved, no one will discover the value of the unknown factors in the equations, the bedspread won't be pulled back, the sheet won't be pulled up snugly to the chest, the bedside lamp will not light the page of a book, what is over is over. Senhor José bent forward, rested his head in his hands, as if he wanted to go on thinking, but that wasn't the case, he had run out of thoughts. The light dimmed for a moment, some cloud passing over the sun. At that moment, the telephone rang. He hadn't noticed it before, but there it was, on a small table in a corner, like a rarely used object. The answering machine came on, a female voice said the telephone number, then added, I'm not at home right now, but please leave a message after the tone. Whoever had called had hung up, some people hate talking to a machine, or in this case perhaps it was a wrong number, well, if you don't recognise the voice on the answering machine, there's no point leaving a message. This would have to be explained to Senhor José, who had never in his life seen one of these machines close up, but he would probably not have paid any attention to the explanations, he is so troubled by the few words he heard, I'm not at home right now, but please leave a message after the tone, no, she's not at home, she'll never be at home again, only her voice remained, grave, veiled, as if distracted, as if she had been thinking of something else when she made the recording. Senhor José said, They might ring again, and nurturing that hope, he did not move from the sofa for another hour, the darkness in the house grew gradually thicker and the telephone did not ring again. Then Senhor José got up, I must go, he murmured, but before leaving, he took another turn about the house, he went into the bedroom, where there was more light, he sat for a moment on the edge of the bed, again and again he ran his hands slowly over the embroidered top fold of the sheet, then he opened the wardrobe, there were the dresses of the woman who had spoken the definitive words, I'm not at home. He bent towards them until he touched them with his face, the smell they gave off could be described as a smell of absence, or perhaps it was that mingled perfume of rose and chrysanthemum that sometimes wafts through the Central Registry.

The concierge hadn't come and asked him where he had sprung from, the building is silent, it seems uninhabited. It was this silence that provoked an idea, the most daring he had ever had, What if I were to stay here tonight, what if I were to sleep in her bed, no one would ever know. Tell Senhor José that nothing could be easier, he just has to go up in the lift again, go into the apartment, take off his shoes, maybe another wrong number will ring, if they do, then you'll have the pleasure of hearing again the grave, veiled voice of the mathematics teacher, I'm not at home, she'll say, and if, during the night, lying in her bed, some pleasant dream excites your old body, as you know, the remedy is to hand, but you'll have to be careful not to mess up the sheets. These are sarcasms and vulgarities that Senhor

José does not deserve, his daring idea, rather more romantic than daring, goes just as it came, and he is no longer inside the building, but outside, what helped him to leave, apparently, was the painful memory of his old, darned socks and his bony, white shins with their sparse hairs. Nothing in the world makes any sense, murmured Senhor José, and set off for the road where the lady in the ground-floor apartment lives. The afternoon is at an end, the Central Registry will already have closed, the clerk does not have many hours in which to invent an excuse to justify having missed a whole day's work. Everyone knows he has no family that would require him to rush to them in an emergency, and even if he did, there can be no excuse in his case, living as he does right next to the Central Registry, all he had to do was go in and stand at the door and say, I'll be back tomorrow, one of my cousins is dying. Senhor José decides he's ready for anything, that they can dismiss him if they want, expel him from the civil service, perhaps the shepherd needs an assistant to help him change the numbers on the graves, especially if he's considering widening his field of activity, there's really no reason why he should limit himself to the suicides, the dead are all equal, what you can do to some you can do to all, jumble them up, confuse them, it doesn't matter, the world doesn't make sense anyway.

When Senhor José knocked at the door of the lady in the ground-floor apartment he was thinking only of the cup of tea he would have. He rang once, twice, but no one answered. Perplexed, worried, he rang the doorbell of the apartment opposite. A woman appeared who asked him sharply, What do you want, No one's answering across the way, So what, Has anything happened to her, do you know, What do you mean, An accident, an illness, for example, It's possible, an ambulance came to get her, And when was that, Three days ago, And you've heard nothing since, do you happen to know where she is, No, I don't, now if you'll excuse me. The woman slammed the door, leaving Senhor José in the dark. Tomorrow I'll have to go to all the hospitals, he thought. He felt exhausted, he had spent all day walking from one place to another, bombarded by emotions all day, and now this shock on top of everything else. He left the building and stood on the sidewalk wondering if he should do something more, go and ask one of the other tenants, they couldn't all be as unpleasant as the woman opposite, Senhor José went back into the building, went up the stairs to the second floor and rang at the door of the mother with the child and the jealous husband, who by now would be back from work, not that it matters, Senhor José is only going to ask if they know anything about the lady in the ground-floor apartment. The stair light is on. The door opens, the woman isn't carrying her baby and doesn't recognise Senhor José, Can I help you, she asks, I'm sorry to trouble you, I came to visit the lady in the ground-floor apartment, but she's not there and the woman opposite told me that an ambulance took her away three days ago, Yes, that's right, You don't happen to know where she is, do you, in which hospital, or if she's with some member of her family. Before the woman had time to reply, a male voice asked from inside, What is it, she turned her head, It's someone asking about the lady in the ground-floor apartment, then she looked at Senhor José and said, No, we don't know anything. Senhor José lowered his voice and asked, Don't you recognise me, she hesitated, Oh, yes, I do now, she said in a whisper and slowly closed the door.

Out in the street, Senhor José hailed a taxi, Take me to the Central Registry, he said distractedly to the driver. He would have preferred to walk, in order to save what little money he had and to end the day as he had begun it, but weariness would not allow him to take another step. Or so he thought. When the driver announced, Here we are, Senhor José discovered that he wasn't outside his house, but at the door of the Central Registry. It wasn't worth explaining to the man that he should go around the square and up the side street, he'd only have to walk about fifty yards, not even that. He paid with his last few coins, got out and when he put his feet on the pavement and looked up, he saw that the lights in the Central Registry were on, Not again, he thought, and he immediately forgot his concern for the fate of the lady in the ground-floor apartment and the fact that the mother with the child had remembered him, the problem now is finding an excuse for the following day. He went around the corner, there was his house, squat, almost a ruin really, clinging to the high wall of the building that seemed about to crush it. It was then that brutal fingers clutched at Senhor José's heart. The light was on in his house. He was sure he'd turned it off when he went out, but, bearing in mind the confusion that has reigned for days now inside his head, he admits that he might have forgotten, if it weren't for that other light, the one in the Central Registry, the five windows brilliantly lit. He put his key in the door, he knew what he was going to see, but he paused on the threshold as if social convention required him to be surprised. His boss was sitting at the table, before him were a few papers carefully lined up. Senhor José did not need to approach in order to find out what they were, the two forged letters of authority, the unknown woman's report cards, his notebook, the cover from the Central Registry file containing official documents. Come in, said his boss, it's your house. The clerk closed the door, went over to the table and stopped. He didn't speak, he felt his head become a whirlpool in which all his thoughts were dissolving. Sit down, as I said, it's your house. Senhor José noticed that on top of the report cards there was a key the same as his. Are you looking at the key, asked the Registrar, and continued calmly, don't imagine it's some fraudulent copy, the houses of staff members, when there were houses, always had two keys to the communicating door, one, of course, for the use of the owner, and another which remained in the possession of the Central

Registry, everything's fine, as you see, Apart from your having come in here without my permission, Senhor José managed to say, I didn't need your permission, the master of the key is the master of the house, let's say we're both the masters of this house, just as you seem to have considered yourself master enough of the Central Registry to remove official documents from the archive, I can explain, There's no need, I've been keeping regular track of your activities, and, besides, your notebook has been a great help to me, may I take the opportunity to congratulate you on the excellent style and the appropriateness of the language, I'll hand in my resignation tomorrow, I won't accept it. Senhor José looked surprised, You won't accept it, No, I won't, Why, if you don't mind my asking, Feel free, since I am an accomplice to your irregular activities, I don't understand. The Registrar picked up the file of the unknown woman, then said, You will understand, first, though, tell me what happened in the cemetery, your narrative ends with the conversation you had with the clerk over there, It'll take a long time, Just tell me in a few words, so that I get the complete picture, I walked through the General Cemetery to the section for suicides, I went to sleep under an olive tree, and the following morning, when I woke up, I was in the middle of a flock of sheep, and then I found out that the shepherd amuses himself by swapping around the numbers on the graves before the tombstones are put in place, Why, It's hard to explain, it's all to do with knowing where the people we're looking for really are, he thinks we'll never know, Like the woman you call the unknown woman, Yes, sir, What did you do today, I went to the school where she was a teacher and I went to her apartment, Did you find anything out, No, sir, and I don't think I wanted to. The Registrar opened the file, took out the record card that had got stuck to the cards of the last five famous people in whom Senhor José had taken an interest, Do you know what I would do in your position, he asked, No, sir, Do you know what is the

237

only logical conclusion to everything that has happened up until now, No, sir, Make up a new card for this woman, the same as the old one, with all the correct information, but without a date for her death, And then, Then go and put it in the archive of the living, as if she hadn't died, That would be a fraud, Yes, it would, but nothing that we have done or said, you and I, would make any sense if we don't, I still don't understand. The Registrar leaned back in the chair, drew his hands slowly over his face, then asked, Do you remember what I said inside there on Friday, when you turned up for work without having shaved, Yes, sir, Everything, Everything, Then you'll remember that I referred to certain facts without which I would never have realised the absurdity of separating the dead from the living, Yes sir, Do I need to tell you which facts I was referring to, No, sir.

The Registrar got up, I'll leave the key here, I have no intention of using it again, and he added, before Senhor José could say anything, There is still one last thing to resolve, What's that, sir, There's no death certificate in the unknown woman's file, I didn't manage to find it, it must be somewhere back there in the archive, or perhaps I dropped it on the way, As long as it remains lost, that woman will be dead, She'll be dead whether I find it or not, Unless you destroy it, said the Registrar. Having said that, he turned his back, and shortly afterwards came the sound of the door to the Central Registry closing. Senhor José stood in the middle of the room. There was no need to fill in a new card because he already had a copy in the file. He would, however, have to tear up or burn the original, where the date of death was registered. And there was still the death certificate. Senhor José went into the Central Registry, walked over to the Registrar's desk, opened the drawer where the flashlight and Ariadne's thread were waiting for him. He tied the end of the thread around his ankle and set off into the darkness.

The translator would like to thank Maria Manuela Lisboa, Maria Eugénia Penteado and Benm Sherriff for all their help and advice.